WHITER THAN SNOW

ALSO BY SANDRA DALLAS

Prayers for Sale

Tallgrass

New Mercies

The Chili Queen

Alice's Tulips

The Diary of Mattie Spenser

The Persian Pickle Club

Buster Midnight's Cafe

WHITER
THAN
SNOW

SANDRA DALLAS

ST. MARTIN'S PRESS

NEW YORK

This is a work of fiction. All of the characters, organizations, and events portrayed in this novel are either products of the author's imagination or are used fictitiously.

www.stmartins.com

Library of Congress Cataloging-in-Publication Data

Dallas, Sandra.
    Whiter than snow / Sandra Dallas. — 1st ed.
        p. cm.
    ISBN 978-0-312-60015-0
    1. Avalanches—Fiction.   2. Parent and child—Fiction.   3. Colorado—History—1876–1950—Fiction.   I. Title.
    PS3554.A434W47 2010
    813'.54—dc22

                                                                        2009040241

First Edition: April 2010

10   9   8   7   6   5   4   3   2   1

This book is for
Forrest Athearn
Our best buddy

ACKNOWLEDGMENTS

William Shakespeare wrote, "I can no other answer make but thanks, and thanks, and ever thanks." I think he understated it. My overwhelming thanks go to Lloyd Athearn, who taught me about avalanches, and to Forrest Athearn, who shared his special knowledge of them; to Arnie Grossman, who critiqued the chapter on Essie Snowball; to Jennifer Enderlin, my splendid editor at St. Martin's Press, and to St. Martin's publicists Dori Weintraub and Joan Higgins; to Danielle Egan-Miller and Joanna MacKenzie at Browne & Miller Literary Associates, who are not only my agents but dear friends. My greatest thanks to my wonderful family—Bob, Dana, and Kendal, Lloyd and Forrest.

Purge me with hyssop, and I shall be clean: wash me, and I shall be whiter than snow.

—Psalm 51:7

CHAPTER ONE

No one knew what triggered the Swandyke avalanche that began at exactly 4:10 P.M. on April 20, 1920. It might have been the dynamite charge that was set off at the end of shift on the upper level of the Fourth of July Mine. The miners claimed the blast was too far inside the mountain to be felt on the surface, and besides, they had set off dynamite hundreds, maybe thousands, of times before, and nothing bad had happened. Except for that one time when a charge failed to go off and Howard Dolan hit it with his pick when he was mucking out the stope and blew himself and his partner to kingdom come.

Still, who knew how the old mountain took retribution for having its insides clawed out.

Certainly there was nothing to suggest that the day was

different from any other. It started chill and clear. The men, their coat collars turned up against the dawn cold, left for their shifts at the Fourth of July or on the dredge up the Swan River, dinner pails clutched in their mittened hands. A little later, the children went off to school, the older brothers and sisters pulling little ones on sleds. Groups of boys threw snowballs at one another. One grabbed onto the back of a wagon and slid along over the icy road behind it. The Connor girl slipped on the ice and fell over a stone embankment, hitting her head. It hurt so much that she turned around and went home crying. The others called her a crybaby, but after what happened later that day, her parents said the blessed God had taken her hand.

After the children were gone, the women washed the breakfast dishes and started the beans for dinner. Then because the sun came out bright enough to burn your skin in the thin air, came out after one of the worst blizzards they had ever encountered, they got out the washtubs and scrubbed the overalls and shirts, the boys' knickers and the girls' dresses. When the wash was rinsed and wrung, they climbed onto the platforms that held the clotheslines far above the snow and hung up the clothes, where they would dry stiff as boards in the wind. Then because it was such a fine day, as fine a day as ever was, they called to one another to come and visit. There was a bit of coffee to reheat, and won't you have a cup? Cookies, left over from the lunch pails, were set on plates on the oilcloth of the kitchen tables, and the women sat, feeling lazy and gossipy.

"You know, the Richards girl had her baby last week," announced a woman in one of the kitchens, taking down the good china cups for coffee.

"Was her husband the father?" asked her neighbor.

"I didn't have the nerve to ask."

In another house, a woman confided, "The doctor says Albert has the cancer, but he won't have his lungs cut on."

"Then he'll die," her friend replied, muttering to herself, "at last."

It was that kind of a day, one for confidences or lazy talk. The women blessed the bright sun after so many winter days of gloom. Nobody thought about an avalanche. What could cause trouble on a day the Lord had given them?

Maybe the cause was an animal—a deer or an elk or even a mountain sheep—making its way along the ridge of Jubilee Mountain. The weight of the beast would have been enough to loosen the snow. That happened often enough. Nobody saw an animal, but then, who was looking?

Or worthless Dave Buck might have set off the avalanche. He'd put on snowshoes and taken his gun and gone high up to hunt for a deer—a fawn, really, for Dave was too lazy to cut up the bigger carcass and haul it home. The company forbade hunting around the mine, but Dave didn't care. He snowshoed up near timberline, where he'd seen the footprints of deer. He didn't find any, and he stopped to drink from a pint he'd put into his pocket. One drink, and another, and he sat down beside a stunted pine and picked off the cones and slid them down the white slope. Then he tossed the bottle into that cornice of snow that dipped out over a ridge.

But perhaps it was nothing more than the spring melt. That storm a few days before had dumped five feet of snowfall on top of a dry, heavy base of winter-worn snow. The wind had driven the snow off ridges, leaving them barren, and piled it into large cornices high up. But now the day was cloudless, the sun shining down as harsh as if it had been midsummer. It was so bright that it hurt your eyes to see the glare on the white, and some of the miners rubbed charcoal under their eyes to cut the sharpness.

But who cared what the cause was? *Something* started the slide that roared down Jubilee Mountain in Swandyke, Colorado, and that was all that mattered.

There was a sharp crack like the sound of distant thunder, and then the cornice of snow where Dave Buck had thrown his bottle, a crusted strip two hundred feet long that flared out over the mountain ridge, fractured and fell. It landed on layers of snow that covered the mountain slope to a depth of more than six feet—a heavy, wet, melting mass of new snow on top, falling on frozen layers of snowpack that lay on a bed of crumbled ice. That bottommost layer, a mass of loose ice crystals formed by freezing and thawing, lubricated the acres of snow lying on top of it just as much as if the bed had been made of marbles, and sent the snow careening down the mountain.

The miners called such a phenomenon a "slab avalanche" because a curtain of snow slid down the slope, picking up speed at a terrible rate, until it reached one hundred miles an hour. Nothing stood in the way of the terrifying slide, because the mountainside was bare of trees. They had been torn out forty years earlier in the second wave of mining that came after the prospectors abandoned gold pans and sluice boxes. Men had trained giant hoses on the mountain, washing dirt down the slope to be processed for precious minerals. Hydraulic mining, as it was called, also rid the mountainside of rocks and trees and underbrush that would have interfered with an avalanche—not that anything could have held back the tons of white that slid down Jubilee Mountain that afternoon. The slide would have taken anything in its path.

This was not the first slide on Jubilee Mountain. The hillside, in fact, was known for avalanches. But it was the worst, and it spilled over into the forest at the edge of the open slope, tearing out small trees by their roots and hurling them into the rushing snow, which turned them into battering rams. A cabin that perched under the pines was wrenched from its foundation, its log walls torn asunder and broken into jackstraws.

The slide rushed onward, churning up chunks of ice the

size of boxcars, gathering up abandoned hoses and machinery and the other detritus of mining that lay in its path. It hurtled on, thrashing its deadly cargo about, not slowing when it reached the bottom of the mountain, but instead rushing across the road, filling the gully with snow as heavy as wet cement and flattening the willows. The avalanche hurtled on until it started up Turnbull Mountain. Then, at last, its momentum came to an end and the slide was exhausted, the front stopping first, the back end slipping down the mountain and filling the gulch with snow higher than a two-story house.

Snow hovered in the air like a deadly mist. The debris caught up in the avalanche rolled a little and was still. A jack pine, graceful as a sled, glided to a stop in the snow covering the road. Clumps of snow fell from the trees still standing at the edge of the deadly white mass, making plopping sounds as they landed. Snowballs broke loose and rolled down the hill, leaving little trails in their wake.

For an instant, all was quiet, as silent as if the slide had occurred in a primeval forest. Then a high-pitched scream came from somewhere in the mass of snow, a child's scream. The slide thundered down Jubilee Mountain just after the grade school let out, and it grabbed up nine of thirty-two schoolchildren in its icy grip. Five of the victims were related, the children of the Patch sisters—Dolly's three, who were Jack, Carrie, and Lucia, along with Lucy's two, Rosemary and Charlie. The slide was no respecter of class, because it took Schuyler Foote, son of the manager of the Fourth of July Mine, and little Jane Cobb, the Negro girl, whose father labored in the mill, and Sophie Schnable, the daughter of a prostitute. And then there was Emmett Carter, that near-orphan boy who lived with his grandfather. All of them were swept up and carried along in that immense swirl of white.

Four of the children survived.

CHAPTER TWO

Lucy Patch was the smart one. People had always said that about her, ever since she was a toddling child. They still did on occasion, although she was a grown woman now, grown and married, with two children of her own. "Lucy's the smart one," they'd remark when Lucy was coming up. It really was not meant as a compliment, because that was only the half of what they told. "Dolly Patch is the pretty one," they'd say at the beginning, and then add, "Lucy's the smart one," as if being smart was honorable mention.

Dolly, whose real name was Helen, wore her hair in yellow-white curls as long as the spiral of a drill and kept her skin as white as quartz. She was plump, with a happy disposition, and her eyes were still the bright blue of a china doll's, just as when she was a baby and her father had called her "Doll Baby," and, when she was older, "Dolly." The name had stuck, even after a packet of doll-size Patch children came along following Dolly. Everyone had called her by those names, even Lucy, who thought they were perfectly dreadful. People still did even now when Dolly was thirty-two, because she was still sunny as a summer's day and lively in step, although she was portly in build. She still wore her hair in corkscrews, the color coming from a bottle, because with her pregnancies, her hair had darkened to the color of a mountain stream during spring runoff.

Only a year younger than Dolly, Lucy had been pretty in her way, if you were partial to dark hair and skin and girls who were too tall and angular, which most folks weren't. Nobody remarked then or now on Lucy's looks, although they were generous in their praise of her intelligence. She believed it herself and had always been a bit of a show-off about it. Whatever she did in school could not be done better. Lucy couldn't help herself. If being smart was her only attribute, why pretend to be stupid? There was this thing about Lucy: She'd been told so often that she was intelligent, she thought she was smarter than anybody else. It got a little tiresome.

And incidentally, Lucy did not care for her own name, either. She wished she had been named Lucia, after the saint the Swedes in Swandyke honored with a parade each Christmas, although the Patch family was not Swedish. Lucia was romantic and exotic, and it would have been silly on someone as plain and straightforward as Lucy. Only Dolly knew Lucy preferred that name, and Dolly sometimes called her sister Lucia when the two were alone.

Although the distinctions might have pitted the girls against each other, the fact was that during their coming-up time, the two were inseparable, as close as any two sisters could be. Lucy helped Dolly with her schoolwork, because Dolly was not much taken with learning. And Dolly, who collected beaux the way an old woman collects blue columbine on a June day, was sensitive when it came to Lucy's feelings. She told a boy on a hayride once that he ought to sit next to Lucy. "At conversation, she beats it all hollow," Dolly said.

"Lucy's okay if you want to hear the Gettysburg Address. Come to think of it, she *is* the spit of Abraham Lincoln," he replied.

"And you're the spit of Theodore Roosevelt," Dolly replied, pushing him off the wagon.

Dolly was smart enough to know that her looks would fade in time—in the bright, harsh mountain sun that turned a woman's skin into a wrinkled brown paper bag, there wasn't a woman over thirty-five who didn't look as if she'd worn out four or five bodies with the same face—but Lucy would always be smart.

By the time she was fifteen, Lucy had skipped two grades

and was in her last year of high school, something for which she was sorry after she realized she would be just sixteen when she graduated. Life didn't hold much for her after that. She would get a job in the office at the Fourth of July Mine—her father had already discussed it with the mine manager—and that would mean long hours performing boring tasks. Her only option was to marry, and she shuddered at the idea of being the wife of somebody who mucked out a mine.

"I wish I could go to college," Lucy confided to Dolly that spring, only a month before graduation.

"What in the world for?" her sister asked. For Dolly, who was made after the timid kind and never contemplated a life that went beyond marrying and raising three or four dandy-looking boys and girls, the idea was shocking. She'd never known of a Swandyke girl who had gone to college, although a few boys had done so. They'd never come back.

"There's got to be something more than working at the mine office."

"It'll only be till you're married."

"But I don't want to be married. I want to go to college, someplace that's green, where I don't have to see a brown mine tipple or a yellow mine dump every time I look up."

"You'll be terrible lonesome away from Swandyke," Dolly said, then frowned. "You'd come back, wouldn't you? I couldn't bear it if you didn't. You wouldn't leave forever, would you?"

"It doesn't matter, because I'm not going anywhere."

"Why not, if that's what you want? We both want something better, and we have to get it the best way we can."

"Unless I can order a college diploma from the Sears, Roebuck catalog, there's no way I'll ever have one. We haven't got a dime for school, what with all the little kids Mama and Papa have to take care of."

"You must ask Papa to send you," said Dolly, who had not the slightest idea what a college education cost.

Lucy scoffed. "How would he do that? He's no good with money. Papa's already spent his wages from now to Christmas. Mama would like for me to go. She told me so, but she won't stand up to Papa."

"No, he wouldn't allow that," Dolly agreed.

"Besides, Papa expects me to go to work to help him carry the family."

While their father, Gus Patch, worked suitable, he made little, and his wages slipped through his fingers. He was a sucker for a hard-luck story, and many a time, he was skinned out of his pay envelope. So the family lived from hand to mouth, and in the few days before payday, there wasn't much to put into all those mouths. In the past year, they had heard their father say often enough to this or that debtor, "When my girl Lucy goes to work at the mine office, I'll pay that bill right off."

The afternoon of their discussion, the sisters were sitting on a rock in the willows that filled the gully at the bottom of Jubilee Mountain. Lucy leaned back so that she could look up the mountainside, up past the barren slope that had been washed clean of rocks and topsoil by hydraulic mining, to the Fourth of July Mine. That was where their father was employed. "I told Papa I wouldn't work there until I finished high school. Graduation's on a Friday night. So he's fixed it up that I start on Saturday morning."

"You must talk to Papa anyway," Dolly insisted. "If you explain it to him, he's sure to go along with you. That's what I've found."

Lucy didn't reply that as the favorite daughter, Dolly usually got her way with their father. "I did talk to him, Dolly. He said I have a responsibility to him. His exact words were, 'I don't care for nothing about college. I got no more use for it than one of those airplanes.' He told me while I was in high school that he'd let me do as I pleased, but now that I'm done with it, I'll have to do as I can."

Dolly flung back her yellow curls and stood up. "I'll talk to him."

Not more than a week later, Gus Patch announced at the supper table that if Lucy could get a job in Denver to pay her way through college and would live with her aunt Alice, a sour old woman whom no one in the family cared for much, he thought he could spare her for a few years. "I expect with a college degree, you could make two or three times what you'd get typewriting letters in the mine office," he said, stirring his potatoes and green beans together, then leaning over his plate and using a spoon to shovel the mess into his mouth.

Later, when the girls were alone, Lucy asked, "It was you who gave him the idea I could be a bookkeeper, wasn't it, Dolly? What did it cost you?"

"I don't know what you mean." Dolly looked down at a ribbon she was ironing between her fingers. "Besides, it was Mama's idea."

"I know Papa as well as you do. It was you, not Mama, who had to promise him something. He's not for giving away a thing for nothing." Lucy grabbed Dolly's hand so hard that her sister dropped the ribbon. "You're not quitting high school, are you?"

"It cost less than it was worth. Besides, I don't care so much for school."

"I won't let you quit."

"Well, there's nothing you can do about it. They keep asking me at the Prospector if I won't come and be a waitress. I've made up my mind."

"So have I, and I won't go to college if you quit school."

The next morning, Lucy picked up Gus's lunch bucket and told him she would walk him to the mine. That was what the children did when they wanted to talk to their father or ask for a favor, since the old man was usually hungover in the early mornings, and his mind was a clutter. "Dolly's not quitting high school," Lucy said.

"Oh, she don't mind."

"Well, I do, and I say she's not."

"I guess when you're head of this family, you'll have a say."

"Papa, I won't go to college if she has to wait tables at the Prospector."

"Suit yourself."

The two walked along in silence until Gus said, "Doll thinks you might not come back if you go below to school."

Lucy didn't reply.

"I don't reckon we could let you do that."

"I don't reckon you could stop me."

"Oh, I guess I could."

Lucy slowed down a little as she mulled over her father's words. She knew then what he was after.

"Wages aren't going up at the mine. I need you to help carry us in these scarce times."

"I could send you money. I'd do it every month."

Gus stopped and put his foot up on a rock to tie his shoe. The leather was scuffed and worn, the toe capped with metal. Lucy stared down at the top of his head, where the hair was thin and the scalp scaly from the mountain dryness. He was asking her to help support the family, maybe carry it all herself if he lost his job. He'd barter that for college. She thought it over before she replied. If she didn't go to college, she'd work at the mine and hand over her paycheck to her father. If she got an education, she'd do the same thing, but at least she'd have been away for four years, and she would be getting a better job. "What if I promise to come back? Will you let Doll finish high school?"

Her father pretended to think it over, but his head hurt too much for him to put much effort into it. "Well, I expect so. If you'll promise, promise no matter what, you'll come back."

"Oh, I will," Lucy said.

Gus sighed. "Then I reckon I could spare you."

It was only later that Lucy thought she had been bought too cheaply. Both Gus and Dolly had gotten what they wanted. Lucy would be bonded to Swandyke, where she'd supplement her father's salary and be a companion to Dolly for the rest of her life. Still, she told herself, she'd have those four years.

And so in the fall of 1905, Lucy registered at the University of Denver. At first, school wasn't easy for her, what with classes, working as a counter girl at a drugstore on Colfax Avenue, and cleaning and cooking for her aunt Alice, who wasn't so bad once Lucy got to know her. Still, in later years when she looked out at the yellow waste dumps on the mountains or the waist-deep snow that covered Swandyke six months of the year and heard the screeching of the gold dredge on the Swan River, she remembered those years at the University of Denver as the happiest ones of her life.

She did not major in math, which had been her intent,

because the school directed girls to more feminine subjects. So she took courses in bookkeeping and business on the side and studied to become a teacher. She was surprised that she had not thought of teaching on her own, because teachers rarely lasted long in the Swandyke schools, and there was a great demand for them. The ones who came from the outside were tired out by the long winters and the harsh landscape and the noise of the mines and the gold dredge that dug up the Swan River high above town. Only half of the new teachers returned the next year.

She studied hard—on the streetcar, during respites at the drugstore, at night, after her aunt went to bed. Aunt Alice insisted that the lamps were to be blown out at 9:00 P.M. to save on kerosene, so Lucy waited until she heard her aunt's snores, and then she relit the lamp in her room and worked on her lessons until midnight. Only later did she realize her aunt had known all the time what she was doing, had gone to bed precisely at nine so that Lucy could get to her books.

With most hours occupied by work or study, and living with her relative, Lucy had no time for social activities. She hadn't the money to join a sorority and didn't care, because the sorority girls she met seemed less interested in education than in clothes and parties and getting married. She was not jealous of them, because she thought them meek as sheep and dumb as burros. Nor did she feel sorry for herself, although she was careful not to mention her family or the circumstances of her young life. At that time, when so few women attended college, the girlfriends Lucy made on campus simply assumed that Lucy's family was no different from their own and that her reason for living with a relative was not due to lack of money but to her parents' insistence that she not be exposed to the temptations of school life. Hers would not have been the only parents who disapproved of dormitories.

With the demands on her time, Lucy took part in only a few of the social activities on campus. But she cherished the discussions after class in a coffee shop off campus, where she spent some of her hard-earned nickel tips. Such gatherings included both boys and girls, but Lucy was not interested in boys, because, as she'd told Dolly, she did not care to marry. Besides, her father had forbidden her to date, telling her aunt, "There'll be Old Nick to pay if some boy fools with her and she comes home with an armful."

Lucy's dedication paid off, and at the end of her first college year, she was awarded a scholarship. The girl did not tell her family about her good fortune. She was afraid that her father would insist she send him part of her wages. It was not that Lucy wanted to keep the money for herself, but she hoped to cut back on her hours at the drugstore once school began in the fall, so that she could enjoy herself a little. After all, she thought with some sense of sorrow, a quarter of her college years was already spent.

That summer, she stayed in Denver, still living with her aunt Alice, who had softened a little. The old woman had come to depend on Lucy, not just to clean and cook but to provide a bit of company. And on her part, Lucy had become fond of the old woman. That summer, the two sat on the porch of the little house, shaded by trumpet vines, and listened to the evening sounds of children playing hide-and-seek or to that of the trolley as it rumbled along the next street. In the evenings, while the light was still good, Aunt Alice mended while Lucy read aloud from a poetry book. Sometimes the two popped corn or made divinity candy and shared it with their neighbors. Or they walked to the creamery, where Lucy spent her tips on ice cream for the two of them. Once, as they walked home in the darkness, stopping to smell the honeysuckle next door, Aunt Alice said, "I expect you miss your sister. I wouldn't complain if she came for a visit."

Lucy was so tickled that she wrote a letter to her sister that night, enclosing twenty dollars for the train fare. A week later, Dolly wired that she'd be arriving the next day. Lucy met her at the depot, met three trains that day, in fact, because Dolly had not told her which one she'd chosen. Although Lucy was exasperated, she had to admit that one of her muddled sister's endearing qualities was that she assumed everything would turn out all right. And for Dolly, it always did.

The two girls had not been together in ten months—the price of a ticket to go home at Christmas had been too dear—so now they were overjoyed at seeing each other.

Dolly said college made Lucy look smarter than ever, and Lucy observed that her sister was as plump as a ptarmigan and even prettier than she had been when Lucy had bid her good-bye in the fall.

"I thought you'd be spoken for by now," Lucy said.

"Oh, there's plenty that's spoke to Papa about me, but they don't do to suit me. However, I ever remain hopeful I will meet a management man, even though they are mostly married. Of course, that wouldn't stop them from foolery, but I won't have it. If I slept on my rights and had an illegal baby, Mama would cry her eyes out, and Papa would bust out my brains."

Both girls laughed, because each knew that while Gus himself had led a corruptible life, he did not intend to let his daughters stray.

"I refuse to marry a man who will give me the life I'm accustomed to, and a hoistman or a cager won't do," Dolly continued. "I want someone who has more than two pair of britches to his name."

"Do you have your eye on anybody?"

"Mr. Bibb, who is the second-level boss at the Fourth of July."

"You mean Henry Bibb, the one who's bald and straddly-legged? He must be more than thirty."

Doll shrugged. "Mr. Bibb's not so bad. He's solid as granite, although I can't follow him when he talks about books and learning. There's not so many to choose from as you'd think, and I can't wait around too long. I'm in my eigh-teenth year, and there's wrinkles starting around my eyes. Mama says it's time enough I was married."

Lucy looked but could see nothing but perfection. "Don't sell yourself too cheap, Doll."

"I won't. I don't expect a man as rich as cream, but he's got to earn more than a mucker does. Besides Mr. Bibb, there's a couple of men who work the gold boats I've got my eye on. They come into the Prospector and leave me twenty-five-cent tips, sometimes fifty, even though they order only a five-cent cup of coffee. Imagine that! One of them's a bounder, I expect, but there's another—he said he's been to college—and he thinks I'm swell. I have hopes." She turned to Lucy suddenly. "What about you, Lucia?" she asked, us-ing the childhood name. "You have any sharp luck meeting boys? You won't find anybody in Swandyke smart enough for you."

Lucy shook her head. "There's nobody—not that I'm looking. You know I made that promise to Papa to go back to Swandyke when I'm done here, and where am I going to find somebody who'll move up there with me? I never knew of a person to live in Swandyke by choice." In fact, Lucy had given the subject a certain amount of thought. It wasn't that she didn't care to marry one day. She did, but, like Dolly, she didn't want a penniless miner for a husband, a man who stank of dynamite and mine mud and who'd grab at her at night with hands that would never wash clean of grease and black grit. Nor did she care to live in a cabin that smelled of cabbage and dirty diapers. No, she, too, hoped to marry a management man who'd build her a house with an indoor bathroom and a dining room so that they wouldn't have to eat in the kitchen. But if Dolly hadn't found such a man in Swandyke, how could she? And it was sure she wasn't about to meet a boy in school who'd agree to live at the top of the world. "I don't think I'll ever marry."

"Doesn't that bother you awful bad?"

Lucy shrugged. "I'll be just frank. I'm not like you, Doll. There's things worse to me than not having a husband. And I'll have you. I think I can stand Swandyke if you're living there."

"Well, where place else would I live?" Dolly replied.

The girls had taken the trolley to the university so that Lucy could show her sister the campus. Dolly had never ridden in such a conveyance, and she slid on the hard seat each time the streetcar came to a stop. When they reached the school, Lucy reached up to pull the cord, but Dolly said she wanted to do it and yanked on the cord until the big yellow car came to a stop, its steel wheels screeching against the steel rails.

Holding on to her skirts, Dolly stepped off the car. "Imagine that, paved streets and a cement walk. I wonder wherever does the water go when the snow melts if there isn't any dirt for it to go into." She stood on the sidewalk a moment and looked around, her mouth open, a little like Lucy had been just ten months before.

But Lucy was used to the city now and felt herself worldly next to her countrified sister. "It goes into the sewer," Lucy replied, about to explain how the storm-sewer system worked, but Dolly wasn't listening.

"Will you look at that." Dolly pointed at a woman whose dress was inches above her ankles. "Is she a slut?"

The woman heard the remark and gave Dolly a hard look, while Lucy shushed her sister.

"Well, she's dressed naked," Dolly said. "You could put all the clothes she has on into your pocket."

"There's lots that dress like that here."

Dolly watched the woman walk away. "I might could try it. I've got good legs, but nobody knows it. Of course, Papa would be killing mad and slap me down for a hooker." She thought for a moment. "Do you dress like that?"

"Living with Aunt Alice? What do you think?" Lucy laughed.

"You have to admit it would be nice not to wear long skirts that drag through the snow and dirt. I get awful tired of sewing strips of material around the bottom of my hems to keep the muck from ruining them."

Lucy led the way across the campus, and Dolly forgot her hems when the sisters passed a trio of boys. Eyeing Dolly, the young men stepped off the sidewalk to let the two girls pass. One bowed as he took a pretend cape from his shoulders and threw it across the muddy walk in front of the girls. Dolly was confused, although Lucy understood the gesture and smiled.

"Are they fresh?" Dolly whispered, and when Lucy shook her head, Dolly gave the boys a brilliant smile.

"You a freshman?" one asked.

"What?" Dolly replied.

"She's visiting," Lucy said.

"Just our luck." The boy pretended to pick up the cape and put it back over his shoulders.

The two girls walked along silently, Lucy thinking nobody had ever done a Sir Walter Raleigh impression for her. "Doll, why don't you go to college, too?" she asked.

Dolly looked up at her sister, startled. "Why would I do that? I never even liked high school."

Lucy didn't hear the reply, because the thought, which had come upon her suddenly, now took hold. It was a splendid idea. "In three more years, I'll be finished. You could enroll then. Despite what Pa says, Aunt Alice is a dear, and I know she'd let you live with her. You could study anything you wanted, maybe home economics, and you'd have your pick of boys here. You wouldn't ever have to go back to Swandyke." For Lucy, the idea was perfect. Because of the promise made to her father, she herself was tied to the mountains, but her sister would get away, and such was Lucy's nature and the affection the girls had for each other that instead of being jealous, she was glad for Dolly. One of them would have a chance.

"But I'd want to go back to Swandyke. I wouldn't live anywhere else on God's earth."

Lucy stared at her sister.

"I wouldn't be happy where there weren't mountains. You think they're a cage, but they make me feel safe, like they're putting their arms around me. If I lived out here where it's flat, I'd be afraid I'd blow away."

"But Doll, you don't know that. You've been here hardly two days. You'd grow to like it."

"That's a thing you know in your bones."

"You could try it, sign up for just one quarter of college. I know you'd change your mind about Swandyke."

Dolly shook her head. "I don't care about learning, and besides, I'd never be happy anyplace but home. It's a thing I know about myself."

And then Lucy understood. She hated Swandyke, but to her sister, the town was home. Dolly had never been ambitious, never wanted to leave, and where Lucy did indeed think of the high mountains as prison walls, Dolly took comfort in them. While Lucy thought of Swandyke as endless mountain winters and the cold and the mud, Dolly saw the town for its short, sharp summers, so hot that you could get sunburned walking to the privy. Dolly reveled in the wildflowers, like bright jewels, and the wind in the jack pines, which sounded like running water. "You could meet dozens of boys here," Lucy said in a last attempt to change Dolly's mind.

"But like you said, what one of them's ever going to live in Swandyke? No, I'll find a husband at home."

Dolly went back to Swandyke after a week, saying she had had a fine time, but as they got off the trolley at the depot, Lucy saw her sister turn a moment to the far range of mountains, just a thin ridge of blue, still dotted in spots with white snow, and Doll's eyes lit up. Lucy knew her sister's heart was glad to be returning there.

Doll promised to visit again, and Lucy promised to go home at Christmas, and the two girls separated, Dolly boarding the coach, then waving from a window as the train pulled out, waving until Lucy could no longer see her.

That night when Lucy went to bed, she found a note on her pillow. "Here's your $20 back. I make my own money now." But there were twenty-five one-dollar bills in the envelope. "Papa doesn't know how much I make in tips. I'd be glad for you to spend it on books—gladder than if Papa gave it away."

After that, whenever Dolly wrote to Lucy, she enclosed a dollar or two. She never returned to Denver.

Lucy went home at Christmas, as she had promised, happy to see her family. She loved Dolly, as well as her father and mother and all the little ones. But she was happier yet to return to school. The cold and the ugliness of the mountains affected her, made her gloomy. She would get used to all that again when she had to. She might even be happy there, since her childhood had not been an especially harsh one by mountain standards and she could force herself to look at the bright side of things. But she didn't want to think about Swandyke until she had to, and she concentrated on her studies, making top grades, and once again, she was awarded a scholarship. When she began her third year at DU, she realized that she was half-finished with college. She was on the downhill side of her education.

In the fall of that third year, Lucy met Ted Turpin. They did not get acquainted on campus, and in fact, Ted was not even a student at the university. He attended the Colorado School of Mines in nearby Golden, and he came into the drugstore to buy a bottle of Mercurochrome. Then he sat down on a stool at the soda fountain and ordered a Coca-Cola.

Ted reached for the glass that Lucy set down in front of him, and she saw an angry cut on the back of his hand and said, "I can get you some cotton if you want to swab that thing with the Mercurochrome."

"Pretty ugly, isn't it?"

Lucy shrugged. She'd seen worse.

"I got it on a gold dredge. I'll bet you a dollar you don't know what a gold dredge is."

Lucy put the tip of her tongue on her upper lip and cocked her head, narrowing her eyes at Ted. She'd never cared for boys who assumed they knew more than she did, and she thought to show up this one. He was tall and thin, with a lean face and sandy hair, and appeared so sure of himself. "And I'll bet you two dollars I can name the dredge. It was the Liberty, wasn't it? The other two are shut down for repairs, and there's not but three gold dredges in Colorado."

Ted stared at her, then reached into his pocket for the two bills. "How'd you know that?"

"I lived in Swandyke in my growing-up years."

"Well, aren't you the lucky one!" Ted grinned so broadly that Lucy softened a little.

"You work on the dredge?" she asked.

"No, at least not yet. I'm majoring in mining engineering. I went up to the Swan River with a class that's studying gold mining. We wanted to see how a dredge worked."

"It's noisy," Lucy told him.

"That's for sure. But it's a fine way to mine gold. Besides, you can't beat the location. I never saw a thing as pretty as those mountains. I'd sure like to climb them one day—you know, with ropes and all."

Lucy studied Ted a moment to see if he was joking. She'd never known anyone who'd climbed the mountains for fun. You just climbed them because they were in the way.

"You ever done that?" he asked.

"I never wanted to."

"Maybe if you'd grown up where it's flat, you would."

Maybe not, she thought, but she said, "You want that cotton?" Ted nodded, and Lucy pinched off a piece from under the counter, then opened the bottle of Mercurochrome and swabbed the cut herself with the orange stuff. She blew on the medicine, not that she needed to dry it, but she liked the touch of Ted's hand.

Business was slow that day, and the two young people talked for an hour, Lucy leaning her elbows on the counter. When the owner of the drugstore frowned at them, Ted ordered a grilled cheese sandwich and, later on, a soda. But finally he said it was time to go, and he picked up his bottle of medicine and swung around on the stool, then swung right back. "Say, would you like to take in a moving picture on Saturday night? There's a theater downtown that shows them, you know."

Lucy fiddled with the tie of her apron. She'd never seen a picture show. "Well, I'd like to, but I can't."

Ted's face fell. "I guess you think I'm a masher. Or maybe you already have a boyfriend. That's it, isn't it? A girl as pretty as you."

Lucy liked that, because nobody ever called her pretty. "Oh no! I don't have a boyfriend. And I don't think you're a masher. It's just that I'm not allowed to date."

"Really? You promised your parents you wouldn't go out with boys?"

"Papa told me I couldn't. I didn't really promise it."

Ted thought a moment. "If you just happened to run into

me when we were both going to the pictures and we ended up sitting together, it wouldn't really be a date, would it?"

Lucy thought that over. After all, she *hadn't* promised. She looked at Ted slyly. "I guess it wouldn't."

Ted grinned. "Okay, then how about if I run into you on Saturday at the theater, the Novelty? It's on Curtis Street. Your father didn't tell you that you couldn't go to the pictures, did he?"

"He's probably never heard of the pictures."

"Then how about it?"

"Maybe," Lucy said, knowing her father would be boiling mad if he learned she had disobeyed him. But how would he find out? She'd tell her aunt she was busy at school. "I could try. But you'll understand if I don't show up, won't you?"

"Not one bit. And I'll be mighty disappointed."

They agreed on a time, and Lucy fretted all week, wondering if Aunt Alice would somehow discover what she was up to and tell her father. The old woman would have a vexation about it. But by the weekend, Lucy decided to chance it. And Ted, it seemed, decided to take no chances at all, for when Lucy left work on Saturday to catch the trolley downtown, he was waiting for her outside the drugstore.

Lucy did not know that life could hold so much joy for her as it did in that third year of college. She had her classes, and she had Ted. She did not let herself think that it would all end. Because their schools were at far sides of the city— Lucy's in the south end of Denver and Ted's in Golden, a town to the west, they did not see each other as often as they would have liked. Besides, since Aunt Alice did not know about him, Ted could not call at the house, so they had to plan their meetings in public places. Sometimes he brought his books and studied at a table near the soda fountain or dropped by at the end of Lucy's shift so that the two of them could walk to the corner near her aunt's house. Ted would leave her there and take the trolley and then the interurban back to Golden. In the late autumn, when the leaves fell, they walked in Washington Park and around the lake, and after cold weather came, they continued to walk. Lucy was used to mountain cold, so the low temperature in Denver did not bother her. Nor did it affect Ted, who loved the brisk weather.

Neither one had much money—Ted's parents had died, and his small inheritance barely covered tuition and living expenses—so they did not go to the movies often or to restaurants for dinner. Ted invited her to a dance once, but Lucy turned him down, because there was no way she could keep such an outing secret from her aunt. Mostly, they talked, sometimes stopping in drugstores for coffee. And talking seemed to satisfy both of them. Ted told Lucy, "I can talk to you about anything. You're as smart as a fellow."

One day as they sat on a bench in Washington Park,

feeding stale buns from the drugstore to the ducks, Ted remarked, "God put gold in the ground for us to find, and I intend to do it. I can just imagine how those old fellows felt fifty years ago when they discovered gold. I guess they're all living the life of Riley now."

"Not so's you'd notice," Lucy told him. "Most of them sold out cheap and spent the money. It was the finding of it that mattered."

"I guess I understand that." He sat back on the bench and grinned. "I never thought I'd meet a girl who knew so much about mining."

"There's not much else to know about in Swandyke. Some of those old prospectors are still around, you know."

"I'd like to meet them."

"You'd be disappointed. Oh, they tromped around mighty for a while, but today, they're no better than ragpickers, living off other folks' leavings. Most people think they're no account for nothing," Lucy told him.

"Well, I wish I'd grown up hearing their stories."

"I wish I hadn't."

Ted turned to stare at Lucy. "If you dislike Swandyke so much, how come you're going back?"

"I don't have a choice. I promised my father I would." She thought a minute. "It's not all bad up in the high country. There's nothing prettier than a mountain summer. And in the fall, when the leaves turn, you'd swear you were inside a gold vug." She added, "That's one of those little pockets filled with pure gold. Every prospector in the world hopes to find one."

"I know what a vug is. Remember, I'm a mining student?"

Lucy smiled. "The aspens are that bright—so bright that they bring a hurting to your eyes. And the people in Swandyke are as good as you'll find anyplace. Why, when there's a cave-in or somebody's hurt on the dredge, there's not a soul in town that won't pitch in. Old Mrs. McCauley, who lives alone, always keeps a bed turned down in case there's an accident and somebody needs tending. At times she has two or three at a time in her house. People who haven't spoken to each other in years come together when there's need."

"Why did you promise your father you'd go back?" Ted broke off a piece of bun and threw it into the water, and they watched as a duck swam over to it and picked it up with his bill.

"I have to help carry the family. Papa made me promise if I went to college, I'd come back to help him out. There are half a dozen little ones at home. My sister's the only one who works now, and she'll likely get married soon."

"What if *you* get married, Luce?"

"I can't. I gave my word I'd go back, and there's nobody on the Swan River I'd want to spend my life with."

"It sounds like you made the devil's bargain."

Lucy laughed a little. "I suppose it will seem so after I

graduate, but right now, I'm grateful I'm away for a few years." She threw the rest of the buns into the lake, and they watched the ducks swim over to them and gobble their dinner. Then they rose and walked out of the park, Ted warming Lucy's fingers in his own. She left him at the streetcar stop, then continued on home. When she arrived, Aunt Alice was mending a stocking in the light from the window.

"It's awful cold to be outside," she observed, weaving her needle in and out over the darning egg.

"I'm all right."

"You're liable to catch your death out there."

Lucy shrugged and took off her coat.

"I don't mind if you ask your young man to come inside next time."

"What?"

"I'd hate to be the cause of you getting pneumonia, you or him."

Lucy sat down on a footstool and stared at the woman.

Finally, her aunt looked up. "You think I don't notice how you leave here all primped up and come back looking like you met the king of England himself?" She chuckled. "I know your Papa don't want you to go out with a boy, 'cause he's scared you won't go on back home, but I think he's terrible mean about that." She put down the darning egg and leaned forward in her chair. "I never had the chance. Maybe you don't know my mother died, and my father said I had to raise up the little ones, made me take charge of the house and be the mother to my brothers and sisters. I was the oldest. Your papa was the youngest. When he was grown sufficient, I was an old maid. I never had no good time. I was used up before I could marry. None of my brothers and sisters cared the least thing about me after they were growed, and Gus is the worst, never so much as sending me a postal, except when he wants something. So I don't care much to keep his commandments. Lord have mercy! He ain't God. Nobody in the family but Margaret—your mother—and you has ever took a liking to me, and I've become right fond of you. You've been a blessing to me every day since you been here, so I guess you can see a boy, and I won't tell."

Lucy grabbed the old woman's hand and squeezed it, and Aunt Alice said, "Now, now." But she seemed pleased, and after that, Ted called at the little house, and the two young people sat in the living room, sometimes by themselves, other times with the aunt. When spring came, the couple took her to Washington Park, or they all walked to the creamery for ice cream. Aunt Alice approved of the young man, and she knew long before Lucy did—or Ted, either, for that matter—that he would propose.

And of course he did. The day he was offered a job as assistant dredgemaster on the Liberty Dredge, up the Swan River from Swandyke, Ted asked Lucy to marry him. The proposal came as a shock to the girl, because she had refused to let herself consider the possibility of marriage, and she was so surprised that she couldn't speak. Ted was sitting across the counter from her at the drugstore, and he said, "I guess I should have been more romantic, taken you to dinner or brought you flowers. But I got the job only an hour ago, and I was so excited, I couldn't wait." He grinned and added, "I expect at the least I should have taken a bath."

"No, oh no . . ."

"No? What do you mean, no? I've got it all figured out. I'll support us, and you can turn your wages over to your folks, the whole paycheck, if you want to. You'll go back to Swandyke like you promised, but we'll go together."

"I meant you didn't have to take a bath." She smiled at him for a long time, then frowned. "I won't quit school."

"You won't have to. We'll get married next year, after you graduate. By then, I'll have the hang of the job, and I'll have time to find a house and maybe get to know your family, too. Don't you see, Luce, it's perfect. You know I've been crazy about you ever since that day you painted my finger with Mercurochrome. I didn't wash it for a week. I must have eaten a hundred grilled cheese sandwiches here, and I don't even like cheese. Promise me you'll never fix me another grilled cheese." He grinned. "I hope you feel the same way about me."

Lucy nodded. "I guess I swabbed that cut so I could hold your hand." She blushed and added, "Now I can hold it for the rest of my life."

"Then you'll do it."

"Of course I'll do it. I'll marry you."

Ted leaned across the counter and kissed her. He'd never done that before, and Lucy drew away. But then she reconsidered and kissed him back.

The drugstore owner came over then and asked, "What's this about, Lucy? You can't do that in here."

"It's about we just got engaged," Ted told him.

"Oh, I guess that's different. Isn't that fine!" the man said, and, as the store was empty, he went behind the drug counter and took down a bottle and poured shots of whiskey into three Coca-Cola glasses and handed them around.

They told Aunt Alice right away, and she said it was about time.

"Now that I have your approval, I'll have to get Lucy's father's," Ted said. "I guess I'll go to Swandyke and ask him."

"No," Aunt Alice said. "No, you won't ask him. I know Gus, and he'll put conditions on it, just like he did about Lucy going to college. You two just tell him you're getting married, so that there'll be nothing he can do about it."

Lucy admitted her aunt was right. So not until the day she stepped off the train in Swandyke at the end of the school year, Ted behind her, did the family have the least knowing of her plans. It was a Sunday, a day off for both Gus and Dolly, and the entire family had gathered at the depot to meet the train. Lucy hugged her mother and Dolly and the little ones, then shook hands with her father, all before anyone became aware that Ted was waiting beside her. They looked him over, thinking perhaps that Lucy had met him on the train. But before they could wonder about it, Lucy blurted out, "This is Ted Turpin. Ted's my fiancé."

"He's what?" Dolly asked, not understanding the word.

"My fiancé. That means we're engaged."

"Oh," Margaret, Lucy's mother, said. "Oh."

"You mean you're getting married?" Dolly's eyes were wide with surprise, her mouth open a little. "Oh, Lucia!" She grabbed her sister's wrist and squeezed it so tightly that Lucy thought the blood would stop going into her hand. Then Dolly turned to Ted. "Mr. Turpin, you are the luckiest man ever I met."

"I am that." Ted grinned, but he looked at Gus when he said it.

Gus was frowning. "I guess I'll say who my daughter can marry."

"I guess you won't," Lucy told him, and Gus's face turned red.

Father and daughter stared at each other, neither turning away until Doll said, "Mama has a fine dinner all ready, and you can bring Mr. Turpin so's we can all get acquainted."

"I expect we could do that," Gus said, finally turning his head to look at Dolly.

Then while Ted made arrangements to store his trunk at the depot, Dolly whispered to Lucy, "You let me talk to Papa. He'll come around."

"I never promised I wouldn't get married," Lucy said stubbornly.

"I'll tell him that."

As they walked back to the shabby house, Ted and Lucy lagging a little behind, Lucy whispered, "Dolly will talk to Papa. She has a way with him. She's the sweetest of us."

"Is she?" Ted replied. "Well, you're the prettiest."

Lucy stayed in Swandyke for only a few days, since she had to return to her job at the drugstore. By the time she left, however, Gus had accepted Ted. Dolly and Margaret had convinced him that Lucy would keep her word about supporting the family. Ted would live in a boardinghouse operated by the dredge company while he looked for a little house. Lucy saw him whenever he was sent to Denver on some errand. He'd go into the drugstore and surprise her, or she'd return home from school or work and find him sitting in the front room with her aunt, who would excuse herself, saying she had forgotten about some urgent business that required her attention.

They wrote to each other, of course, and Lucy revealed herself in letters as she had not done in conversation, quoting bits of poetry and writing her innermost thoughts. Once, she wrote that she would like the bedroom of their house painted blue "for the sky and your eyes," and he wrote back that he had already found a house and would paint every room in it blue.

She had been shy about discussing children with him

but felt no such hesitation in her letters, saying she hoped they had two, a boy and a girl. "I want to name them Jack and Helen—Jack because I like it, and Helen for my sister. That's Dolly's real name," she wrote.

Ted responded, "Jack's a favorite of mine, too. And your sister's a crackerjack."

The time passed quickly, and now Lucy did not mind that her school years were coming to an end, because she had a future ahead of her. When a neighbor of her aunt's moved away, Lucy bought the woman's pots and pans and a set of dishes, all for two dollars, and shipped them to Ted for the house. Aunt Alice helped her hem sheets and tablecloths, and when Ted gave the measurements of the windows, the two women made curtains. Ted reported that he had hung them and they looked splendid.

At first, the two engaged people wrote each other every week, but after a while, Ted's letters came less often, because he spent long hours learning about gold dredging, Lucy knew. Besides, what was there to write about in Swandyke? Dolly and Margaret filled her in on what was happening with the family. The months passed. Lucy had hoped to go home at Christmas, but two employees quit at the drugstore, and the owner had been so kind to her that Lucy stayed on during the holidays.

Late in January, on a day when the cold and wind in Denver were as bad as in Swandyke, Lucy got home late. The streetcar had been caught in a snowdrift, and she had

had to walk a mile. As she turned in at the walk, she saw fresh footprints, a man's. Whoever it was had just arrived, and Lucy thought it must be Ted. She went inside, and as she slipped off her coat in the hall, she heard her aunt ask, "So that's for what intent you have come here."

"Hell done broke loose." The voice was not Ted's but her father's, Lucy realized. He had not been to Denver since the day more than three years earlier when he had brought her down from Swandyke to start college.

"Papa!" Lucy said, dropping her coat on the floor on her way into the front room. "What's happened?" Someone in the family must be sick—awful sick, if her father had come to tell her about it. Or maybe one of them had died. Not Dolly, she prayed. Then she thought of Ted and put her hand to her mouth. The dredge boat was a brutal place to work. Men got mangled in the machinery or fell into the water and drowned, although by now, the Swan ought to have been frozen and the boat shut down. For a second, she wondered if Ted had written her about that, but then she realized she hadn't had a letter for a long time.

Gus turned and stared at his daughter. He worked his teeth on his lip, agitated, then blurted out, "The ways of a woman and the ways of a snake are deeper than the sea. She captivated him."

"What are you talking about?" Lucy asked. She could not imagine.

"I'll say it slow so's you can catch it," he said, not talking

42

slow, but loud. "They had a rambling time, him and she. I'm not easy in the heart about it. But like I say, she captivated him, primping like she did, stripping her shoulders and baring her legs so she could catch him. I told her he was yours, but did she mind? She was my favorite, but she shamed me." He shook his head and slumped down into a chair.

Lucy stared at him, shaking her head a little as if to shake away the thought that had come to her. The old woman, standing, put her arm around the girl. "Tell it to her, Gus," she said.

But Gus was still caught up in fury and shook his head. So Aunt Alice said, "Your father came here to tell you that Ted and Dolly went over to Middle Swan and got married day before yesterday. Dolly's his lawful wife now." The old woman gripped the girl, propelling her to the sofa.

Lucy would have fallen if her aunt had not held her, and she let herself be dragged. She was numb, all the way down to her feet, and fell against the cushions. "No," she whispered as if talking to herself. "He said I was the pretty one."

"She said love cried out to them," Gus said. "I believe he smothered her down. Dolly wouldn't have gone after him."

"Well, it's disgraceful," Aunt Alice said. "I won't give them even a good wish."

Lucy's mind began to work a little, not much, but enough to know a thing. "No, it was Dolly," Lucy said. "It wasn't Ted; it was Dolly."

Gus ranted, and her aunt clucked, but Lucy paid no

attention to them. She lay against the sofa for an hour while they talked in tones that were both angry and soothing. She did not say a word, but only hugged herself to keep from freezing. She was as cold as if she were outside in the blizzard. After a while, the aunt took a crocheted afghan from the back of a chair and put it over Lucy's knees, but it fell off, and Lucy left it on the floor. Then she stood up, and the two older people stopped talking, and the room was quiet. The girl announced she was going to bed.

"Ain't you going to have supper?" her father asked. Nothing had ever upset him enough to miss a meal.

Lucy did not answer, only went into her room and closed the door, then lay down on the bed with her clothes on. After a time, her aunt came in with a tray containing Lucy's dinner, setting it on the table beside the bed. And later, she came back and removed the untouched tray and spread a blanket over Lucy. The girl didn't respond, only stared at the ceiling.

The house grew quiet, and Lucy lay there, listening to the wind batter the walls and send cold seeping through the boards, because the little cottage was poorly built. But the cold did not numb her thoughts. She did not sleep, and when morning came and she heard the sounds of her father and aunt in the kitchen, she threw aside the blanket and went out to face them.

"I've thought about it," she announced. "I'll have my teaching certificate in May, and I'll get a job here in Denver and live with you, Aunt Alice, if you'll let me. I will pay you room and board, and I'll send Papa half of my paycheck each month."

"Of course you can live with me," the aunt said quickly. "It's the best plan all around. Isn't it, Gus?"

Lucy's father sat gobbling his food, reminding Lucy of how the ducks in Washington Park had snatched up the stale buns that she and Ted had thrown to them, and she felt a stab of pain as she realized how many times each day something would remind her of Ted.

Gus stopped eating, his fork over his plate, and told Aunt Alice, "Lucy's promised to go back to Swandyke. It was our agreement if she went to college."

"God my deliverer, Gus! You can't expect her to go back. Not now," the aunt said.

"A promise's a promise."

Lucy gasped. "How could I face them? How could I face anybody?"

Gus took a bite of his eggs. He must have two or three scrambled on his plate, Lucy thought. She and Aunt Alice were frugal and ate eggs only on Sunday. "You made the promise to me. It's not my fault what's happened. It taken place without my knowing."

"But I couldn't go back," Lucy said.

Gus shrugged and repeated, "It ain't my fault."

"No, Papa, please," Lucy begged.

"The family needs your help more than ever, now that

Doll's wages'll go to her husband. I never made her promise nothing. I can't spare you, too."

"Well, you'll have to spare her," Aunt Alice said. "You're asking her to let the devil take a mortgage on her. What does Margaret say about it?"

"Oh, she don't hold with me. She thinks I ought to let the girl go, but she's not the one Lucy's made the promise to." He paused to swallow his food. "You won't go back on your word will you, Lucy?"

The two older people looked at the girl, who thought for a long time and finally assented, for giving your word was a solemn commitment.

After breakfast, the women walked Gus to the trolley, and when it pulled away, Aunt Alice said, "At least he came to tell you. You have to give him that. He didn't write. He took two days off work to tell you in person. That has to mean something." She paused and added, "Or maybe Margaret made him do it. She couldn't come herself, what with all the children to look after, and she didn't want to tell you in a letter. So maybe she made him come. Whatever it was, he did come."

Lucy nodded, but in her heart, she knew her father had not made the trip to Denver because he was sensitive of her feelings. No, he'd come to bully her into returning to Swandyke.

· · ·

Lucy had a few suitors after she returned to Swandyke, but none to compare with Ted Turpin. She eventually married Henry Bibb, the second-level boss at the Fourth of July Mine, a man who'd once courted Dolly. He was a little older, a good person, clean in his ways, solid, as Dolly had once said about him. He had had an education, and he loved Lucy. And what did it matter if she did not care as much for him as he did her? She was not happy, but neither was she caught up in sadness. When the children came— Lucy quit her job, no longer earning a paycheck to turn over to her father—she had a good life, as good as could be expected in Swandyke, at any rate, and in time, she could go for a day without thinking about Ted. She missed him dreadfully at first, but later it was Dolly she missed, because the two never spoke now except when it couldn't be helped. And when that happened or when it was necessary to refer to her sister, Lucy called her Helen—Dolly's real name.

But Lucy's marriage came later, after she had been back in Swandyke for a while. Lucy went home the day after she graduated from college, to a job in the office of the Fourth of July Mine. She had planned to teach, but her father wanted her at the mine, and it didn't seem to matter what job she took. Ted and Dolly had not been at the depot with the family to meet her, and she did not see them for several days. Dolly came by the house one evening after supper to loan their mother a pan—her pan, Lucy thought, one that she had bought from her aunt's neighbor, but what use did she have for it now? Lucy went outside and sat on a rock to keep from facing her sister. After a time, Dolly came out and called softly in the dark, "Lucia?"

Lucy didn't reply, but Dolly found her and sat down beside her. Lucy moved as far away from her sister as she could and turned to look at the mountains.

"I'm sorry, Lucia. I love him, honest to God I do. I didn't marry him just to have a husband. I know you think I did, because I was desperate. But I love him. I wish you'd understand." When Lucy didn't reply, Dolly continued. "There wasn't anybody else. There wasn't going to be. You have your education, but I wasn't going to have anything."

Lucy stood and walked a little ways off, glad that in the darkness Dolly couldn't see the tears running down her cheeks. "Couldn't we be friends? I miss you so much," Dolly pleaded.

Lucy's throat closed up. How could she be friends with the woman who had robbed her of her happiness? She didn't reply, and Dolly went home. Later that year, Dolly's first child was born, a boy, whom they named Jack. Dolly told her mother that Ted had picked the name.

Ted never sought out Lucy, and they never said more than hello if they passed on the street or happened to meet each other when Ted and Dolly visited the family. It was nearly two years before they had a real conversation. Lucy

avoided the street where Ted and Dolly lived, but that particular evening, she wasn't thinking and found herself in
front of the little house Ted had rented after he moved to
Swandyke, the house he had meant for her. The walls of the
front room were painted blue, Lucy noticed as she looked
through the curtains—curtains that she had made.

She hurried on, but not soon enough, because Ted came
out of the house then. She shrank back into the trees, but he
spotted her and said, "Luce?"

She didn't answer, but neither could she run. She was
rooted to the spot and let him come up to her. He smelled of
whiskey, and Lucy knew he drank too much, knew because
Dolly had complained to their mother about it. "It's you. I
knew it was," Ted said. He didn't sound drunk, only sad.

He took her hands, but Lucy pulled them away. "How
dare you!" she said.

"Do you hate me?"

"I don't know," Lucy told him.

"I did a terrible thing, and I'm paying for it. I knew six
months after we were married that it was a mistake. I don't
know why I did it. We're both unhappy, Dolly and me. We
never talk, not the way you and I did. I might as well talk to
a turnip."

"I don't want to hear it." Lucy turned to go.

"Wait. I wronged you. I'm sorry."

"Sorry for yourself, or sorry for me—and Dolly?"

"Sorry for all of us. Sorry for the mess I made. If I could go back—"

"Well, you can't. You did this to us, and now you have to live it. We all do." She said it mean and ugly, and it broke her heart to talk to him like that.

"Could I see you sometime, maybe just to talk?"

"No."

Ted bowed his head, wounded. Then he said softly, "I still love you."

Lucy turned abruptly, running a little until she was away from the house. She did not turn back to see that Ted watched her, although she knew he did. He loves me yet, she thought, but that did not make her happy, only bitter, for what good did it do either one of them, or Dolly, either?

It was not long after that that Lucy married Henry Bibb, married him in part because what else was there for her in Swandyke? They had two children. Rosemary, seven, was a sweet girl, blond, like Dolly, and Charlie, eight, was like his father—serious, thin-haired, and straddly-legged, but as smart as Lucy. The children brought joy, but somewhere in her heart, Lucy still carried the ache that had come on her the night she learned that Dolly and Ted were married.

Dolly had three children. Besides Jack, who was ten and looked mostly like Gus, there were Carrie, nine, a pretty child, thin and lanky, like Ted, and Lucia, only six.

As she stood at the kitchen sink washing dishes and listening for the school bell that fateful day of April 20, Lucy thought once again about Dolly's sad attempt to win her over by giving her daughter Lucy's pet name. She thought it something of an irony that her daughter, Rosemary, looked like Dolly, while Dolly's daughter Lucia was the spit of Lucy.

CHAPTER THREE

On his eighth birthday, Joe Cobb saw them lynch the schoolteacher. That was in Alabama, in 1896, more than thirty years after the end of the war that had freed the slaves, and Joe knew then that Negroes would never be free, that the world would always be a brutal place for black people.

The men forced the children to watch. Without warning, they entered the tobacco barn that served as a schoolhouse and grabbed the teacher, blocking the door so the students could not run away. The men marched the children outside, behind the teacher, and the little ones stood silently, twitching, shifting from one foot to the other as the men put the noose around the teacher's neck. Joe looked away. It didn't seem fitting to watch, but a man prodded him, and he turned his head back. Still, he did not look directly at the teacher, but made his eyes blur and looked over the condemned man's head.

"You little *negras* pay attention," one of the white men said, pronouncing *Negro* in the southern way, with as much loathing as if he had used the other word, the uglier one. The men hadn't bothered to put white hoods over their heads, so the students were aware of who they were. But it hadn't been necessary for them to disguise themselves, because the men knew the children would never tell. Their parents wouldn't ask, and the children wouldn't say. And who would they tell if they did? One of the six men was the sheriff. Another owned the sawmill that employed several of the students' fathers, and a third ran the store where the colored families shopped. That one was also the town mayor. The other members of the mob were farmers, mean men who would as soon chop off the foot of a Negro child who failed to step off the sidewalk while they passed as they would squash a toad that got in their way. Lynching a Negro in that small Southern town was sport, and the men wouldn't be punished even if their names were printed in the newspaper. There was one law for white people and "Negro law" for black ones.

The teacher pleaded, promised he'd leave the small backwoods town and return north and never come back. He asked what he'd done wrong and apologized for it, even though he didn't understand how seriously he had offended them. Joe reached out a hand as if to help his teacher, then stopped, for what could one little black boy do? He would likely get a whipping for making that small gesture.

"He teached them *Latin*," one of the farmers said with disgust.

Then Joe understood what had set off the men. And he understood, too, that he and his friend Little Willie were responsible. They had talked Latin in the store, feeling smug, a little proud of themselves, although it was only three words, and enraging the owner, the mayor. "What you little niggers think you're doing sassing me?" He brought a broom handle down hard on Joe's head, and the two boys ran out into the dusty street. But they'd giggled after they got away. Imagine, they told each other, they knew something a white man didn't.

Joe's hands began to shake, and he put them into his pockets, feeling the mouth harp he had received just that morning for his birthday. He did not have to be a man grown to understand how much the white people hated the schoolteacher. He understood now, although his mother, Ada, had warned him, told him what the whites said.

The colored people had been delighted when the teacher showed up, a man who had been to college and whose father was a doctor. But the whites hadn't liked it. "You take your boy out of school, Ada, before he forgets who he is," said the white woman who employed Joe's mother to sweep and clean, wash and iron, and cook for a dollar a week.

"The Negroes were put on this earth to be of the servant class, and it's not right, them learning to talk and think like white people. It unfits them. You elevate a darky, and next thing your young bucks'll think they're as good as we are, and we can't have that. It will upset the natural order of things."

When Joe overheard his mother tell his father of the conversation, he knew she'd said "Yes'm" to the woman and maybe repeated it, "Yes'm."

"Now, Ada, if you could read and write, you wouldn't be content to work for me," the woman had continued. "Then where'd you and me be?"

"Yes'm."

He'd heard other whites in town put it less delicately. "It's as foolish to teach a *negra* to read as to learn a monkey to shoot a gun," a farmer had said, learning against the feed store, looking at the boy and laughing.

"You can't teach 'em not to be black," his friend had replied. Even at that age, Joe knew that most whites believed learning was the ruination of a good Negro and that an educated darky was more likely to be discontented and lust after white women.

There'd been incidents in town before the lynching, so the teacher should have known better. Someone had thrown a rock through the schoolhouse window, and the teacher himself had been splattered with mud and told he was to wear overalls like any other black man. Suits were for white men. They had broken the teacher's spectacles, saying he wouldn't need them if he kept his eyes to the ground. Then two white boys had grabbed the teacher's books and tossed them into a hog pen.

The treatment brought a bad feeling to the black people who had been so hopeful when the teacher arrived from the North, full of stories about how Negroes had been kings in the Bible and how the black race had produced men like Frederick Douglass and Booker T. Washington, who were superior to most white men. The teacher dressed and spoke like a white man. He walked like one, too, his head high, his step sure, instead of using the shuffling gait of slavery days. The parents warned him to be deferential to whites, to tug at his cap when he passed one and not to look him in the eye. They told him there might be trouble with that Latin motto he gave the school. The students were proud of it, but the older folks, they knew it meant trouble.

But the teacher had laughed when they warned him, replying there were worse things than the taunts of rednecks. He'd said the word out loud, and the black people had cringed, warning him to watch his tongue, because a white man might overhear him. A black man could be castrated for less.

The teacher hadn't changed his ways, and finally, when the two boys said the school's Latin motto that day in the dark store that smelled of oiled floorboards and rotted wood, molasses and soft moldy bread, repeated the words, saying loudly that they were in Latin, the storekeeper said he'd had enough. He went to the saloon and rounded up the three farmers, drunk as they were, and the sheriff, who was a bully, and the mill owner, who'd said often enough that he was tired himself of the way black workers thought they should get as much for a day's work as a white man.

The men went to the school and grabbed the teacher, who must have thought he was in for a flogging, because he yelled to the children not to be afraid. And the men did indeed whip the teacher, whipped him until the blood ran down his legs. But then they got out the noose, and at last the teacher seemed to understand that he would be hanged. He reared and pitched and looked mortal afraid, and his eyes bugged out like the white people in blackface at the minstrel shows.

The men strung him up. It wasn't an execution where the condemned man had a final word, but just a sloppy lynching where the teacher mumbled the words of the Lord's Prayer before he flopped around at the end of the rope like a catfish out of water. It took a while before he stopped moving, because the fall didn't break his neck, and he'd had to strangle himself to death. Then the body turned round and round because of a twist in the rope. Joe put his hand in front of his mouth, hoping he wouldn't throw up. He looked down and saw that Little Willie had wet his pants. A girl was sniveling, another shaking so hard that Joe thought she might tip over. He could smell the fear among the children.

When the teacher at last was still, his head over to one side, the men, silent now, the bravado gone, got on their horses. "Now, don't you little *negras* never forget this," one of them said to the children. As if we ever would, Joe thought.

The students were afraid to cut down the teacher, afraid to touch him, and they ran home and told their parents what had happened, although they didn't tell the names of the lynch mob. And when dark came, the fathers took down the dead man and buried him deep in the woods. They knew better than to mark the grave. They searched the teacher's room and found an address, and a woman who could write penned a note to his family: "Your son don get cilled, and we bureed him. Hes a good man. We sory." She took the letter to the post office and purchased a stamp. But the postmaster must have wondered why a colored woman was sending a letter to Boston, because he opened it, read it, then threw it away. The mothers said weren't they lucky that the schoolhouse hadn't been burned down.

The school board didn't shut down the Negro school, as many expected. Instead, the school board found another teacher, a local girl who hadn't gone further than the third grade and who understood what was expected of her. She resumed classes in the tobacco barn, a drafty building with no stove and cracks between the boards big enough to let a cat through. But Joe never went back, because there was nothing the young girl could teach him.

What Joe learned that terrible day the teacher was murdered was not hatred as much as sadness and a knowing of the world, and, of course, that was exactly what the white men had intended. Joe was a smart boy, and when he first met the teacher, he'd decided he wanted to learn everything he could so that he, too, could be a Negro who stood tall with white men. He was embarrassed at the way his father, Riley Cobb, bowed to the whites, docile, obedient, laughing when they made fun of him, never protesting when he was shortchanged at the mercantile. Joe could count, and once he'd spoken up when the change came back two pennies short. His father had smacked him and said, "Shut your mouth, you little fool."

"But Pappy—" the boy said after they left.

"Don't you never tell a white man he's wrong, boy, if you want to live. That's the way of it."

School had been different. The teacher told them they were as good as anybody, and that they could own stores and farms just like white men. All they needed was an education. So Joe sat up straight and listened.

The lynching was the end of Joe's boyhood. He no longer walked along the dusty roads, barefoot as a duck, with his fishing pole over his shoulder. Nor did he play baseball with a broomstick and the ball his mother had made from rags. With no school to attend, Joe was sent to the fields to help his father, who was a share-tenant on Hogpen Lane. "He's old enough to work," said the landowner, who claimed part of the crop Riley made and wanted all the field hands his black families could produce. So now the boy rose before daylight and worked until dark.

It was not an altogether unhappy time. Joe loved the smell of the earth, freshly turned, and the touch of the dew on his feet. There was pleasure in seeing the tips of the corn poke up from the earth and the white cotton peek from the boll. Riley sang songs from slavery days that had been passed down to him from his own father, and as there were no white men to oversee them, the father straightened his shoulders and lifted his head as he stood in the shade of a tree, explaining the workings of nature to the boy. Sometimes, when the sun beat down hot enough to melt a person's eyeballs, his father waved Joe off, telling him to put down his hoe and take off his overalls and swim in the pond. Riley Cobb was a kind man who alternated between beating blackness into his son to teach him how to survive and wanting the boy to have a little time of joy before he understood what a burden it was to be a black man at the turn of the century, some thirty years after emancipation.

Following the harvest, when the cold weather came and there was no work in the fields, the family—there were also a mother and four younger children—sat in front of a fire in the former slave cabin where they lived and listened to the grandpappy, an old, twisted, muscled man, tell about the bitterness of slavery days. "They'd treat you like you was no more than mules," he said. "They'd whip you, break your jawbone, and they'd've cut off your head for a soup bowl, only you was worth money to 'em. You think you have it poorly, Joe, but you don't know what hard times is." He'd sink into his memories, then say, "Freedom cried out to us. We thought if we was just free . . ." And then he'd shake his head and add, "I wish I had went before I had so much to grieve over."

"We thought if we just had education," Joe's mother would say, letting the thought drop. Then she would add, "Well, trust in God and hoe your row, and better times will come."

Joe liked it better when his grandpappy told him stories about Br'er Rabbit and Br'er Fox and would laugh and say, "White man's took everything else away from us, but we keeps our humor." The stories were about how the weaker animals always got the better of the stronger ones. Joe knew without having to be told that the weaker animals were the colored people, and he gloried in their cunning and trickery. As he weeded under the hot sun, the sweat pouring off his back, he pretended he was Br'er Rabbit, getting a white boy to wield the hoe in his place. And when he watched his mother plod off to work, a laundry basket in her arms, he thought of what it would be like if the old white lady washed *their* clothes.

But at the same time that he dreamed of revenge for the schoolteacher's death and the daily acts of humiliation that he and other colored people faced, Joe learned to survive, and that meant acting the way the white people expected him to—good-natured, stupid, lazy. He let the white men make fun of him just as his father did, seething inside but not showing it. Only rarely did he flare up, and then it was in such a way that the white man did not fully understand that he had been bested. When the man who owned the land Joe and his father worked complained about the responsibilities of being a landowner and remarked, "You have an easier time of it than I do," Joe replied, "Yessir, and so do your hogs."

Joe turned into a handsome young man, certainly by white standards—broad-shouldered, well muscled, light-skinned, with a straight nose and hair that curled instead of kinked. That was not altogether a blessing, because white women glanced at him with approval, which infuriated their men. Joe knew he should never be alone with a white woman, never look her in the eye when he passed one on the street, never brush against her, or he'd fare no better than the schoolteacher. So he shuffled off the sidewalk into the street if he saw one coming. And if she called to him, "Boy, do you want to earn a nickel to chop my wood?" he'd look foolish and shake his head, and she would make a re-mark on the shiftlessness of colored people.

Not all white folks were like that, Joe learned. Some were kind, and a few even respected the Negroes. The white minister at the Friendship Church buried Negroes at the colored cemetery, asking God to make their lives easier in heaven. One of the teachers at the white school helped the colored teacher plan lessons. And several white women in town put together food baskets, which they took to the shacks where colored people were stove up. Sometimes they brought medicine, too, and sat awhile with the sick person to let the family rest. And they weren't uppity about it, but were kind instead. "You mustn't believe we're all like the sheriff and the mayor, Joe," one of them told him. Joe knew that, but the trick was you didn't know which ones you could trust, so you didn't trust any of them.

When he was sixteen, Joe was arrested for fighting a white boy, and he was sentenced to prison. The fight wasn't his fault. Joe had been carrying the laundry basket for his mother when the white boy ordered him to put it down. Joe did as he was told, hoping that would be the end of it. But the boy upended the basket, kicking the clothes into the dirt and stomping on them.

Joe's mother begged the white boy to stop, for she would have to wash the clothes again, and her fingers were so crippled from rheumatism that she could barely rub the cloth on the scrub board. Joe tried to stop the boy by pushing him away, but the fellow turned and slugged Joe, hit him twice—left, right—causing a hurting in Joe's stomach.

Joe let the anger that had built up in his young life take over then, and he kicked the boy. Joe might have gone to prison for five years, maybe ten, because white people would not abide a black boy who hurt a white one. But as it turned out, Joe's mother's employer was the wife of the mill owner, who had just fired the boy for stealing. So Joe was sentenced to only two years in prison. Of course, the white boy was not punished. It was Negro law.

Instead of going to prison, however, Joe and half a dozen other convicts were "sold" to a turpentine operator, the rights to their labor traded by prison officials for a few dollars. They were shipped off to a camp deep in the piney woods. Because he was sizable, Joe was assigned a job as a woodcutter, and he was worked like a mule, because what did the operator care if one black convict was broken? It wasn't like slavery days, when a black man had some worth. If Joe was worked to death, he'd be easy enough to replace.

The men were roused before sunup and taken to the field in chains, where they worked until it was too dark for the guards to see to shoot them. Slackers were beaten. Joe was cautious, not only at work but in the camp, a dark and dangerous place where the prisoners mixed with the regular turpentine workers. The first month he was there, Joe glanced at a black woman who was swaying near a fire, a sweet singer whose voice was smooth and silky and ripped through his heart, making him so lonely, he wanted to hug himself like a baby. He took a step toward the fire and found a knife at his throat. "You look at my woman again, and you don't know what you will come to before you die," said a voice that was low and ragged in his ear.

Joe put out his hands and said, "Easy," and the man drew back the knife, but not before he scratched it across Joe's throat, drawing a line of blood as fine as a thread. "I just got here. I mean no trouble," Joe told him.

"Stay away from the women," the man warned. Joe recognized him as one of the regular turpentine workers. "There's girls enough from the juke house for you."

"I got no money. I came from the prison."

The man relaxed a little. "Then you got to stay out of trouble." He stepped back and looked at Joe. "You work hard, and you keep away from Sykes over there, and when you can't, you mind your back. He is treacherous." He pointed with his knife at a fat white man with eyes like a pig. "He'd rather whip a man to death than eat breakfast. And if you run away, you better hope you make it, 'cause you won't be worth nothing if they bring you back."

Joe thanked the man and went to sit with the other new turpentiners who had come from the prison. One of them was Little Willie, who had stood next to Joe when the schoolteacher was lynched. Little Willie, a runt of a man, had been sentenced to five years of hard labor for killing a dog that was the property of a wealthy farmer. The farmer sicked the dog on Little Willie every time he passed. "And one day, I fixed up not to take it again, and I kicked that dog till I broke his neck," Little Willie told Joe.

As the two men sat near the fire, shivering, because it was cold in the woods and neither had a coat or a blanket, Little Willie said he'd rather die than spend his sentence in the turpentine camp.

"You've got to bear it," Joe told him.

"I can't suck sorrow for five years. Maybe I'll run away."

Joe shook his head. "Where'd you go? They've got dogs to track you down. You'll never make it, never under God's kingdom."

"I'll just go where they can't ever find me."

Joe looked out for Little Willie, because the small man was treated mean, but there wasn't much Joe could do. Oh, he might threaten another black turpentiner for bothering Little Willie, but he couldn't do anything when the bully was a white man. One guard dropped an ax on Little Willie's foot and nearly cut off his toes. Another knocked his tin plate of food to the ground. His shoes were stolen. He was whipped for not working hard enough. Little Willie turned morose, and there was a gleam of madness in his eyes, so Joe wasn't surprised when one morning the man wasn't there.

Guards went after him with dogs, and in less than a day, he was brought back, beaten and trussed up like a pig, thrown onto the ground as a lesson to the other prisoners. The white men joyed in the prisoners' fear.

After the others turned away from Little Willie, Joe crept up to him and held him while he sipped a cup of water. "There wasn't anyplace to go," the man said through broken teeth.

The next day when the turpentiners returned from work, Little Willie was gone, and one of the men who had been there a long time told Joe that most likely Little Willie had been thrown into a swamp to drown, if he wasn't dead already. "You dare not talk about it," he said.

Those two years in the turpentine camp were a plague of misery for Joe, but he lived through them, which was something to be grateful for, since many of the prisoners didn't make it. They were killed in fights with the other turpentiners, knifed by the women, beaten to death by the guards, or died from the poor food and brutal working conditions. Joe had a deep scar across his cheek, where a guard had cut him after Joe refused to kneel down for a whipping. "I only get on my knees to pray," he'd said, and the guard went after him with both the knife and a whip. The black man learned meekness from that encounter, and during the rest of his stay at the camp, he was whipped no more than the other prisoners.

When he was released, Joe returned to his parents' farm, a wiser young man now, but one devoid of hope for his future. He figured he wasn't going to have anything, so nothing could hurt him. But Joe was wrong. He knew it when he met Orange, a good-sized gal of seventeen with smooth skin and fancy hair—red hair. Joe knew the first time he saw her at the church that he had to have her and that in the end he'd be hurt in some way.

Orange was a quiet woman, serious, with a fierce desire to learn, and she reawakened that same yearning in Joe. Teaching him appealed to her, and when Joe called on Orange, the two sat outside on a log with a ragged primer she'd picked up somewhere, and she helped him with the words. She opened an arithmetic book, and discovered that Joe could figure. Maybe that was why he was good with mechanical things. There wasn't anything he couldn't fix, and Orange encouraged him to get a job working with the blacksmith. But Joe wouldn't do it. He wanted to be as far away as possible from white people.

When he was in his early twenties, Joe married Orange, and they set to housekeeping in an old slave cabin on the farm on Hogpen Lane that Joe worked with his father. It was a one-room shack fit up with a door and a single glassless window with a heavy wooden shutter to keep out the cold and rain, but they treasured it up, and for the first time since he was eight years old, Joe knew real happiness. At night, as they looked out a hole in the roof at the stars, Joe satisfied himself with his wife's smoky body, and in the first year of their marriage, Orange gave birth to a little girl. They named her Jane. She was a sweet child, obedient, and pretty, which caused a confusion in Joe's breast. He was proud of his daughter's fine looks, but he knew they would be a burden to her when she was older and white boys came sniffing around. He would not borrow trouble, however, not in the early years of his child's life. So he gloried in the little girl. And when Orange became pregnant again when Jane was five, Joe looked at his wife's protruding belly with gladness.

Orange had given birth the first time with so little trouble that Joe did not worry. Her labor had lasted only an hour or two, barely enough time for him to fetch his mother, who had grannied many of the birthings in the neighborhood. So when Orange went into labor with their second child late one afternoon, Joe sent Jane across the fields to fetch Ada, instead of going himself. He feared the baby might come before his mother arrived and he'd be needed.

Orange was still in labor when Jane returned with her grandmother, Ada, Joe's father coming behind them. Ada went into the house while Joe sat in the shade with his father, thinking he ought to have a nice bottle of whiskey to celebrate after the baby was born. It would be good to share the bottle with the men who'd stop by, and to brag a little about the fine baby boy he'd produced—for it would be a son this time. Or so he hoped, because he didn't believe he could love another little girl as fiercely as he did Jane. The two men sat on a bench that Joe had fashioned from a log and talked about crops and weather, stopping when they heard Orange's cries. Joe wrung his hands at each moan, the sweat dripping down his face. "Don't worry," his father

told him. That was the way it was with women in childbirth, paying for Eve's sin, as they must. Every so often, Joe
went to the door and looked in at his wife writhing on the
bed, but then his mother would wave him away.

After several hours, when the baby did not come, Ada
went outside and said she didn't like the looks of things and
asked Joe to go after an old lady down the road, the oldest
liver in the area, who'd seen more childbirth than anyone.

Joe fetched her, and the two women worked with Orange through the night. From time to time, one of the old
women came out of the shack and asked Joe to go to the
creek for water. Or she'd rest a minute on the bench in
the cool night air, her head against the rough boards of the
cabin. When Joe asked to see Orange, he was told to stay
away, although the old granny woman cackled once and
said, "Might be a good idea you see the hurting you brought
on your woman by pleasuring yourself."

On the following morning, Ada leaned against the outside cabin wall, her head resting in her hand. "She's got a
hard time of it. The baby's turned," the woman explained.
"It's tearing up her insides, and she might not bear again.
Some women are not meant to have but so many babies."

"I don't care about babies. You save Orange," Joe told his
mother, who nodded. She went back inside, and Orange
cried out. But the cries grew softer, weaker during the day,
and on toward evening, Joe's mother told him she didn't
expect Orange would live through the night. "We can't get

the baby out, and she's weak as a rag doll. You best prepare yourself, Joe."

"You mean she'll die?" Joe himself felt weak. "Can't you do something?"

"I can't, but the white doctor might. You go fetch him, Joe, ask him would he come, please."

"He'll come. I'll make him come," Joe said. He knew where the doctor lived—not far, maybe two miles—and he ran all the way. The doctor was sitting on his front porch with his wife, and Joe thought it was a good sign that the man was at home instead of out tending to some white patient. He ran onto the porch and tugged at his cap. "Please, sir, my wife—"

"What you doing on this porch, boy? Don't you know you're supposed to go to the back door?" the woman said.

"But I saw the doctor—"

The woman pointed to the back of the house. "You march right on over there."

"Yes'm." Joe turned, his shoulders slumped, and hurried to the kitchen door and knocked.

The woman ignored him as she remained in her rocker, saying something to her husband. After a few minutes, the two of them stood up and went inside, and finally she answered his knock at the back screen door.

"What do you want?" she asked Joe.

"Please, ma'am, my wife's in labor, and the baby's turned

and won't come out. Could the doctor come and see her? Please."

"The doctor's just sitting down to dinner now."

"Yes, ma'am. But my wife's about to die. She can't hold out much longer."

"Dinner will get cold." The woman reached up and hooked the screen, then called, "Louis, this darky says his wife's in labor. You want to tend her?"

"Oh, those people don't have much trouble with it. I'll have my supper first."

Joe stood on the back stoop, smashing the fist of one hand into the palm of the other in anger. He watched while the woman dished up the supper and carried it into the dining room. Then the couple bowed their heads and gave thanks. After a while, the woman came back with the plates and filled them again. When she returned with the empty dishes, she took down two cups and saucers; then, remembering Joe, she said, "He says he'll be along directly, soon as he has his coffee and his cigarette."

Joe seethed. He thought of smashing through the screen and dragging the man out to his buggy. His pride told him to leave, but he couldn't do that when Orange needed the doctor. So he waited, hating the man inside, who held Orange's life in his hands. At last, the doctor came into the kitchen, unlatched the screen, and told Joe to go hitch up his buggy.

When Joe came out of the barn, leading the horse, because the doctor had not invited him to sit in the buggy and Joe thought he might have to trot alongside the conveyance on the way back to the farm, the doctor picked up his bag and climbed into the buggy. "Well, get in, boy," he told Joe. "I can't find your wife in the dark." The doctor clucked at the horse, which started up at a slow pace. "I wouldn't worry too much about her. The *negra* women generally get on just fine. Why, back in slavery days, a woman just stooped down in the field and the baby came out. Then she scooped it up and went on hoeing." He chuckled. "I expect by the time we get to your place, it'll all be over." He leaned back and let the horse plod along.

The doctor was right. It was over. Orange lay on the bed, one old woman on each side of her. The granny woman mopped Orange's forehead with a rag dipped in water while Ada prayed. "Well, it can't be all that bad," the doctor said, and took off his coat. But he left his hat on, and Joe forever remembered that. The doctor did not take off his hat for Orange. The doctor's jovial expression turned sour, and he said, "Why didn't you tell me this was serious, boy? Your woman's already dead. I'm past doing anything."

Tears streaming down his face, Joe knelt down on the floor and raised his hands to heaven. "Please, Lord," he begged.

"Even the good God can't do anything," the doctor said, putting his coat back on. He started for the door, then turned to Joe. "I don't suppose you got anything to pay me for my trouble."

Still on his knees, Joe looked up at the white man and asked, "How much?"

"A dollar."

"I'll bring it to you." He laid his head on the bed beside Orange's body and cried. Later that day, they buried Orange and the baby, a girl.

Joe thrashed over in his mind about that doctor, let his feelings fester. He thought not to pay, but then the doctor would tell it about that Joe was shiftless, just like all the other Negroes. So after a few days, Joe took the money out of a can that was buried under the front steps of the house, a dollar in nickels and dimes and pennies, and that evening he walked into town and went to the back door of the doctor's house. The woman was away, and the doctor himself answered, pushing open the screen. "What you want?" The man frowned at Joe.

"I brung your money. You said a dollar."

Then a look of recognition crossed the white man's face. "Oh, it's you. I didn't think you'd pay."

"I said I would."

He held out his hand. "What have you got for me? I charge white folks two dollars but Negroes only one."

Joe looked at the greedy hand and the smug look on the doctor's face, and suddenly he could not control himself. The hurt from Orange's death and the hatred that he had saved up since he was a boy welled up inside of him, and he could not stop it. He threw the money at the doctor, and before the white man could react, Joe said, "I got something else for you." He made a fist with his hand and smashed the doctor in the face, knocking him to the stoop. "You killed my wife, who wasn't any harm to you. You did it as sure as if you'd stuck a knife in her. You had your supper, and you let Orange die. I'll kill you and go to hell and pay for it." Joe stood over the man, ready to hit him again, to stomp on him. But for the first time in his life, he saw that a white man was afraid of him, and that was victory enough.

He took a step backward, and then the awful realization of what he'd done hit him as surely as if the doctor had stood up and punched Joe in the stomach. He'd struck a white man, and he'd threatened to kill him. A lynch mob would come for him, just as it had for the teacher. Joe turned and ran home as fast as he could, dug up the money can again and emptied its contents into his hand. He filled a sack with corn bread and fatback and wrapped it in his second pair of overalls. He shoved his knife and his mouth harp into his pocket. Then after he went to the door to listen for the dogs and horses but heard nothing, he snatched up Jane's extra dress and Orange's old primer and added them to his pack. Not even stopping then to look around for anything he might have missed, he made for his parents' house, where Jane was staying, and snatched up the girl. "We got to run," he told his mother. "I'm a wicked fellow. I hit the doctor. He'll be killing mad."

"I dread to see that, though he deserved it," Ada replied. "Oh yes, that white man deserved a whipping." Then she became aware that Joe had picked up Jane, and she said, "Leave the girl be. You can't do for her. Besides, they catch her with you, they'll string her up, too."

"They'll do that if they find her here."

"We'll hide her."

"I got nothing else. I'd as soon take a beating as leave her behind."

The old woman understood, and instead of protesting further, she asked, "Where are you going?"

Joe shook his head. "As far away as ever I can get."

Ada looked around frantically for something to give her son, but all she saw was the stack of flapjacks she'd fried up for dinner. "Take these," she said, putting them down his shirtfront. Then she watched as her son ran off across the field, the small girl on his shoulders. When she could no longer see him, Ada sank down on her knees and blessed God and said a prayer to keep her kinfolks safe.

Joe did not know that the doctor never told another white person what the black man had done to him. He blamed a screen door for slamming against his face, and because townsfolk knew that the doctor's wife was a big chunk of a woman who was handy with a frying pan, they didn't believe the story, and they snickered behind his back. Nobody even considered that the doctor might have been hit by a colored man.

A week later, the doctor went out to Hogpen Lane, to the cabin where Joe's mother was clearing out the few things that her son had left behind. She looked up with alarm, but with confusion, too, because she did not understand why white men had not come there earlier, hunting Joe.

"Joe's gone. Don't ask me where, for I'm not knowing. He'll nevermore be back," she said.

The doctor nodded, for that was the way when a black man broke Negro law. Only whites got justice. Blacks got lynched. He took off his straw hat and wiped his forehead with the back of his hand. Then he sat down on the dirty bench by the door and twirled the hat in his hands. "When I started my practice, I swore to uphold the Hippocratic oath. I don't expect you know what that is, do you, auntie?"

"No, sir."

"It means I swore to treat people who needed me, no matter who they were or whether they could pay. Somewhere over the road I've traveled, I forgot about that, and I let this woman, this Orange, die."

The old woman waited while the doctor looked out across the fields. The cotton was up and the white just beginning to show. The work would be harder for the family without Joe.

"I guess I'm saying Joe doesn't have to worry on my account. I told it about that I walked into that fool screen door and broke my nose." He stood and brushed off the seat of his pants with his hat, then stepped down off the porch and climbed into his buggy. "Good day to you, auntie."

Jane squalled and squalled as Joe ran through the cold night, and at last he set the girl down. "Baby, your mammy is dead, and we are running away and won't ever come back home," he said, rubbing her bare feet, for the child had never had a pair of shoes in her life, and her feet were cold. "If the white men catch us, we'll get a killing. If you squawk like that, they'll hear us. So you have to be still. Do you understand what I'm saying?"

And Jane did, because while she was only five, she was a black girl, and she'd already known meanness. She nodded, and Joe relaxed a little, thinking it would be good to eat something and then realizing that he'd held the flapjacks in his shirt for hours and hadn't even known it. He shared them with the girl, and they ate the cold dinner and drank water from a stream. Joe fashioned his overalls into a sling and tied the child to his back, and while she slept, he ran on. In the night, he passed one town and then another, and when he crossed the railroad track of a third, he waited just beyond it for a westbound train. He didn't know where he was headed, only that it would be far away. The white men would look for him going north, so he figured he'd head west, and he and Jane could cover more miles in a train than by foot. Besides, he couldn't tote the girl forever. Although Jane was a little spare-made child, Joe's back hurt from the carrying of her.

He sat in the grass as the sky turned gray in the east, hoping a train would come through before the light was up. Jane was awake now, and as they sat in the weeds beside the track, they ate the corn bread Joe had snatched up, although he did not build a fire to fry up the fatback. Just before the sun broke the horizon, they heard a long whistle and felt a rumbling along the rails. They ducked their heads as the engine passed, although an engineer wouldn't think much about a Negro man and child sitting beside the track watching the train. Joe scanned the boxcars of the slow-moving freight train until he saw one with its doors open. Carrying the child, he ran along the train, letting the open car come up beside him. Then he pushed Jane into the boxcar and pulled himself up.

In the dark of the car, Joe thought the two of them were alone. But as his eyes adjusted, he saw two men in the corner of the freight car, one of them holding a bottle, and both of them looking at Jane. They were colored, although Joe knew a black man could be as treacherous as a white one. Jane, frightened, curled up beside her father, and Joe put his left arm around her. Then he reached into his pocket with his right hand and removed the knife with its long, narrow blade, which caught the morning light.

The two men looked at the knife and then at Joe, and Joe

could sense their fear. "You can put it away," one said. "We don't mean no harm."

"Glad of it." Joe scratched his face with the blade, scratched it where the men would see the ugly scar on his cheek. Then he flexed his muscles and put down the knife. At least if the men attacked him, they'd know they were in for a fight.

One of the men offered Joe the bottle, which he'd corked and was ready to roll across the car, but Joe shook his head. In a while, the two men finished the whiskey and tossed the bottle out the car door; then they lay down and began to snore.

"Pappy, I'm not sleepy," Jane whispered. So Joe slept, too, while Jane kept watch.

Later, when they were all awake and Jane slept, the two men told Joe they were running off because they'd robbed a white store. "What'd you do?" one asked.

Joe didn't trust them, so he said, "I've done nothing. My wife let me go, said I wasn't ever going to see my girl again. So I fooled her and snatched up the baby, and now it's my wife that can't see her."

One of the men chuckled and asked, "Where you headed to?"

Joe scratched his head. "Can't say. Maybe New York City."

"Well, you ain't going to get there on this train. It's going all the way to Kansas City."

. . .

So that was where Joe ended up for a time. He found a job there, working in a warehouse, leaving Jane to care for herself in the room in which they lived. But he was restless. He saved up a little money, and after a time, he and Jane caught another freight, letting themselves off at Topeka for a while and then at Hugo, in eastern Colorado, and finally in Denver. Joe liked Denver, was surprised to discover that black people lived in houses there as nice as the ones white people owned back where he came from. But more than that, he was intrigued with the mountains that rose up to the west. He'd never seen mountains before, and the blue range drew him. So one day, he and Jane climbed aboard a train whose last stop was a town on the Swan River—Swandyke.

As soon as his feet touched the ground, Joe knew Swandyke was where he would stay. He couldn't say why, and later it seemed odd to him that he liked it so much, because Swandyke was different from home, and there weren't any farming jobs, just mining. It might have been the town's bustle, compared to the laziness of the South, or the dry air and cold nights, instead of the everlasting heat and damp he was used to. Or perhaps it was the white man on the platform at the depot who had accidentally shoved Jane up against the wall when he turned around with his suitcase. He'd stopped and taken off his hat and said, "I'm sorry, young lady. I hope I didn't hurt you."

Joe stared at the man in astonishment, because he had never heard a white person apologize to a black one. Then he said, "Naw, boss, she's tough."

The man fished in his pocket for a nickel and handed it to Jane and said, "You buy yourself a treat now."

Joe asked the man outright if he knew of any jobs for a black man. "I can't say as how I know of any especially for a Negro, but there's jobs at the Fourth of July Mine for a man who'll work. You go up to the office there and tell them Jim Foote sent you." So later in the day, after he had set up a campsite under a pine tree, he left Jane and went up to the mine.

"You ever worked in a mine before?" the man in charge of employment asked Joe.

"No, sir, but I work hard. I'm stout enough to pull a freight car, and I'm a good hand to fix machinery. Mr. Jim Foote sent me."

The man nodded. "I'll start you up top, unloading ore carts. If you work out, I'll move you into the mill. No drinking on the job. It's a fireable offense."

And so for several weeks, Joe worked in a white man's job, while Jane stayed in the camp by herself, picking wildflowers, watching the squirrels and camp robbers, building villages of pine needles. From time to time, she saw other children, but they were white, and she was afraid of them, so she hid herself.

Toward the end of summer, Joe came back to the

campsite and found a white woman talking to Jane. He looked at her warily, but she didn't seem to notice. "I've come to make a proposition," she said.

Joe narrowed his eyes as he stared at the woman and tugged at his hair, a gesture he'd put aside after he'd started at the mill, because the workers there expected him to act like a man, not a shiftless darky. But this was a white woman, and they were alone, and he wished she'd go away.

She ignored the deferential manner and said, in a businesslike way, "I've noticed you living out here in the meadow. That's fine for summer, but cold weather'll catch us soon, and you might want a warmer place to stay."

"Houses are scarce and hard to find for coloreds. There is plenty of land here, but no houses. I expect we can fix up a tent, stay here till the new year."

"No, you'll be perished by then. By Christmas, the temperature'll get to twenty below, and there'll be snow-drifts as high as a house. A tent's no place for you, and certainly not for your girl." Joe started to object, but the woman went on quickly, "Mittie McCauley's my name. I'm a widow woman, and I need somebody to cut my wood. I own a prospector's cabin. It's not big, just one room, but it's tight, and there's a good fireplace to it. If you'd just help me with my wood, I'd be pleased to let you live there."

"How much wood you want chopped?" Joe asked. White people had tricked him before.

"Oh, I've got enough for this winter, I expect, but I'd like some help for the next winter."

"People here might not like that. A white man here told me, 'Uncle, you stay away from the white ladies.'"

"Nobody speaks for me." The woman cocked her head and added, "I didn't know you had a white nephew."

Joe had to chuckle at that, and then Jane whispered, "I'd like to live in a house, Pappy." So Joe guessed they could take a look.

Mittie led them to the cabin, which she had cleaned just that day, and let them look around at the beds, covered with quilts that the old woman had made—not new quilts, but they were clean—and two straight chairs that stood beside a homemade table. A kerosene lamp with a bright metal reflector hung from the ceiling. Jane looked at her father and smiled, then asked, "Can we stay, Pappy?"

Joe relaxed a little. If the old woman was tricking him, they could always move out. It wouldn't hurt to stay for a little while. "I guess so."

Mittie held out her hand. Joe stared at it a long time. He'd never shaken hands with a white person, especially not a white woman. "It's a deal, then?" the woman asked.

Joe reached out his huge hand and barely touched the woman's. "Deal."

He moved their few things into the cabin that night, and when he returned from work the next day, he found that the woman had stocked it with flour and cornmeal, salt and potatoes and cans of beans. And she'd left a cake on the table, "a welcome-home present," she told him when he returned the plate.

After Joe and Jane were settled, Mittie McCauley showed up at the cabin, asked Jane's age, and was told the girl was seven. "Then she's got to enroll in school," the woman said. "You don't want her to grow up in ignorance."

Joe snorted. "I'd be glad for her to go, but there aren't any colored schools in Swandyke."

"Of course not. You're the only coloreds here. We've got one school for everybody."

"They won't take her."

"They'll take her. You leave it to me."

"She's got nothing to wear. She's got no shoes. Her feet are on the ground."

"I have a plenty of clothes my daughter wore when she was a girl."

"I'm not putting her anyplace white kids can beat her down."

"And you think they'll treat her better if she's ignorant? This is not the South, Mr. Cobb."

"I want to go," Jane said, and so Joe let the old woman dress the girl in a red dress and a blue coat brightened up with brass buttons, and enroll her in the Swandyke school. There were some who did not like it. A few parents went to the school board and said God didn't intend for black and white to mix. But when the principal said the only way he knew to separate them was to build a separate school just for Jane and assign her one of the teachers, they grumbled but said no more.

After he had lived in the cabin a year, Joe went to Mittie with a can of silver dollars and asked if he could buy the house. The old woman looked stern. "I'd have to have a hundred dollars for it," she said. "Not a penny less. Don't think you can cheat me, Mr. Cobb." Joe tried not to let his surprise show, for the house was worth far more. He counted out the money and handed it to Mittie, who gave him a paper saying the house was his. Only later did Joe realize that the old woman had expected him to buy the house, had wanted him to, and that she knew better than he that the place was worth twice what she had charged. That evening, Joe went to the store and bought a bottle of Coca-Cola, and he and Jane celebrated their own home. Neither one of them had ever tasted Coca-Cola before.

Every year after that, Joe went to Mittie's house and chopped her winter's wood.

Jane loved that cabin, simple as it was, because it belonged to them, and her father said that nobody in the family had ever owned a house before. With Mittie's help, the girl learned to cook a few things—stir up corn bread, boil beans, stew apples. Mittie supervised the girl in making curtains. In the summer, Jane filled a quart fruit jar with wildflowers for the table, and in the winter, she replaced the flowers with a basket of pinecones. Jane gathered them with Rosemary Bibb, her schoolmate.

One April day as he labored in the mill, Joe stopped to look out at the bright sunlight glaring on the white slope of Jubilee Mountain, and he reflected on the change in his life from only a few years before. He had a job in which he was paid as much as a white worker, a fine house next door to a white woman's, and his daughter Jane had a white girl as her friend. Life had turned out pretty good.

CHAPTER FOUR

Lately, Grace Foote had been thinking about the ghosts. When Grace was a little girl of seven or eight, the laundress, an old black woman who'd been born a slave, told her about ghosts as the two sat in the wash room, heavy wet sheets hanging around them like a spectral fog.

"I seen a little boy standing behind you just now, Miss Grace, dressed all up in one of them white suits young'uns wears back long years ago, and with pretty curls. Fine-looking boy," the old woman said, staring past Grace. "He's gone now. He walked through that wall easy as you please." She fingered a charm on a string around her neck.

Grace knew the woman was talking about her father's brother, who had died as a little boy in that very room, drowned in a washtub when he was three years old. Her father kept a picture of him. Even at that young age, Grace *knew* the old woman had not seen a ghost, had only seen the tintype of the little boy in the study, where it sat in a velvet frame on the library table, a black ribbon pinned across the corner to tell that the boy was dead. The woman had made up the story to scare her. But maybe it really was true, because Grace *had* been a little frightened. She had felt chills down her spine and something like a wisp of a breeze behind her when the old woman spoke.

Then Grace remembered that Father had dropped the picture and broken the frame and put it away in his desk until he could have it repaired. Well, maybe the woman, who had come to work for the family only that week, had been snooping. That was it. She'd found the old image and known the boy was someone in the family and saved up the knowledge to scare Grace. Maybe.

"*I've* never seen any ghosts. I don't believe in them," Grace said. If she said a thing out loud, she truly would believe it.

"You will when you see one. What time was you born?"

"At midnight. Mama heard the clock strike just as I came in the world, and they don't know if my birthday is the ninth or the tenth of April. That's why we celebrate two days."

"Then you's born between the lights, between dark and dawn. That means you ought to feel things other folks don't. There's things can't be explained in this world, but they happen. I know it. I'm born in the dark, too. Once, I was sleeping, but I looked up when I heard a woman walking past the bed in high-heel slippers. I got up and went over that whole room, but she ain't there. Another time, I hear somebody sweeping, but there ain't nobody. And the worst time, I waked up in the night and knew there was a bird in the house. That's a terrible thing, 'cause a bird in the house means death's a-coming. But there wasn't no bird." She shook her head. "Didn't matter. Next day, my sister's youngest drowned in the river."

Grace shivered. She hadn't seen the little boy in the room, but she had to admit, if only to herself, that she'd sensed other things in her short life, things she'd never told anyone about, and they had scared her. Maybe the old woman was right about her sensing things you couldn't see. She'd wake up in the night, sure that someone or something was beside her bed. She'd cry out, and her mother would come and shush her, asking where she got such ideas about spirits and creepy things, because there were no ghosts under creation. Grace had thought something was wrong with her then, because her mother was always right. So when the girl felt chills, she told herself that a window was open somewhere in that vast house, and when she sensed a presence, she believed it was her imagination. But now, here was this old Negro woman telling her that ghosts were real. Grace pondered that.

The laundress, sensing she had an audience, took her

hands out of the laundry tub and dried them on her apron, then sat down on a bench. "Some say it's my blood stop circulating that brings on spells. But they ain't spells. I know what I see. Now I tell you some things, but you got to promise you won't let on to nobody." Grace wouldn't tell anyone, especially her mother, who would chide the old laundress, maybe even let her go, for scaring the girl with such foolishness. Grace crossed her heart.

"First off, never eat nine persimmons in a row, or you'll turn into a boy."

Grace looked at the woman with wonderment. "It's true as the Bible. I've seen it myself. There's an old lady that died, and me and another woman laid her out, and we saw she's a man. They say when she was a girl, she was awful fond of persimmons." The laundress nodded to emphasize the truth of what she'd said. Then she got up and lit the fire under the wash water. "And here's another thing: If you wear red when you're a-carrying your child, you'll have a boy."

The old woman went on with a litany of superstitions, which the girl found to be queer and not quite believable, but she liked the laundress and liked sitting in the steamy wash room, where her skin felt cool and damp and her hair curled up into ringlets, so she listened. Of course, she did not really believe any of the stories. Her mother had said superstitions were for the ignorant, and the washerwoman could neither read nor write. But the superstitions went down into her subconscious, and after that, she never ate persimmons. And when she was pregnant with Schuyler, she bought a red dress, not that she especially wanted a boy, but she knew she didn't want a girl, because girls had a harder time of it. She also put a knife under the bed when she went into labor—another of the old Negro's superstitions, that a knife or pair of scissors left under the bed during childbirth would cut the pain. But Grace didn't think that had helped much.

Now as she looked out at the everlasting snow on the godforsaken slope of Jubilee Mountain below her, Grace wondered why the thoughts of ghosts and superstitions had come on her again. She hadn't remembered the laundress in years, the foolish old woman who'd both charmed and frightened her with stories of haunts and curses. She had warned Grace never to cut out a dress on Friday, or she wouldn't live to wear it out, and said if tea leaves floated to the top of her cup, Grace would come into money. One time, the woman had taken Grace's hand and started to tell her what lay ahead in her life. Then she'd stopped and wouldn't go on, although the girl had begged and promised to give her a quarter.

"You best give me a quarter not to tell," the old woman had said darkly, and Grace, frightened, had obliged. Sometimes, she thought that she should have made the woman tell her what she saw. Or maybe it didn't matter. Maybe she was already living the life the laundress had seen.

Once, the woman had put a little bag containing something that smelled frightful about the girl's neck. When Grace's mother discovered it, there'd been a row. "I've told you again and again not to pass on your ignorant ways to my daughter, Sabra. I'm going to have to let you go." The laundress had pleaded, saying she had no family and would starve without the work, but Grace's mother was firm. "I warned you twice before."

The old woman stood then, the washing still in the tubs, and took a sprig of something from under her head rag and waved it around, shouting a curse with such vehemence that Grace's mother blanched. After the laundress left, Grace's mother laughed and said that the curse meant nothing and that in the future she'd hire only Irish girls to do the washing. Her mother, Nancy, had been right about the curse, because if anyone had led a blessed life (and still did), it was Grace's mother. Oh, there had been that setback with Grace's father and the Schuyler fortune, but the unpleasantness hadn't lasted long, and her mother had married a man who was even wealthier.

Once again, as she shaded her eyes against the glare of sun on snow below the Fourth of July Mine, Grace wondered if the curse had been meant for her.

It was seeing the black man that brought up the memories of the laundress and made her restless, as though the witches were riding her, Grace thought. Her husband said the man had worked at the mill for nearly two years, but

Grace had never encountered him. There was that dark little girl in the school, but Grace had assumed she was a Mexican. Then Grace had seen the girl and man together and known they were both Negroes. And when she asked, she was told there had been talk at the school that the girl ought not to attend. "But where else could she go?" Grace had asked, because she had a few virtues, among them a lack of prejudice. Besides, before long, her son, Schuyler, who was seven, would go east to school, so what did it matter who attended the grade school at Swandyke? Oh, Jim fought her over the idea of boarding school, and she couldn't really blame him, since after Schuyler left, Jim would have only her for company, and she hadn't been much of a wife. Perhaps the laundress had seen that in Grace's hand.

She wondered if the Negro here in Swandyke had a wife. Grace would be curious to talk to her, find out if she believed the things the old laundress had told. Then she laughed out loud—not a laugh really, but a snort. What would people think if they knew that the wife of the superintendent of the Fourth of July Mine was swapping superstitions with an ignorant colored woman? That would give them something to talk about, those busybodies who gossiped about her over their quilt frames. Not that they hadn't been friendly in their way. When Grace arrived, they'd brought their cakes and cobblers and told her about the beautiful summers, as if they were a reward for living through the hateful months of snow. They'd asked her to quilt with them.

But Grace detested quilts, those ugly covers made from fabric leftovers.

The Swandyke women were a queer lot. She remembered the fat woman with the ridiculous curls like Mary Pickford's, and another, her estranged sister (or so she'd been told), who read books and newspapers and might have been somebody to talk to, except that she kept to herself. Grace hadn't known how to be easy with the women, and she'd told Jim that she thought it wasn't her place as the superintendent's wife to mix with them. So she'd been aloof, not because she'd wanted to be, but because she didn't know how to be friends—with them or with just about anyone else, because she'd never really had friends. They probably had been hurt, those well-meaning Swandyke women, thinking her "airish," and gradually they'd left her alone. Grace had only herself to blame for her loneliness. But she was used to it. She had been born lonely.

She encountered the women in the store and on her long walks, and remarked about the weather, asked about families she couldn't keep straight and didn't care about, and in recent weeks, she had shown a curiosity about mining superstitions. One miner had told her that women were bad luck in the mines. Another mentioned it was bad luck to kill a rat underground, because rats, like canaries, served a purpose, letting miners know when deadly gas was accumulating. But most of the miners didn't pay attention to that particular superstition. Some miners ran from a mine when they heard a peculiar knocking, believing the Cornish Tommyknockers, or mischievous spirits, were warning them of a cave-in.

The superstitions fascinated her. She couldn't seem to hear enough of them, and she wrote down the snippets of information whenever she heard them. She realized others had noticed her obsession the day she encountered Mittie McCauley in the post office and sought to engage her in a conversation, because the woman had lived in Swandyke since its beginning in the 1860s. She inquired how the old lady was feeling.

"I'm doing very good, except I'm all stiffed up," the woman replied, looking a little surprised, because pretty nearly every time she went to the post office, Grace ignored her.

Grace remarked on the snow, and then in an offhanded way, she said that she had heard that the woman always kept a bed turned down. "Is that for good luck? I mean, do you believe that if you're prepared for an accident, it won't happen?"

Mittie looked bemused, as if she understood that Grace was pumping her for information, and replied, "No, it's in case somebody's hurt and needs a bed."

"Oh." Grace tried then to look as if she were only making mail-time conversation.

"But if you're interested in superstitions, I know a plenty of them, although I never put much stock in them, or conjurations, either. They say if a hawk flies over your house, there'll be a death, but then, there's some people thinking that waking up in the morning means death, and who can argue with the truth of another day putting you closer to the end? You could come and talk to me sometime. I'd welcome a visit."

"I'll do that," Grace said, hoping her tone told the old woman not to expect her.

But why not talk to her? Grace thought now. She could claim she was writing a book, or, if that sounded too pretentious, a magazine article, and who knew, maybe she would write one, because she was good at writing, better at it than at conversation with those people. She liked the idea of being an author. Besides, writing would be something to do, and God knew, talking to the old woman would be more interesting than making needlepoint seats for her eight dining room chairs. That was boring work, drone labor that caused her to dwell on her life too much as she stitched.

She would ask about mining superstitions, but perhaps she would learn others, something that would explain her own life. And that, she decided, was the reason she was so taken with old wives' tales. Perhaps there was something that explained what had happened to her, why she felt things. Grace had always blamed herself for making bad decisions, but maybe it was "in her stars," as people put it. She wondered if the laundress had indeed seen something in the little girl's hand that foretold an unhappy life.

Has it been an unhappy life? Grace asked herself, stopping and reconsidering. There were some who thought her the luckiest girl in the world, married to a successful mining executive and the mother of a bright little boy. Perhaps her life had not been all that unhappy. Still, there was little joy in it.

Of course, Grace's life had begun well enough, because the family was wealthy beyond most people's dreams. Her grandfather had started the family lumber business in Saginaw, Michigan, by acquiring vast tracts of timberland just after the Civil War. As the money flowed in, he built an enormous three-story house with turrets and long, narrow windows, a porch that wrapped around three sides, and trim that dripped from the eaves and corners of the house like wooden lace. There were two parlors with huge crystal chandeliers, a music room, a billiards room, study, five bedrooms (not counting the servants' rooms), and five white-tiled bathrooms, one so large that it was turned into a delivery room, where Grace's mother gave birth to her only child in 1892.

Outside were the stable, with the names of horses on brass plates in each stall, and a playhouse that was an exact replica of the big house. It was set in the back in a formal garden with rose beds and a fountain and statues of barely clad women. Grace treasured the little house, because it was hers alone, and she went there when the slights of child-hood were too great for her to bear. A governess came in each day, and a groom hitched up Grace's pony to a dogcart whenever she wanted to drive it. But with all this, Grace grew up a lonely and discontented child, sure that people did not like her. Her father, John Schuyler, preferred ani-mals to children and spent most of his time hunting or watching his own horses race. The family stable was known all over the East. Grace's mother, Nancy, was engaged in social affairs.

The parents took frequent trips, leaving Grace in the care of a nurse and, later on, a governess. Nancy paid little atten-tion to Grace as a baby and young girl but was more atten-tive when Grace reached eighteen and the mother could plan her daughter's debut. Nancy urged Grace to find a suit-able husband before she turned twenty and lost her youth.

But no one pleased Grace—or perhaps it could be said that Grace pleased no one—and once the coming-out fes-tivities were over, Grace asked her parents to send her to college. College might have been the girl's salvation, be-cause she was bright and independent and comfortable with her studies, and an education could have brought her out of the shadows that seemed to hover over her. But in 1910, it was unthinkable that a young woman of Grace's social standing would consider a profession. The idea of college gave Nancy great concern, for she did not believe that a four-year education at the University of Michigan or even at one of the women's colleges in the East was desirable. It would stamp Grace as even more of an oddity, make her too intellectual to be attractive.

But Grace begged, and at last the two agreed on a compromise: Grace would attend a two-year finishing school. Even that was not pleasing to Nancy, although it would allow her to explain away Grace's lack of a fiancé by rolling her eyes and saying, "You know modern young women; they simply are not satisfied to go from mother to husband, but must be out on their own for a time." In Grace's case, "out on her own" meant living in nunlike strictness in a dormitory with dozens of other girls who, like her, had settled for finishing school instead of a real education.

While such a school was not her first choice, Grace found the experience satisfying because she enjoyed literature and art. She did think later on, however, that learning to work a needlepoint canvas, plan parties, and flirt in French and English did her little good in a mining town at the top of the world. The French and Italian she had perfected so well that anyone who heard her speak one of the two languages believed she was talking in her native tongue were useless in a blue-collar town. Better if she had studied Spanish or Polish or one of the Slavic languages that the miners and their families spoke.

Still, the finishing-school polish did come in handy on occasions such as entertaining Jim's business associates—visiting engineers, mining consultants, and the company officials who traveled to Swandyke and stayed in the superintendent's house. Grace was a touch of sophistication in that town of women worn down by overwork and hardship. Tall and willowy, her light brown hair fashionably bobbed instead of knotted at the back of her neck, Grace dressed in smart clothes that were not ordered from the catalog at the general store.

She was a good hostess, chatting about mining, since she had picked up enough information to sound knowledgeable, and telling amusing stories about the townspeople or occasionally admitting her own foibles, such as drinking a little too much. "I ought to live right, but I wouldn't have any friends if I did," she confided.

Jim was proud of her in those moments, she knew, and that drew the couple together. She had never loved her husband, but she liked him, and he liked her, although she knew he was disappointed that she had never fit into Swandyke. But she hadn't known how to, and now it was too late.

She was a whiz at fixing cocktails (although most of the visiting dignitaries and business associates preferred the illegal Tenmile Moon that was manufactured locally), and visitors marveled at the wine-and-cream-sauce dishes with the French names that Grace prepared. She hadn't learned to cook at school, of course, but had taught herself from necessity, because where could one engage a decent cook at ten thousand feet? She gave her dishes exotic names, especially when the ingredients were second-rate. A can of peas became *petit pois* and a tough chicken soaked in wine was *coq au vin*. And there was her *pièce de résistance, mousse au chocolat,* whose primary ingredient was a five-cent Hershey bar. Jim, who was as easygoing as Grace was high-strung, thought the mousse a great joke.

Grace could make darling little cocktail sandwiches, too. When she arrived in Swandyke as a bride and discovered that she had to pack her husband's lunch bucket every day, she put in some of her sandwiches, cucumber or egg salad or cream cheese with pimento, cut into triangles and trimmed of crust. Jim had had to tell her that he preferred roast beef or meat loaf between two full pieces of bread. Grace cringed later on when she recalled how naïve she had been in those early days and how Jim's associates must have teased him about his lunch bucket.

It was the Christmas of 1911, during her second year of finishing school, that Grace discovered the Schuyler fortune was gone. She came home to find that the household staff had been cut. That was not unusual, for from time to time, her mother had rows with the servants, let them go, then kept their positions vacant for weeks until she found others who suited her. Still, the cutback in staff was odd, because the family usually had a full contingent for holiday entertaining. The stables were empty, but again, that had happened before. Her father had numerous ideas about racing, and on occasion he sold off all his horses so that he could indulge himself in some new theory.

What tipped off Grace was Nancy's ruby-and-emerald necklace, or, rather, the lack of it. The necklace, with its matching earrings, had been a wedding present from Grace's grandfather, and her mother wore it every Christmas Eve. It was a magnificent piece, with rubies shaped like teardrops suspended from a gold chain that was entwined with emeralds. And it was as much a Christmas tradition as the ten-foot tree in the front parlor or the spectacular party her parents threw each Christmas Eve. To be invited to that fête was to be stamped a member of Saginaw's elite.

"Your necklace, Mother. My goodness, you've forgotten it," Grace said as she encountered her mother in the hall, poised to descend the staircase to greet the guests below.

"Oh, I'm tired of wearing it every year," her mother replied.

"But you always wear it. Grandfather would be crushed if you didn't."

"How can he be?" Nancy laughed. "Your grandfather's been dead for years."

Grace frowned at her mother.

"Well, if you must know, I broke the clasp."

The two women gave each other a long look, until Grace asked, "You don't have it any longer, do you?"

"Our guests are waiting."

"Did you lose it?" When there was no answer, Grace recalled the servant shortage and the empty stable, and then as she stared at her mother, Grace was startled to observe that Nancy was wearing last year's gown. She always ordered the latest fashion for the Christmas Eve ball. And then Grace knew. "What happened?"

"It's best you don't worry your head about it. Besides, it's only a little reversal. Your father will acquire more timberland. We aren't to let it spoil Christmas Eve. We have guests." And Nancy smiled and began her grand entrance, and Grace knew her mother had already forgotten the setback.

Grace followed a few steps behind, clutching the railing, because no finishing school could teach her to hold up under such circumstances. She looked out over the upraised faces, which were happy with anticipation, the men in their tails and women clad in shimmering satins, with tiaras and necklaces sparkling in the light of the chandeliers, and she thought that this would all end. John Schuyler had no head for business; he'd never worked in the lumber company. Besides, Grace knew for a fact that most of the vast forests of virgin lumber had already been clear-cut, and there were not many left. Her father would be no more able to acquire new timberlands than she.

Nancy turned as she reached the bottom of the staircase, smiled brilliantly at Grace, and took her daughter's hand in an iron grip as she moved about the room, welcoming people. After a few minutes, the girl became aware that nearly every person her mother greeted had an eligible son. Her mother was matchmaking, hoping to find Grace a husband while everyone still believed the girl to be an heiress. The idea would have amused Grace if she had not been appalled. Her mother, who had never paid much attention to her, now seemed driven to find her a suitable husband before the family was disgraced. And what if she didn't find one? Grace had never worried about a husband, knowing she could live in the family home on her father's money until she found someone she liked. Now, she realized, she had no choice. She was aware that her father did not know how to cut back his spending, and it would be only a matter of time until every cent was gone, and where would that leave her? And her parents? They were counting on her. She knew as surely as her mother did that she would have to find a husband—a rich one—and soon.

She wondered which unsuspecting young man she and her mother would settle on. And then Grace was introduced to George Amter, stocky, handsome, with hair like ebony, and Grace's life was changed forever.

A year earlier, George might have been considered beneath Grace's notice. His mother was pedigreed, but his father was new money and had a whiff of scandal about him, something to do with a young widow who had sued him for alienation of affection. It was rumored she dropped the suit and disappeared after being paid a generous sum—someone had seen her on a train, carrying an infant—but no one knew the circumstances, and it was all so sordid that the family would not have been welcomed in Saginaw's best homes were it not for the goodwill extended to Mrs. Amter. There was the belief that morals, or the lack of them, were inherited, which caused concern that George might be cut from the same cloth as his father. The mothers of Grace's friends treated the young man with a certain caution, which made him all the more attractive to their daughters. Grace was not the only one who was smitten.

To the girl's great delight, George seemed equally attracted to her, and she could not believe her good fortune. He monopolized her that evening, then called on her each day until her Christmas vacation was over and she returned to school. And after that, he wrote her notes and sent her nosegays. Whenever Grace returned home for a holiday, George was invited to the house for cocktails or for dinner. There was a time when Nancy would have discouraged George's attentions because of his father's sullied reputation. But now she was thrilled that Grace had attracted such a catch, because it was rumored that the Amters were as rich as the Schuylers were thought to be.

"We can still afford to give you a proper wedding. We may be able to keep up appearances until the end of the year," her mother whispered to Grace following the girl's graduation, which George attended. "But you had better plan the event earlier rather than later."

"Mother! He hasn't asked me."

"Then you must get him to, because we can't hold out forever. Fortunately, it's summer, and I've never worn jewels in summer. If I did, you would notice they are all paste now."

School over, Grace returned to Saginaw, where George took her sailing and to summer dances. They rode horseback together and went for long walks in the dusky evenings, all alone, so that they could talk, because George had told her she kept him on his toes with her ideas. He loved a girl with a head on her shoulders, he said. George would lead her down some shaded trail, and when they were alone, he would take her hand. Once, he pinned her against a tree and kissed her and said, "You know I'm nuts about you, don't you, Gracie?" She'd always despised being called Gracie, but now she liked the intimacy of the name.

Once or twice, she thought George was going to propose. They often went about with a group of people their age who formed Saginaw's young smart set, and on occasion, George stole her away from the others so that he could put his arm around her. During one of these times, when they had escaped from a picnic and were sitting on a bench by a lake, looking up at the stars and the wisp of a moon, he put his thumb under her chin and lifted it so that he could look into her eyes. "I can see my reflection. It's like I'm part of you. I hope I can always be a part of you." He smiled and leaned in to kiss her. But they heard voices, and he quickly moved away, to Grace's disappointment, because she was sure he had intended to say more.

"There you two are. We keep losing you. Honestly, I thought you'd fallen into the lake!" exclaimed Charlotte, who was Grace's closest friend, and a group of young people burst in on them and swept them back to the picnic.

Because Grace was sure after that evening that George would propose—it was just a matter of when—she wanted to tell someone, and Charlotte was the only friend with whom she'd ever exchanged confidences. But Charlotte was a dull girl, not much for keeping secrets, and it would be an embarrassment if people thought Grace had set her cap for George. So she kept still. Besides, she admitted to being just slightly superstitious and would not jinx the situation by talking about it. Thinking about that decision later, Grace wondered if things might have turned out differently if she had told Charlotte. Perhaps that was another of her bad decisions.

And then everything was over. Grace's aunt died, and the family went east for a month to attend the funeral and participate in the rituals of grief. Grace did not receive any letters or wires from George, which she attributed to the Schuylers' moving from relative to relative. Any missive sent to her would have been delayed, if not lost altogether. Besides, men were unsure about interfering in family intimacies. She returned home the day after George and Charlotte announced their engagement.

Nancy, who was rarely sensitive to Grace's feelings, called George a "cad" and said Grace was lucky she hadn't married into such a family. He might have money, but he had no breeding, and weren't they lucky they had discovered it before it was too late?

Grace, of course, was brokenhearted. For days, she stayed in her room, crying and refusing to see anyone, while her mother gave it out that she had caught a dreadful head cold on the train and remarked how fortunate it was that with all those foreigners riding on the cars these days, Grace hadn't picked up some terrible contagion.

Grace couldn't stay in bed forever, however, and when at last she emerged from her room, she and her mother made the obligatory call on Charlotte to extend their best wishes. As Charlotte basked in the attention, simpering and saying George's proposal was the surprise of her life, Grace studied her friend and wondered what in the world George saw in her. Charlotte was sweet enough, never saying a harsh word to anyone, but she was as placid as a brick, and thick— thickheaded and thick in body, with a sort of porcine cast to her face. George was as wealthy as Charlotte and had no need for her money. So that didn't explain Charlotte's attraction. There were no ties between the families that would have caused the parents to pressure the two into the match. Perhaps George had taken advantage of Charlotte in that way that girls were warned about. He'd have felt honorbound to marry her then. But Grace thought that unlikely, because George had never approached her with an improper suggestion. And Charlotte was afraid of sex. She'd once told Grace that her greatest fear was her wedding night. Besides, Grace thought uncharitably, Charlotte couldn't dress or undress herself without her maid's help.

Grace and her mother admired the wedding gifts that had already been delivered, including their own, a sterling silver coffee urn, which Nancy claimed had been ordered from a New York store the minute she heard of the impending marriage. That wasn't true. The urn was an abominable thing, a wedding gift to Grace's parents, which they'd never used. It had been polished and boxed up and delivered to Charlotte so that the family would not have to purchase a present.

"I am so dreadfully sorry we can't entertain for our Charlotte," Nancy told the bride's mother. "But with a death in the family . . . well, I know it's old-fashioned, but I just don't think it's proper. I hope you understand." That would save not only Grace's face but part of the dwindling fortune, as well.

Charlotte's mother did understand and replied, "But you won't let that stop Grace from being a member of the wedding party, will you? Charlotte would be heartbroken, and George, too, for she is dear to both of them. You will agree, won't you, Grace?"

"You have to say yes," Charlotte added. "I couldn't get married without you."

Because saying no not only would have been a breach of etiquette but would have caused talk in Saginaw, mother and daughter exchanged glances, and Grace accepted.

And so for the next few weeks—the couple was anxious to marry; "You know how impatient young people are today," the bride's mother confided to Nancy—Grace and George were thrown together at dozens of parties and outings given for the wedding couple. George was not overly friendly with Grace, but neither did he avoid her. It was as if the two of them were old friends, as if nothing more than polite conversation had ever passed between them. George never gave her a word of explanation, and, of course, Grace never asked for one.

Grace threw herself into the festivities, partly to show George—if he cared to observe it—that his marriage meant nothing to her, and partly because Grace was now desperate to find a husband. She remembered the old laundress's curse and her frown after examining Grace's hand and wondered if somehow, she, not her mother, had been the recipient of that curse. Or perhaps one of her poor decisions had been not following her mother's advice and marrying before twenty, because at twenty, she found many of the young men frivolous and unappealing. But what she thought of her young swains did not matter now. She must marry before anyone found out about her financial state. She wished that she had insisted on attending a university, where she might have learned enough to find a respectable job. But that option was closed to her now. She looked over the men in the bridal party and singled out two or three as husband possibilities. She flirted with them, let one or two pet her, but she was not enthusiastic about any of them.

Two days before the wedding, Grace attended an outing held in the bridal couple's honor at an estate in the country. There was dinner and dancing and champagne, and because the guests by now were bored with all the entertainments, they drank a great deal, and by the time the evening ended, a number of them were swacked, among them Grace's escort, who was so besotted that he passed out. Charlotte's mother, a bit befuddled herself, asked George to see Grace home.

George replied he'd happy to be of service, and Grace, although greatly agitated, said that she would be pleased to accept his kindness. "You'll be safe, darling Grace," Charlotte called as she sped down the road with her parents.

George and Grace were the last to leave, and George let the dust from Charlotte's car settle before he helped Grace into his own motorcar and turned on the engine. "Darling Grace," he muttered as he started slowly down the dark road. "Darling Charlotte. Darling everybody." He seemed in a foul mood, and Grace suspected that he did not want to be alone with her any more than she did with him. He must be furious that he had been put in the position of escorting her home. Well, she would make it as easy as she could for both of them by keeping a shut mouth.

She wished George would drive faster and was surprised he didn't, because he liked a boiling pace, but he poked along, looking straight ahead and keeping silent himself. Grace concluded that he was a little drunk. She, too, had imbibed more champagne than she should have and was light-headed.

"Gracie," he said at last, and the name stung her.

She thought to rebuke him by pointing out that her name was Grace, but she couldn't. She just let the old name slide over her, and in a minute, tears ran down her face. George looked over at her and touched her cheek. "Darling Gracie," he said, this time with tenderness. He pulled off the road into a grove of weeping willow trees and turned off the engine. "Darling Gracie, don't you know I love you?"

Grace turned to him in astonishment, thinking for a moment that the voice was in her head, fueled by the champagne. But George repeated the words. "I love you, Gracie. I'd give anything if it was you I was marrying." He drew her to him and kissed her. "Say you love me, too."

"I—"

"Say it."

"I won't."

George stared out into the darkness. "I suppose I can't blame you. I've treated you horribly. I wouldn't be surprised if you hated me. But I think you love me at least a little."

Instead of looking at George, Grace focused on the branches

of the willow tree that draped over the car. Stars twinkled through the leaves. "I don't understand."

"It's all so complicated. I can't explain it. I just wish you were going to be my wife instead of Charlotte."

Grace did not know what to say. His words did not make sense, but then, she had had a great deal to drink, and she could not think properly. "Then why are you marrying her?"

George sat pensively, as if searching for the words to explain himself. But instead of answering, he suddenly reached over and drew her to him. "It hurts me to see you and know I can't hold you." He took her chin between his thumb and forefinger, but Grace turned her head aside and would not look at him. So George put a hand on either side of her face and forced her head up, and he kissed her. He held her so tightly that she couldn't move, and he kissed her face and her neck and her shoulders. Then his lips moved down until he was kissing the cleavage between her breasts. "Oh, Gracie, Gracie," he said, and he began to push down the top of her dress.

"George, no," she said, making little fluttering gestures at him, wanting him to stop and not to stop. He moved his hands slowly down her body, pushing the dress with it. The gown gave easily, for Grace was slender and did not wear a corset as Charlotte did, and the dress was diaphanous and loose.

When he had pushed the dress nearly to her waist,

George maneuvered Grace back on the seat and began to slide his hands over her breasts, her waist, and then Grace felt the silk fabric of her skirt as it inched up her legs and over her hips. She made little sounds of protest, which George silenced with kisses, and she felt his hands loosen her undergarments, and then his body was on top of her, and she was pinned to the seat of the car. Through the fog of champagne, Grace knew she should stop him. She knew about boys who forced themselves on girls, and she was aware of what she must do, but to her surprise, she did not want George to stop. His hands were warm and soft, and they made her body tingle. For an instant, she thought that Charlotte was a fool to dread this, and then she saw with sudden clarity that George was engaged to Charlotte, and that she must not let this happen. She tried to shove him away, but by then it was too late.

When it was over, George pushed himself off her and helped her sit up. Grace, embarrassed now, straightened her clothes, fastening the snaps and buttons that had come loose, touching a rip in the fragile fabric. She combed her hair with her fingers, then sat demurely on the seat, her hands clasped together, not able to look George in the face.

"Gracie . . ." George said. "He placed the tip of his index finger on the bridge of her nose and slid it down to the tip. Then he kissed her nose. "I will remember this all of my life."

"I think we'd better go home," she told him. "My mother

will wonder where I've gotten to." In fact, her mother never waited up for Grace, but the girl felt strange, and she had turned prim.

"Right," George said, and he turned on the engine. They motored in silence until they reached the house. George walked her to the door, which Grace unlocked herself, because there was no servant to open it. "I'll see you in the morning, darling. We'll talk then."

Grace nodded, then went inside and up the stairs to her room, where she sat in the dark in the wrinkled gown. She felt disoriented, but not from the champagne this time. And then she felt a sense of happiness creep over her. She threw the dress into the back of the closet, where it could be examined and repaired later. As she got into bed, she wondered what George would tell Charlotte. For an instant, she felt sorry for her friend, but the feeling didn't last long. The knowledge that George would marry her now, would have to marry her after what had happened, enfolded Grace in a softness as thick and warm as a bed of feathers.

In the morning, Grace bathed and dressed in a thin summer frock, since the day was already hot, and then she went outside and sat beside the fountain, listening to the quiet sound of the water as it fell from tier to tier into the huge iron basin, then was piped up to the top of the structure to make its way down again. She ran her hand through the water and flicked the drops onto the flowers nearby. The yard was well maintained, because her mother had kept a single gardener. After all, what would people think if the gardens went to weeds? Grace dried her hand on her skirt and walked to the playhouse. It had always been a place of refuge. Whenever she'd felt lonely or her little playmates had abandoned her, she had used the playhouse as a hiding place. But she had not been inside in a long time—years, really.

She pushed open the door and saw the children's furniture there, the table and chairs, a doll carriage, some books, all covered with a layer of dust. She would have just such a playhouse for her own child, and then she touched her stomach. Good God, she thought, could I be pregnant? They would have to marry right away, just in case. But they should marry quickly anyway, elope, and probably that very evening, because George and Charlotte's wedding was planned for the next day. If they ran off, people would talk, of course, but that would be preferable to having a seven-months baby. She could never deal with the stigma of that.

Grace glanced at the little tin dishes on the toy table and remembered the tea parties she and Charlotte had given there, pretending to be grown-up ladies with houses and servants of their own. And then she was shaken out of her reverie by the sound of a motor. She looked across the garden and saw George getting out of his automobile. She wanted to run to him, but instead she went only as far as the fountain and waited demurely. He saw her and came over to her quickly.

George did not sweep Grace up in his arms as she had expected, but stood awkwardly in front of her. Well, of course, she thought. He did not know how she would react after last night and who might be watching. So Grace took his hand, and they sat down beside the fountain, and she whispered, "I love you."

George wrung his hand away and stood up. "I'm sorry for that. It doesn't make it easier for either one of us. I've done you a terrible wrong, and I ask you to forgive me."

Grace was confused. "Last night—"

"Last night was a dreadful mistake. I hope you will blame it on the champagne and that you are all right." When Grace didn't answer, George said, "Of course you're not. Maybe I shouldn't have come. I had to apologize before the wedding tomorrow. You deserve that much."

"The wedding?" Grace asked.

"I'm marrying Charlotte tomorrow. Surely you didn't forget." He added softly, "I wish it weren't so."

"But last night, I thought . . ."

"Thought what?"

"That you and I . . ." She would not be so bold as to say it.

"You thought we would get married?"

Grace was greatly embarrassed and turned away. "I thought in situations like that . . ."

"But we can't, Grace. Don't you understand?"

Grace shook her head.

"I guess you don't, do you?" He took her hand and sat down again beside her and stared into the fountain. "The fact is, Charlotte's family has money, and yours doesn't."

Grace went rigid and looked at George in shock. "All you cared about was my money, then?"

"That's not true. I couldn't have married you without it, but I do love you." He leaned forward, his elbows on his knees. "I'd planned to ask you to marry me. I almost did once or twice. Then while you were away, my father found out that the Schuyler fortune is gone. I should have figured it out on my own, what with all these economies your father has effected, but I merely thought he was being eccentric." He gave a mirthless chuckle.

"Why does the lack of a fortune matter if you love me? You have money."

"Not a cent. We're as broke as you are. My father lost everything on a business venture, and it's up to me to restore the family fortune." He laughed a little at the irony of it. "Isn't it funny that we're a pair of penniless fortune hunters and we fell for each other?"

Grace did not find it funny at all, nor did she consider herself a fortune hunter, although maybe she was. "You could work."

George shook his head. "And just what could I do, Gracie? My education is as useless as yours. I was brought up to fish and play golf and mix a mean cocktail. Who'd hire me?"

"But you're clever. You could do anything you wanted.

I don't need servants, and I could learn to cook and keep house." The idea of being alone together, just the two of them in a little cottage not much bigger than the playhouse, appealed to her.

George took a deep breath. "The truth is, I don't want to work. And I don't want to live in a nasty little bungalow. There it is. I like my life too much to give it up. I suppose it means I'm weak, but I'd rather live off someone else's money than work for it."

Grace looked out across the garden at the playhouse. She had left the door open. "Does Charlotte know—about your family, I mean?"

George shrugged. "I suppose her father does, but she wants me, so it doesn't matter to them. They must feel I'm better than that sorry lot of young bucks sniffing around her."

"But last night . . ."

"I'm sorry—for your sake, that is, but not for mine." Without looking at her, George stood, but Grace could not. Her knees were weak. He squeezed her hand. Then he raised it to his lips. "I wish it could be different."

He turned then and walked to his car, slowly at first, then, straightening up, faster, as if he had put his evening with Grace behind him. She watched him go, let the dust settle behind his motorcar, then got up herself and went to close the playhouse door. But she went inside instead and sat down on the dusty little chair, her knees almost to her chin. She put her arms down on the dirty table and rested her head on them. She did not sob this time; she did not have that luxury. Instead, she let the agony and then the shame and finally the horror of what she had done wash over her. She did not know much about pregnancy, but she was aware that she had taken a terrible risk, and that she must find a husband at once. She sat on the little chair for hours, and when at last she stood up, her legs cramped, she knew what she must do.

The wedding was a brilliant affair, and why not, because Charlotte's family had spared no expense. But Grace barely noticed the flowers that covered the altar of the great cathedral or the lavish wedding supper prepared by a chef imported from New York. Tents were set up on the lawn of Charlotte's family estate, in case it should rain on the guests, who had arrived from all over the country in private railroad cars.

Grace had grown up with such entertainments, and this one did not make an impression. She had participated in the wedding ceremony as if in a dream, a smile frozen on her face as she watched the couple exchange vows. Did she wish she was marrying George at that moment? Grace wondered. She now had a very different opinion of him. Did she still love him? Grace did not know. But those were not the thoughts that occupied her mind as she moved across the lawn in search of one of the groomsmen—James Foote, a distant cousin of Charlotte's.

She had met him at the bridal parties, danced with him, flirted a little when she thought George was watching. He had found her intriguing, she knew, had told her she might be the only person in the room who'd ever read a book. He'd seemed flattered that Grace had taken an interest in him, and he'd even tried to kiss her, although Grace had slipped from his embrace and called him a bad boy. Jim had given her an odd look at that point, as though he found the "bad boy" cliché too brittle for her to use.

Jim Foote was older and already established as a mining engineer. He did not have money beyond what he earned himself, Grace realized, but she did not care, because that meant they would live wherever his work took him, instead of in Saginaw. She did not want people there to see her disgrace. Of course, he was not handsome like George, who had thick black hair and an almost pretty face. Jim was thin, with gray eyes, protruding ears, and long arms, and was already as bald as a brass doorknob. Grace liked him the best of the bunch of unattached males who were wedding attendants and even found him somewhat appealing, not that it mattered much.

She saw him standing by himself, an empty glass in his hand, and she picked up two glasses of champagne and went over to him, handing him one. "It's awfully hot. I brought you this to cool off," she said, watching him gulp the wine, then handing him the second glass. "Are you enjoying yourself?"

He looked down at her, because although she was tall, he was that much taller. "Not really."

Grace acted taken aback. "It's such a lovely party."

"Oh, if you like this sort of thing." He studied her a moment. "Do you really want to know what I think?"

She nodded.

"I think spending all this money on a wedding is appalling. Do you know what that money would do in the mining town where I work?"

"You're a spoilsport," Grace told him.

"Yes, I'm sorry."

He looked away, and Grace, remembering how he had not liked being called "bad boy," decided to be less lighthearted. "What would you do with it, the money?"

"I'll tell you." He led her to two chairs that were a little ways away from the rest of the guests. They sat down, and Jim leaned forward earnestly and began to tell her about the poverty in Swandyke, Colorado, the town where he was superintendent of the Fourth of July, the area's largest gold mine. He talked about the poor schools and the hard lives the miners lived. Grace looked at him wide-eyed, although she did not pay much attention to what he said. Each time a waiter came by, she nodded at the champagne, and the waiter took Jim's empty glass and handed him a fresh one.

At last, Grace said, "It's awfully hot here. Would you mind terribly if we went over to the pond, where it's cooler?"

"I've bored you."

"No," Grace replied, lying. "I want to hear more. You're the only person here who is serious about life, and I would like to hear what you have to say. But it's very hot here." They stood, Grace taking his arm and leading him to a secluded spot, where they sat down in the grass. It was quite dark now, and while they could hear the sounds of the orchestra and the chatter of the guests in the distance, they could see nothing but each other.

"I've never met anybody who is as concerned about other people as you are," Grace said, putting her hand on his arm.

"Well, I never expected to find a girl at Charlotte's wedding who would listen," he replied.

They talked softly, Grace making sounds of sympathy and interest, because she knew how to flatter a man. Finishing school at least had taught her that. When he said something funny, she fluffed her hair and gave a tinkling laugh, and at last, Jim whispered, "Miss Grace—"

She put her finger on his lips and said, "It's just Grace, Gracie if you like." And she leaned in so that he could kiss her. After that, it was easy. She let him put his arms around her and caress her, and after a time, he pushed at her skirt, and she moved a little to make it easier for him. He knew what to do, and Grace thought later that she was not his first. Well, she probably had not been George's first, either, because his father would have introduced him to brothels. Jim must have visited them, too, but likely on his own.

When they were finished, they lay on the grass beside each other for a long time. Grace was in no hurry to go home this time. At last, she sat up and said softly, "My God, Mr. Foote, what is it we've done?" It was the champagne, she told him, since he musn't realize she was sober.

He put his head in his hands and apologized, saying he had had only the noblest intentions toward her when they'd found this place to talk. He seemed contrite, more than George had been, and Grace was forgiving, saying boldly that she shared the fault, for she had liked the way he'd touched her. And so she played him along, making him feel guilty but at the same time a little grateful for her understanding and forgiveness.

The next day, Jim called on Grace. "I haven't slept," he said, "and if anything . . ." He could not finish the thought. But he added, "I know my responsibility." He left that afternoon, giving Grace his address, and a few days later, she received a letter from him, a formal one telling her how much he had enjoyed meeting her and saying he hoped she was well.

Two weeks after the wedding, Grace did not bleed as she had every four weeks since her nature first came to her, when she was fourteen. She did not tell Jim until another month passed and she knew for sure she was pregnant. She wrote, and within the week, Jim was in Saginaw. They eloped that day, Grace leaving a message for her parents that she could not bear going through the weeks of engagement festivities that had consumed Charlotte. Her parents were relieved. They could not stretch their declining fortune to cover the cost of a wedding like Charlotte's. Perhaps they believed that Grace had eloped solely to save them the expense. So Nancy only sighed when her friends said how thoughtless it was of Grace to deprive her of the joy of planning her only daughter's wedding.

Grace herself was glad to be away from Saginaw, although she had no idea of what lay ahead for her. She had read the popular Zane Grey novel *Riders of the Purple Sage* and thought Swandyke must be set in a glorious southwestern desert of sagebrush and piñon trees, with desperadoes and Indians. The two of them would go about on horseback, and Jim would be proud of her riding skill. He had written that the town was in a mountain valley, and she pictured pretty cottages and quaint people. The residents would be poor—she remembered that from the conversation with Jim—but they would be happy and would see her as Lady Bountiful. She envisioned herself visiting them when they were sick, taking along custards and beef tea that her cook had prepared, and handing out presents to the children at Christmas, just as her mother had done to the children of the servants.

When she arrived in Swandyke, however, Grace was stunned at the brutality and the ugliness, and then at the harshness of that first winter she spent at the Fourth of July. Still, she told herself, it was better than giving birth in Saginaw to George's off-child, his bastard. Nothing could be worse than that. She had made a bargain with the devil, and she would keep her part of it.

Grace went into labor on a spring day, when the snow had stopped and the warmth of the sun and the sounds of birds came into the house. She was attended by the company doctor, a man who assured her he was well acquainted with childbirth. No society doctor for Grace Foote. Nor was there a white-tile bath to be turned into a birthing room. She gave birth in an old brass bed, tended by the doctor and a nurse, who later gave up the job to become an inmate at a whorehouse up the river in Middle Swan. The labor was an easy one, and the baby was a boy. The doctor held him up, and Grace blanched when she saw him, for he was the exact image of his father. And then the fruit of her deceit hit her, and she gave a bitter laugh. The joke was on her. The big ears, the eyes, the long arms, and even the bald head identified him as Jim Foote's son.

Now, Grace stood at the window of the superintendent's house, holding back the curtains with her long fingers, the nails perfectly varnished, looking down the treeless snow-covered slope below the Fourth of July Mine, remembering the irony that Jim, not George, was the father of her son.

She had tricked her husband into marriage, when it hadn't even been necessary. Poor Jim, she thought. He was so honorable. She had tried to be a good wife, but she was ill-prepared to be married to a mining man in such a dreadful place.

With Schuyler in school now, she had time on her hands and brooded about why her life had turned out the way it had, wondered if everything that had happened had been preordained, and whether the old black woman had seen that in her hand. And if the past had been set for her, the future would be, too. That was what concerned her now. Would she spend the rest of her life staring out the window at the endless snow?

A few weeks earlier, Grace had asked her mother to send her books on the occult, explaining that the local people were taken with superstitions. Grace wrote her mother long letters about the mine and the mountains and the towns-people, fantasy letters describing the beauty of Swandyke and the gentleness of its inhabitants. The letters were so entertaining that Nancy passed them around among her friends, and everyone said that Grace ought to have them published. Her mother had never been to Swandyke, and Grace saw no reason to let her know the real circumstances of life there.

John Schuyler had died—or had he committed suicide?—in a hunting accident not six months after Grace left Saginaw, and Nancy had married just a year later. The new husband was immensely wealthy, and the couple spent much of their time in Europe. Grace visited them in Saginaw, always taking Schuyler. She loved the boy and did not want to be away from him. He was the one good thing that had resulted from the awful mistake that had begun with George. She often encountered George and Charlotte on the trips. They seemed perfectly suited for each other now, because George had grown fat and dull, and Grace could not imagine what her life with him would have been.

Now, Grace glanced at the horseshoe that hung over the door; she'd explained to Jim she'd placed it there to ensure that spring would come. She set aside the needlepoint to stare out the window again, looking out at the long white slope sparkling in the sunlight, waiting to catch a glimpse of Schuyler coming home from school. And slowly, a sense of foreboding came upon her, and she thought again of the long-ago curse.

CHAPTER FIVE

This time of year, the sun did little to warm the graves under the pine trees of the Mountainbrook burial ground. Minder Evans stood in the shadows and shivered a little, because he had seen some years. At seventy-five, he was too old to tramp the cemetery each day in the winter's cold. But he came, even these past few days, when he'd had to wade through the heavy snow the storm had dumped on Swandyke. It was a pact he'd made with himself when he sold his interest in the Fourth of July Mine—to visit the cemetery every day instead of just on Sunday, as he had for years. People thought it was a little odd, he knew, this remainder of the Grand Old Army coming to the graves so often, but then, the Civil War veterans were a strange lot. Folks had grown used to seeing Minder wandering among the stones, not just those of the Union soldiers but of the Confederate ones, too, for in the end, the two sides had enough in common to override their differences of long years ago.

There were not many Civil War graves, just twenty-two, but the tending of them took time. There may have been more, undoubtedly were, but these were the ones marked with the names and ranks and units. These were the graves of soldiers who wanted to be remembered for their part in the conflagration, men for whom the war never ended. Minder stopped at each one, said a word or two to the dead, swept the gravestones clear of snow in the winter and pine needles in the summer, repaired and painted the five wooden markers, cleaned the marble and stone ones.

The number of veterans was of no consequence to Minder, because he had nothing else to do except, of course, to care for his grandson, Emmett. The boy was ten now, and Minder walked him to school each day, because Emmett was timid, and his grandfather was all he had. And Emmett was all that Minder had. They were like two old men together, and precious to each other. Minder thought he would not live if anything happened to the boy. He had lost everyone else. His wife and his daughter had both taken the pneumonia and died on the same day, when Emmett was not yet old enough to walk. And then Emmett's father had taken out. Minder hadn't heard from him since the day the man had gone off to work, saying he'd come home for dinner, but he'd never come home for dinner. Instead, he'd left out, and they'd never seen him again. The deaths had put Minder himself in misery so deep that he could hardly blame the young man. But the father should have put aside his sorrow for the sake of the boy. He hadn't, and that meant Minder had the care of Emmett. No one else would take him, and Minder wouldn't give him over to an orphan asylum. So he'd raised the boy himself, taught him to work and have good manners. "Just doing those two things will keep you out of trouble," he told Emmett. But Minder knew better.

Minder wasn't thinking about Emmett now as he stood in front of the grave of Junius Cable ("Co. D, 18 Ohio Inf."). The plain marble stone, rounded at the top like a church window, was surrounded by an iron fence. He hadn't known Junius Cable, who had died in 1869, and Minder wondered again if the man had perished from the lingering effects of the war. So many of them had, especially the Southerners, like Cyrus Cheek ("Virginia"—the rest of the identification had worn off). He'd died in 1872 and was buried on the other side of the cemetery. Minder didn't know for sure if the war was the cause of Cyrus Cheek's death, either, but he'd known the man a little, and he'd come to believe it was. Either that or he'd died of plain meanness. Cyrus wouldn't give a person the sweat off a black cat's eye, and he acted as if the Virginia cavalry, of which he'd been a member, had won the war.

Minder trudged on to Theodore Wesley Arden's grave

("7th Ohio Inf."), which was marked by a red sandstone obelisk, broken off at the top, decorated with sandstone leaves. He'd known Ted Arden, too, a righteous man who thought he was a sinner because he loved to dance, and indeed, he could cut a step like nobody else. But the poor old fellow was stroked, and at the ending up, he could barely talk. His last words to Minder were, "I never was arrested, and I never was a juror. I never rode in an automobile, and I have one tooth left. You think I'll go to heaven?"

"I believe you'll go on past heaven," Minder replied, and the old man pondered that as he took his last breath.

Minder walked the same route every day, beginning with Lieut. S. P. Key ("Co. K, 3rd Colo. Cav.") and ending with Sgt. Frank Comb ("Co. B, 1st Minn. Inf."). He'd made a path through the snow from grave to grave, half of them clustered together, the rest spread out in family plots. The cemetery was deserted that day, as it usually was in winter. The ground was so hard that you had to use dynamite to blast out a grave, and folks wished the dying would hold out just a little longer, until spring, so the burying would be easier. Few came to visit the dead when the weather was bad, only the old widow, Mittie McCauley, and she did not intrude, just nodded, because she had her own ghosts to ride. Or maybe she liked the solitude, too.

In the summer and fall, the cemetery was filled with women tending the graves, for women were the survivors. They came with their bouquets of columbine and lupin summer's-half-over set in jars of water and propped them beside the markers. Women in Swandyke were charged with caring for the departed, most of them dead from accidents in the mines or on the gold dredges, much the way the widows of the South carried on what they called the "noble cause" after that terrible war. They had forgotten there was nothing noble about war, about the killing and the maiming. Minder'd never forget the dead men, nor the smell of rotting flesh that had risen up when he'd stepped on a severed leg or guts that had spilled out onto the red dirt. Or the sounds—the guns, the cries of the wounded, the rebel yell, which could chill a Union soldier to the bone. And the silence when it was all over. That had been even worse, the silence as you walked among the dead and praised God that you were still alive, although you never knew why. Why had God spared him and not the rebel boy who had lain at his feet, his head lying off to the side, the skull cleaved as cleanly as if it were a split melon? Why had God saved Minder and not his pard? It made a man wonder if God cared or if there really was a God. Over the years, Minder had decided there wasn't. And even if there was, Minder didn't like him much.

Then there were the worst sounds of all, the noise of the explosion and the screams of the men burning, drowning, calling out as they sank into the water and then were still. Those were the sounds of Minder's own personal hell, the sounds that he believed would follow him into eternity.

The old man walked on to the next grave, stopped, and greeted Alfred Totter. He'd known Al Totter, worked beside him for five years at the old Irish Queen Mine in the 1870s before either one mentioned he'd fought in the war. And then they'd considered each other warily, like dogs circling, before they found out they were both Union volunteers. They'd talked about the war as only two men who'd shared a terrible time could do, because no one else understood. Neither wives nor children, especially not wives. Minder had never told his wife about the worst of the war. She was a good woman and had suffered, too, but she hadn't seen her friends dying around her, their faces torn off, their limbs severed.

Nor had he ever told anyone else about that terror he relived every day.

Minder picked up a pine bough on the Totter grave and shook off the snow, then replaced the branch. He thought of those branches as quilts, and in winter, he placed them on the graves reverently, as if to keep the occupants warm.

Now, he looked out at the sun shining on the snow and saw Mittie McCauley trudging up the trail to the graveyard, and suddenly he felt the need of a human voice. The day's work at the cemetery made him gloomy, and he wanted to shake off the feeling before Emmett came home, bursting through the door with news of his day. Emmett didn't like going off in the morning, was afraid of the new day, but he was happy when he walked home with his little friends.

Minder waved to Mittie and watched as she came through the iron arch with MOUNTAINBROOK CEMETERY spelled out in big iron letters. Seeing Minder waiting for her, the old woman went over to him, adjusting her scarf, retying it under her chin. Her face was brown from the sun, but smooth, and she was as fit as anyone her age—my age, Minder thought, maybe a little younger. She ought to marry again, her being a widow for ten, fifteen years. He himself had given it a little thought. The boy needed a woman around. But Minder didn't want to adjust to someone else. Besides, better men had courted the woman and had no luck, and he'd known his chances were poor.

"You do them proud," the woman told him now. "You don't let them be forgot."

"It's little enough. I'm the lone sentinel around here." He had a sudden thought. "Did Frederick fight in the war? Was your husband a soldier? I ask you: Was Fred one of us?"

She looked off at the far mountains, sky blue in the distance. "He was. Frederick fought for the Union, was at Shiloh. But he wouldn't talk of it."

"I could tend his grave for you, save you the trouble of tramping out in the cold."

"No, it's my job. I can talk to him up here, talk out loud. People must think I'm touched."

Minder smiled. He talked out loud to the graves, too.

"I look at the ground when I tell him things, but I like to think he's up there." She pointed upward with her chin and laughed a little. "I guess I'll never know. There's things can't be explained in this world."

"If Fred McCauley's not in heaven, nobody's there," Minder replied, although he wasn't so sure. The old woman's husband had fallen into temptation at times.

"I wonder . . ." she said, and she stopped, and Minder waited. "I wonder if he finds peace now. I wonder if any of them do."

Minder had wondered that, too; every day he'd asked that question. "I'm not for sure knowing, but I think some of them do. Maybe. But not all. No, I think not all." He was one of those who would never find peace.

Minder was eighteen when he went for a soldier. He'd wanted to join earlier, but his pa said he'd do more good at home, working on the farm, instead of turning himself into cannon fodder for the Secesh. Besides, who cared about freeing the slaves? the old man asked. Minder thought he knew what it was like to be a slave. It was for sure that his father worked him like one, got him up before daylight, rode him like a mule until it was too dark to see, beat him when he felt like it, because the father was that cruel. The difficult life had taken everything out of the old man but meanness and cussing.

Minder was raised hard. The eldest of five boys, he was low like his father and pack-jam full, as solid as a pine knot, and was used to the relentlessness of farmwork. He'd had two precious years of school, had it only because his mother had insisted on it, and then she'd fallen and been disabled to work. She'd taken a fever, and cut off her hair, which was long and thick and as red as cherries, and his father, a Bible-thumper when it suited him, had smacked her for it, saying, "If a woman cut her hair, let her also shave." It was only a matter of time, living with the old man, that she went in meanness, too, and told Minder that, at nine, he was old enough to do a man's work. He'd tried to protect his brothers, especially the one who wasn't just right in the head and almost too sickly that he couldn't be raised up, but the parents had a way of turning the boys against one another, so after a time, Minder looked out only for himself.

He asked his father about joining up. Minder thought it would be a lark, tramping off to the South to fight the Secesh. The old man cussed him out, said he'd beat the starch out of him if he tried to leave, use him like a mule to pull the plow, which was the father's way of punishing the boys, sometimes yoking two of them together. Minder didn't know that, at eighteen, he had the right.

The old man didn't trust the boy to stay on the farm, and he watched him, so Minder bided his time. He waited until he was ordered to the blacksmith with a plowshare to be mended. He went, spent the day in town, waited until dark to go home, met the old man on the road, because the father had thought the son had joined up and was on his way to drag the boy back. Minder felt smug, said the blacksmith had been busy, so he'd had to wait all day. He figured that the next time Minder went to town, the old man wouldn't be so anxious to see him home, and that might buy him an extra day. So Minder buried his few possessions—a knife, a dollar in pennies and nickels, a marble, an eagle claw, a rock he'd seen fall out of the sky—in a stone crock near the road and waited until he was sent on another errand. He collected his treasure then, and instead of walking to the town, he hitched a ride in a wagon with a farmer who was going all the way to the Mississippi River to Fort Madison, Iowa, and he joined up there. It was an easy thing to do. He scratched the pen to the paper, and he was a soldier in the United States Army.

Minder met Billy Boy Forsythe in Fort Madison on that first day. Billy Boy had joined up, too, and his family had come along to see him off—two brothers, three sisters, his mother and father. The women cried, and the men shook Billy Boy's hands and told him how proud they were of him. "I hate to leave you boys with the work," Billy Boy told his brothers, but they punched him in the arm and replied they were glad he was going to do his part to preserve the Union.

"You'll make a brave and loyal soldier," one of them said.

Minder watched them. He wasn't jealous, but more curious, because he'd never seen a family act that way, didn't understand it. He stared at Billy Boy's sisters, and reddened when one turned and caught him looking. He expected her to raise her nose in the air the way the girls at home did, but instead she went over to him and asked if he was part of her brother's unit. Minder didn't know, but Billy Boy said, "If you just joined, I bet you and me are going to fight this war together." And so Minder sat with the family when they opened the picnic baskets and shared the fried chicken and cake and lemonade. And later, he and Billy Boy shared the pint that Billy Boy's brothers passed around as a going-away present. It was a fine day, the finest of his life. He'd met Billy Boy, joined the army with a pay of thirteen dollars a month (more money than his entire family had ever had at one time), acquired the first whole suit of clothes he'd ever worn, and a pair of drawers. Minder had never worn drawers before. He thought he was a swell.

Just before the boys marched off, the girls hugged and kissed Billy Boy, and one gave Minder a peck on the cheek. It burned like fire. "You have a look out for Billy Boy. He's just turned seventeen," she told him.

The army was the time of times for Minder Evans. Billy Boy complained about the food—said it would make a mule desert—and the graybacks and the endless marches where the soldiers tramped for miles in their hot uniforms, buckled and belted with half a dozen straps across their bodies to hold ammunition, canteens, haversacks, knapsacks, and such. But Billy Boy was part of a rich family that had hundreds of acres, dozens of cows, and a hired hand or two, or three. He had come up easy, not overworked like Minder, so he didn't know hardship. Minder did, of course, and in the army, he ate better than he ever had in his life and slept better, too, because he had a wool blanket and a fine bunk in a dog tent instead of a tattered quilt on a dirt floor under a leaky roof. Even the marching was easier than plowing the fields. Oh, it was a swell time—at first anyway.

Minder, who had joined to get away from the farm and because he thought the war would be a great adventure, didn't care about freeing Negroes, and he wasn't sure about preserving the Union, because he hardly understood what the Union was. Billy Boy explained it to him. "You can't tear a country in half. Then it wouldn't be the *United* States, would it?" Billy Boy asked, and Minder guessed not. "A man's life isn't worth much if he allows his country to be torn apart by traitors," Billy Boy continued. Minder liked the pretty words and later used them himself when another recruit as dog-raw as himself asked Minder why he'd joined.

He liked the good times with his compatriots when they raised Old Scratch. After they left Fort Madison on a Mississippi River steamboat, they tapped a keg of beer someone had stolen and smuggled on board and got roaring drunk and sang "John Brown's Body" at the top of their lungs, the whole lot of them, even Billy Boy, who said he'd never had a taste of stimulant in his young life until he joined up. When another of the company made fun of Billy Boy for that, called him a sissy, Minder fisted him.

In camp, they joined a group of Iowans and went off searching for what one of the men, Josiah Hatch, called "horizontal refreshments." Josiah had been to town before and said it was a regular Sodom and *Gomorrow*. Some of the girls were from New Jersey, he explained, as if New Jersey were as exotic as Persia. Minder was game. He'd never had a girl before, never even kissed one, and he thought the girl—a woman, actually—at the place Josiah took them was the most amazing creature he had ever seen. Her hair was a curious yellow, and she powdered her face, the powder mixing with sweat in the wrinkles of her cheeks. When the woman took Minder into her bed, Minder decided she was as old as his mother, and that unnerved him, but not for anything would he quit her, because his friends would have been merciless. When he was done and had paid, he thanked her, and she gaped at him, for nobody ever thanked her.

"How was it?" asked Billy Boy later. Billy Boy had not indulged himself.

"Hurrah for hell!" Minder replied. He felt strange the rest of the day.

They were a pair: Minder, tough and scrappy, ready for adventure, while Billy Boy, slender and quick, thought things through before he committed himself. Minder looked after Billy Boy, while Billy Boy was right clever to Minder, teaching him about books and history and explaining why there was a war against the South. Minder had thought the war pitted the slaveholders against those who did not own slaves.

He was surprised to discover that there were Secesh who were themselves abolitionists.

"My sister Kate says she's of a mind to write you, since you don't get any letters," Billy Boy said after they'd been in the army a few weeks. "She asks if you'd object, says if you have a sweetheart at home who'd fuss about it, she won't."

Minder had no sweetheart and had never received a letter in his life. So the idea thrilled him, and he and Kate began a correspondence. Her letters were chatty and funny, written in a fine hand on writing paper. Barely literate himself, Minder wrote back on slips of paper, scratching out words in the dirt beforehand so that Billy Boy could tell him if they were spelled properly. Kate sent him newspapers, and Minder read them slowly, sounding out each word, until over time, he could read most anything if the words were simple. Once, Kate gave him a tiny Bible, inscribed "May God protect the loyal soldier Minder Evans is the earnest wish of his friend Kate Forsythe." Minder carried the Testament in his pocket and read it by the campfire, asking Billy Boy what the strange words meant. And so the two engaged in many a theological discussion about God's plan for mankind in general, and the Union soldiers in particular, because it was the belief of all that God himself was a Union man.

Minder cherished the letters from Kate and wrote that he'd rather have them than a solid gold watch. As Minder's writing skills improved, he revealed parts of himself to Kate that he'd never shown to anyone. When the war was over, he wrote, he planned to go west, maybe find a gold mine, since he was tired of being poor. He told about the pranks and adventures of the army, such as the time he and Billy Boy, tired of camp rations, shot a cow. Stealing was against the army's rules, so they skinned the animal and lugged it back to camp, claiming it was a slow deer. Much of what he wrote was about food, because by then, the rations were not as good as when Minder first joined the army. Hardtack, so hard that it had to be soaked in water to be edible or pounded into pulp with a rock, was the butt of many army jokes. Minder wrote Kate that he had bit into a piece of hardtack and remarked to Billy Boy that he felt something soft.

"A worm?" Billy Boy asked.

"No, a nail," Minder replied. The incident was an old joke in the army, but Minder didn't think Kate would mind if he appropriated the story for himself.

He also drew pictures of camp life, showing Billy Boy cooking over a campfire and cleaning his rifle. He pictured the officers hiding behind trees, with the bullets flying around them, or drinking coffee as they ordered the soldiers into battle. Minder even drew a series of pictures of himself, first asleep, then wakened suddenly as a bee stung his nose, and finally a picture of his face with the swollen proboscis.

Along with her letters, Kate sent him gifts—a box of cookies, a pen wipe (which he carried in a pocket over his heart, since he had never had a pen to wipe), a housewife that she had made herself, with compartments for buttons and thread and needles, even a tiny pair of scissors. And in time, Minder believed himself in love with Kate. He told Billy Boy that after the war, he intended to declare himself and ask if she would have him. Minder could not remember which sister she was—the one with the blond curls, the brown-haired one, or the girl with the spectacles—and he was embarrassed to ask Billy Boy. But it did not matter. He would have taken any one of them.

After they had exchanged letters for a time, Kate sent Minder her likeness, but it was small, not much bigger than his thumbnail, so he still wasn't sure who she was. He studied the brown-tinted photograph, which he kept in his Bible, and sometimes in his mind, he mixed up Kate with the prostitute. Those were nasty thoughts, and Minder tried to keep them away. Kate had an aura of purity about her, and Minder did not want her sullied in his mind. Nonetheless, at night, when he could not sleep, he imagined Kate, dressed naked, lying beneath him.

Like the others in their company, Minder and Billy Boy chaffed under the endless drilling and the boredom of camp life and itched to get into a fight before the war was over. After all, it was 1864, and the South was made up of degenerates who couldn't keep up the pace much longer. The two feared that the war could end before they had a chance to fight it. From time to time, the Iowa soldiers engaged in skirmishes. One of them was nicked in the elbow. Another broke his rifle. They captured two rebels, who were poorly thin and barefoot and didn't amount to a cuss, and Minder thought it was a fool of a job to fight against such. He told Billy Boy that a bobtail dog with a bayonet on his tail could have captured the Confederates.

"At least we didn't run," Billy Boy told him, and Minder wondered if Billy Boy was a coward, because Minder wasn't afraid. But it was unlikely that Billy Boy was yellow. He was just more of a thinking man.

The two became the leaders of their bunch of Iowa fellows, Billy Boy the brains and Minder the daring. Minder led an assault on a Secesh barroom, where the soldiers liberated the whiskey, rum, brandy, gin, and wine, and got as drunk as the devil. The boys cheered when Billy Boy suggested they take a few bottles back to the officer who was in charge of guard duty, hoping for a reprieve from that onerous chore. And they did not blame Billy Boy when they discovered that the officer they'd picked was an abstainer, who poured the purloined liquor onto the ground and assigned them duty that very night.

Minder and Billy Boy's companions did more than wage war on saloons. Once when half a dozen of the company were reconnoitering, they came across the engine of a Confederate freight train parked on a siding. The crew had gone to mess call in the camp a few hundred yards away and left the train unattended.

"It'd be a lark to capture an engine," one of the soldiers joked.

"Why, that's a fine idea," Billy Boy said. The others laughed, but Billy Boy was serious. "We couldn't take it back with us, but could be we could use it to give a goodly dose of damage."

Minder saw immediately what his friend meant and asked, "Anybody know how to drive an engine?" Minder himself had never been inside a train, had never even seen one before he joined the army, but one of the others said he allowed as how he could. "Then quick, boys, uncouple the cars, and we'll climb aboard," Minder told them. The others followed his orders, releasing the cars and jumping onto the engine. They took off down the tracks, Minder being so bold as to reach over and blow the whistle as they encountered a group of Confederates near the tracks. The soldiers jumped aside, and one or two waved, and the Iowa boys waved back, laughed at being taken for rebels. They passed a Negro, too, and Minder thought it was funny when the black man jumped off the tracks so fast that he fell down and cussed himself in Negro talk. Minder didn't have much use for colored people.

"Now, what are we going to do with this train?" Minder asked after they'd passed the encampment.

"I've pondered that," Billy Boy said. "We can't take it back to camp with us. So we'll get up a good head of steam and derail the engine on that curve just before the bridge. That way we'll take out the bridge and the engine both." And that was what the boys did. They fired up the boiler as good as they could, then slid off, leaving only Minder, who volunteered for the duty, as the engine headed full speed toward the river. At the last minute, he, too, jumped and watched the engine careen into the bridge, then plunge into the water.

It was a bold plan, but with one minor complication. As they had demolished the bridge and jumped out of the engine on the near side of the river, they had to swim their way across to the Union camp. Billy Boy didn't know how to swim, so Minder put him on a log and pushed his friend across the river, Billy Boy shivering a little. Nothing scared him more, he said—not bullets nor fire—than a watery grave. Minder did not understand fear, but he was glad to protect his friend. After all, hadn't he promised Kate (or perhaps one of her sisters) that he would look after her brother?

Capturing lost rebs and even hijacking a steam engine were larks, but the boys longed to be in a battle, to kill their share of cowardly rebels and maybe even get a bead on old Jeff Davis or General Lee himself. They knew it wasn't likely they'd encounter the leaders of the traitorous South, of course, but they hoped to show off their patriotism and their marksmanship by striking down a Confederate or two. And so it was with great excitement that these Iowa volunteers were ordered to a place called Spotsylvania. As the recruits marched smartly into the Union encampment, one of them called out to the weary veterans who had already fought the first day of the battle, "Iowa's here, boys! Iowa's here!"

They were met with catcalls and hoots of derision, one fellow shouting as he squatted beside a campfire, "I-o-way. What way is that? Turn tail and run away is what."

"Fresh fish!" cried others.

One old soldier who was chewing tobacco, drooling juice down his chest, leaned over and spat, then remarked, "They don't know enough to learn a dog to bark."

"It'd take just about three pairs of minutes for them boys to cry for mama," added his companion, a man whose eyes were bright with fever. His mouth hung open, and he sat on a rock, his hands on his thin knees, looking like a corpse.

The Iowans didn't mind the remarks, because they were full of themselves. Nor did the old soldiers really care much about the attitude of the newcomers. Many of them were morose old fellows, fatigued by war, and they were glad for reinforcements. Others found the Iowans targets for jokes and pranks and perhaps saw them as marks for games of chance—if they survived the fighting. A few of the veterans took the Iowans under their wing, however, and warned them about the next day's battle. Billy Boy listened to them, but Minder thought them sour fellows. He itched to fight. "I expect to dispatch a few Secesh to hell to pump thunder at five cents a crack," he wrote Kate that night, too keyed up to sleep. *Dispatch* was something Billy Boy said, and Minder thought it a right smart word.

He almost could not stand the slow and careful way the men prepared for the fight, because he was ready to rush the enemy. He waited impatiently, until at last the chaplain stood before them and said, "Men, remember that you are fighting for a glorious cause. The Lord is on our side, and if by chance you are struck down, you will be with Him this day in heaven. May God be with us in our fight to preserve the Union."

Minder was not much for preachers. Nor were some of the others. One man called, "You be with us, preacher, or you be behind a stout tree?" But he was hushed by others, who said the chaplain was a gallant man who would indeed be with them, and welcome. The day before, he had carried a bottle of brandy into the battle instead of a gun, administering it to those in need, which was just about everyone.

A few of the soldiers read passages in their Testaments or bowed their heads in prayer, Billy Boy among them, and Minder wondered if his friend was thinking again that he might be a coward. Minder promised himself he'd be beside Billy Boy and watch over him—and keep him from running.

The battle commenced in the morning, and it was a strange time for Minder. Later, he would be a little embarrassed by his naïveté, but at the time he could only wonder. He had thought it would be a clean thing—men firing from behind trees or running in a straight line, with the killing swift and simple. But all was dark and confusion, with smoke rising up from the cannons and the guns and white puffs from exploding shells, until a man could hardly see, and the *ssst* of bullets, the scream of shells, and Minder was not prepared for all that. Within minutes, the air was so dense and the action so frenetic that he could not be sure who was reb and who a fellow Union soldier.

Then Minder saw the wounded, not cleanly killed with a single bullet to the head or chest the way you'd shoot a deer, but butchered like hogs. The men lay on the ground, blood and intestines and brains spilling out of them, most of them silent, but a few calling for help, for water, for God. Some tried to staunch the blood that flowed from where their legs or arms had been severed. One soldier looked at the bloody stump of what had once been his hand and cried, "Mother, I can't milk the cow."

The soldier beside Minder called out as he was shot in the stomach, and at first Minder thought the man was Billy Boy. But instead, he was Josiah Hatch, the Iowan who had taken them to the whorehouse. Josiah would never again seek horizontal entertainment.

Minder did not stop to help Josiah or any of the wounded, because he could do nothing for them. Instead, enraged at what had happened to his comrades, he was swept up in a desire to kill the traitorous Confederates who had caused the war, and he rushed forward with his rifle, shooting a reb who stood on the battlefield with his gun aimed at the Union lines. The man dropped as if he'd been a mule shot in the head, and Minder felt no guilt—no elation, either, but only a sense of relief: He had killed a rebel. He was as cool as ever he was in his life as he muttered, "Goddamn son of a bitch gone on down to hell."

Minder dropped down to reload, tearing open the cartridge, then turned over onto his back the way the veterans did to ram the charge home. He got to his knees, firing again, and again the charge struck a reb. Minder heard someone cheer "Hurrah!" at that, and then he realized the shout had come from him. He turned to look for Billy Boy and almost didn't recognize him, because his friend's face was covered with powder from tearing the cartridges with his teeth. They grinned at each other. Then both of them picked their targets and fired into the enemy lines.

They fought like that, side by side, one of them moving a little when someone called "Close up the gap" or "Re-form the line," but mostly, they stayed together, one shooting while the other reloaded. Once, Billy Boy shoved Minder's head to the ground at the instant a minié ball whirled past where the head had been, and Minder knew that Billy Boy had saved his life. He did not feel fear even then, but only rage that the man had tried to kill him, and he raised his rifle, but Billy Boy had already shot the Confederate, who lay writhing on the ground. Billy Boy had raised himself up to do it, and Minder told him, "I guess you aren't a coward."

"I couldn't let him kill a brave and noble soldier," Billy Boy replied, and Minder felt a strange emotion that his friend would endanger himself to defend his pard. He understood now the bond among the old soldiers he had met in camp and felt a pride that he and Billy Boy felt that way about each other. They were closer than brothers, and Minder knew he would sacrifice his own life for his friend's.

Then came the call to fix bayonets, and Minder attached his bayonet to the end of his rifle barrel, and with the others, he rushed the enemy. He thought he would thrust the bayonet through the first Secesh he reached, but instead he used the rifle as a club, striking the boy in the shoulder, then kicking him in the head as he went down. This type of fighting was satisfying to him, because while he had never shot a man with a rifle, he had been in many a fight, and hand-to-hand combat was something he knew. Minder was a rocky chunk of a man with solid fists, and many of the rebs were weakly fellows who could not defend themselves. Billy Boy, however, was not so well prepared to fist the enemy, and Minder found himself swinging his rifle butt against the rebs who swarmed around his friend. He figured he had saved Billy Boy's life, and when the battle ended that day, he thought the two of them could call it even. He did not write Kate that he and her brother were nearly killed, but said instead that they had had enough glory for one day.

The killing did not bother Minder, but the wounding did. In the night, he heard the piteous call of the dying asking for help, asking for water or "Mother"; they would have been better off if they had been killed at once, not left like that on the battlefield to suffer. He heard the chaplain moving among them, listening to the wounded men cuss, and knew the preacher would write their wives and mothers that in their last breaths, the dying had said they were happy to have been called upon to give their lives in the cause of the Union. He wondered how many of their families would believe that. Minder slept intermittently that night, awaking once and crying, "We got to close their sight. We got to put nickels on their eyes."

The harsh voice of another soldier replied, "There ain't enough nickels in the whole world for that."

"They died for a noble cause," one of the officers remarked the next morning, but Minder saw nothing noble about the slaughter, and he wrote as much to Kate in the following weeks. His letters to her became more solemn now that he and Billy Boy were in the fighting. Sometimes, Minder poured out his agony to Kate, as he could not to Billy Boy or any other soldier. He still wrote about the jokes the soldiers played on one another and the adventures of camp life, but increasingly the letters described the battles and the death. And sometimes he drew pictures of the fighting. Minder did not know that such information was not appropriate for a young girl, because he had no sisters. But he had the need to tell her. Writing to Kate kept him sane. Sometimes he thought he was fighting the war for her. He cherished her letters, reading them over and over until he knew them by heart.

During the next months, in which he turned into one of

those weary veterans, Minder became inured to death. Sometimes he was assigned to gather the dead, to shroud the bodies and build boxes for them, or, more often, line them up in a ditch for burial. Seeing the rows of dead soldiers did not affect him. The dozens and dozens of bodies meant little more than piles of fence posts, but if he recognized one of them as a friend, saw the flies and worms feeding on his wounds, Minder turned away and vomited. From time to time, he said a prayer, although he was not sure he believed in God. Still, there might be some power out there that could keep the dead men from taking the horrors of war into eternity with them. Often he carried his rage into the next day's battle, and so he developed a reputation for nerve and daring, because even after months of fighting, he still did not know fear.

Minder and Billy Boy never fell in battle, were never even nicked by a bullet, but in the course of time, they were captured by the Confederates, and that, Minder thought, might have been worse than dying. A Union officer ordered both of them to go in search of his horse, which had not been properly picketed and had wandered away, and the two walked into a nest of Secesh who were spying on the Union camp. It was a fool thing, and Minder was a little ashamed that they had been taken that way. The rebs were decent-enough fellows. They relieved the pair of their weapons and coins and gewgaws and Billy Boy of his gold watch, but they let the two prisoners keep their Testaments. And they shared their supper, which was mostly a cornmeal gruel seasoned with grubs. Then the two captives were marched through miles of rain to a railroad line, where they squatted in the mud with other prisoners to wait for a train.

When the train arrived, the prisoners were herded on board like cattle, so crowded into the boxcar that not all of them could sit. Minder and Billy Boy took turns standing.

The train ride was the beginning of the worst time Minder had encountered in his young life. It seemed they rode forever in the car with its awful stench, for one end of it had been designated a sink. Some of the wounded prisoners died during the trip, but their bodies were unloaded only at intervals. Minder thought he would die of thirst before they reached their destination. None of the men knew where they were going until the train stopped and the doors were opened, and the word went from man to man that they were assigned to Andersonville, the worst of the prisoner-of-war camps.

"It can't be so bad as they say," Billy Boy told Minder, and he was right. It was worse. As the men dragged into the compound, the other prisoners called them "fresh fish" and gathered around. Some asked for information about how the war was going and if the Union was winning. But others eyed the newcomers, looking for the weakest of them, the ones who could be picked off the easiest. As they shuffled through the camp, one of the soldiers was shoved to the ground and cried out, "My shoes!" But he was too late, and his footgear had disappeared. Minder clutched his coat and looked around fiercely to let the others know he wouldn't be taken without a fight. When one prisoner, toothless, with hollow eyes and yellow skin, clutched at Billy Boy, Minder told him to let go or take a beating. And because the newcomers were stronger and healthier, they were left alone—for the time being, at any rate.

Minder knew their survival depended on cunning, and for the first time in his life, he was grateful for his father's viciousness, which had taught him how to protect himself. He saw a dead prisoner being carried out of a mud and stick cave known as a shebang, and he claimed it, pushing Billy Boy inside. "That boy died of dysentery," a prisoner warned him, but Minder didn't care. He knew for certain if they slept out in the rain and snow, both he and Billy Boy would catch pneumonia, and that was as sure a way of death as any.

Without each other, they might have died. Minder had his coat, and at night he put it over both of them as they slept spoon-fashion to keep warm. He scavenged scraps of wood, which they used to make the shebang tighter. Billy Boy acquired a deck of cards, and the two played bluff, or poker, as some called it. As they had nothing to bet, they put up anything they could think of. Minder won the President's House in Washington off of Billy Boy, then lost it after Billy Boy made him put it up against the Capitol Building. Billy Boy bet a herd of elephants and Minder a peck of monkeys. They won and lost General Grant's horse and

Abraham Lincoln's hat, the Comstock Lode and Pike's Peak. The game helped them while away the hours of boredom, which were almost as deadly as the disease and lack of food.

They tried to keep themselves clean, because Billy Boy was of a mind that health depended on cleanliness, but it would be only a matter of time until one of them came down with one of the diseases that pervaded the camp. And strangely enough, it was the stronger of them, Minder, who began to complain that his legs were drawn up and his gums sore. His skin turned a sallow hue, and a tooth popped out. They both knew it was scurvy, and Billy Boy tried to get his friend a place in the hospital. But the wards were full. The only time a place opened up was when someone was cured or, more likely, died. And then the bed was assigned to the sickest man. The only cure for scurvy was fresh vegetables, but where could one find a carrot or a turnip in Andersonville?

"I reckon I'm getting ready to go to sleep for good," Minder said one day when he could no longer stand up.

"You'll not die," Billy Boy told him fiercely. "You're my pard, and you'll not die. Kate's told me I can't go home if I don't take you with me." He smiled at the little sally, his attempt to keep up Minder's spirits. Minder knew his friend tramped the camp, searching for something to treat the scurvy, but he also knew it was hopeless.

Then one day, Billy Boy returned with a sack of onions under his jacket.

"Where'd you get them?" Minder asked, because finding a single onion, let alone a sack of them, was nothing short of a miracle.

"I traded my gold watch to a reb," Billy Boy replied as he cut the first of the onions in half with a strip of metal they used as a knife. Each day, he gave Minder half of an onion, and in time, the symptoms of scurvy abated.

It was only later, after he could walk again, that Minder realized Billy Boy wore no shoes. At first, Billy Boy said he was saving them, but when Minder remembered that the rebels who had captured them had taken Billy Boy's watch, his friend admitted he'd traded the shoes to a Confederate for the onions, a good trade, a satisfactory trade to both sides, he explained. "The reb had enough to eat but no shoes. He said he'd always fancied a pair and was willing to pay high for them. It's near spring, so I don't need the shoes. We'll beat the Secesh before snow falls," Billy Boy said. "And if we don't, why then I'll take one of your shoes, so we'll each have half a pair."

In March, the prisoners were told to ready themselves for an exchange. They would be sent to Vicksburg, Mississippi, and from there, they would go home. Some of them cheered and carried on, but Minder and Billy Boy sat quietly. "Was it worth it, the war?" Minder asked.

"We freed the slaves."

"I don't care much about Negroes."

"We saved the Union, then."

"I don't care much about the Union, either."

"We saved each other, then," Billy Boy said.

Minder nodded. Perhaps it had been worth it for that. He was glad he'd joined up. He'd survived. He'd met Billy Boy. And there was Kate. He knew his life was better than if he'd stayed on the farm.

The prisoners were released, sent by train and steamer from Georgia to Jackson, Mississippi, then marched the miles farther on to Vicksburg. It was not an easy march—walk was more like it, because Billy Boy had caught pneumonia and was feverish and weak, and Minder had to help him along. Still, they were in good spirits. They were going home—to Billy Boy's home. Minder had not written to his home folks since he'd joined up. They didn't know if he was alive or dead and wouldn't have cared, so he saw no need to inform them. But he'd inform Kate. He'd write to her as soon as he got to Vicksburg and tell her that he and Billy Boy were on their way. He'd tell her he had something important to ask her, too, and he hoped she'd want to go west, but he'd stay in Iowa if she was of a mind to live there.

On April 24, 1865, after the war was officially over, Minder and Billy Boy and two thousand other released prisoners boarded the *Sultana,* one of the Mississippi's great steam packets, on a journey up the river to Cairo. The soldiers laughed at the way they were pack-jammed together, and they all crowded to one side of the steamer to have their picture taken, almost capsizing the boat. They had survived the war, survived Andersonville. Nothing could harm them now.

"There's too many of us on board," Billy Boy remarked, but Minder only shook his head, because Billy Boy was one to worry, and he asked as a joke whether his friend wanted to wait for the next boat. The two found a place on the hurricane deck, where they could sit propped against the railing. The steamship backed out into the flood-swollen Mississippi, and Minder felt elation that he was going home to Kate, wondered if his letter would arrive before he did.

"You think she'll have me?" he asked Billy Boy.

"What?" Billy Boy replied. In the moonlight, Minder could see that his friend's eyes were red and glassy with fever.

"Kate. You think she'll marry me?"

"You already asked me, asked me a hundred times. Why'd Kate want to marry up with somebody who smells like he's been dead for two weeks?"

"Maybe I'll wash up first, trim off my beard. She's never saw me with a beard. You think that would help?"

"Naw. Then she'll see how ugly you are. By now, she's bound to be sweet on somebody else."

"You're joking me, aren't you? You better be joking me," Minder said, not sure of himself then.

Billy Boy smiled, and Minder punched him in the shoulder, nearly knocking him over, because Billy Boy was that weak. "I'd be proud to have you in the family," Billy Boy said. "Now don't pester me any more about it."

In a minute, Billy Boy went to sleep, curled up on the deck, but Minder was too keyed up to close his eyes. He stared out at the river, so swollen now that he could see the tops of trees peaking out of the water. The river had overflowed the banks, and the *Sultana*, creaking under its heavy load, sat low in the water. Some of the soldiers had complained that they were packed in like hogs, but Minder didn't care. After what he had been through, he was not afraid of a river. In fact, the Mississippi seemed peaceful to him; the sound of the water lulled him.

He was more worried about Billy Boy, who had grown weaker. But Kate would take care of him, feed him milk and bacon until he was fat as a groundhog.

The next night, when he couldn't sleep, Minder was again thinking about Billy Boy and how needy he was, when he heard the explosion. It was loud and terrifying, and Minder felt the boat heave and then heard the screams of men being scalded and burned and impaled on shards of lumber. Billy Boy woke up, thought he was in battle again, and reached out for his gun.

Minder grabbed his friend's arm and shook him. "It's the boat. I think it's blowed up."

The two saw the fire caused by the explosion of the *Sultana*'s boiler, saw the bodies of the dead and wounded, and then saw the men in the water. Someone tried to fight the blaze with a wet gunnysack but could not stop it. "The boat is sinking!" a man yelled. Another, whose hair was burned off, cried, "Jump. We got to jump, or we'll all be dead alike."

Billy Boy turned to Minder, his face white in the light from the flames. "I can't swim."

"Follow me," Minder replied, although he did not know where he was going. He only knew it was up to him to save Billy Boy, who would never survive in the water by himself. And Minder was sure they couldn't stay where they were. So he led the way to the front end of the deck, where the two grabbed hold of ropes and lowered themselves down to the bow of the boat. The steamer was littered with burned and injured men, and the survivors trampled them in their frenzy to get off the *Sultana*. Minder looked into the water and found it thick with soldiers, horses, and mules. He watched as men sank beneath the water and didn't come up. Some of the survivors fought over planks and sticks of wood, shoving one another away in their attempts to save themselves. A man yelled, "Let go of me, fool, or you'll drown us both." The river was so thick with people that you could almost walk on their heads, and Minder knew it was death to jump among them.

But they did not have any other plan. Minder waited until there was a clear space in the water, then grabbed a panel of a door and told Billy Boy, "Now. We'll jump together. Hang on to the board."

"I'll drown," Billy Boy cried.

A burning timber fell onto the deck beside them, and there was fire all over Billy Boy. They tried to brush it off, but Billy Boy's hair was burned. Minder said, "I'll take care of you, I promise. We're pards to end of the road, aren't we?"

"I'm scared, Minder," Billy Boy said.

"Well, I'm not. I'm not going to lie to you. I'll have to swim hard, but you can hold on to the board, and I'll get us both to shore. It's jump now or die here in the fire."

"You promise you'll stay with me?"

"I said I would, didn't I? I won't let us face the day of judgment yet."

The two climbed onto the railing, each one gripping an end of the panel, and they went overboard. Billy Boy let go as they reached the water, and Minder thrashed around, searching for his friend, diving under the water, but it was so dark and muddy that he couldn't see anything. Then suddenly, Billy Boy popped up beside him, and Minder grabbed his friend with one hand and began to swim with him toward the riverbank.

The river wasn't what Minder had thought it would be. The current was swift and the water cold, and his coat and shoes were waterlogged, dragging him down. He couldn't rid himself of the heavy clothing because Billy Boy held on to him. Minder went under once, then came back up, gasping for air. He looked around for something to grasp and saw a piece of lumber and lunged for it. But with Billy Boy holding him back, Minder couldn't reach it, and the board floated on past. "Let up," he called to Billy Boy, but his friend was too frightened.

Minder saw the men around him slide under the waves and disappear, and now he wondered if that would happen to him. And for the first time in his life, he was afraid. He had been brave in battle and in the fight to survive at the prisoner-of-war camp. But now he believed that death was after him, and he knew fear. He saw part of a tree floating with the current, and with a mighty effort, he shook off Billy Boy and reached for the log. He should have pushed Billy Boy to the timber, made sure his friend was safe, but instead, at that instant, Minder cared only about saving his own life. So he let Billy Boy fend for himself while he lunged for the log. He grasped it, then turned and shouted to Billy Boy, watched his friend struggle in the water, reach for the log, reach for his pard, his fingers touching Minder's coat. Minder should have reached out to him, let go of the timber and grabbed his friend, but he didn't. And then Billy Boy was gone. His head slid under the waves.

Minder yelled for his friend, reached out, but the log was moving downriver with the current, and Minder wouldn't let go to dive into the water to search for Billy Boy. Instead, he floated along with the log, and as he did, he told himself that he couldn't have saved Billy Boy. It would have been foolish to try. But in the end, he knew that he had let Billy Boy drown. He should have shoved Billy Boy onto the log first, but he'd been afraid, and so had saved himself instead of his friend.

Minder clung to the log for a long time, fighting off others who tried to appropriate it for themselves, and then he was alone, moving down the river. He no longer could see the flames on the *Sultana,* and he wondered if the boat had sunk, but the sky was lit up, and he thought the packet must be still burning. After a time, the screams and pleas for help stopped, and all Minder could hear was the sound of the waves. He floated with the current for a long time, past Memphis, where the *Sultana* had docked only hours earlier to off-load cargo. He was not frightened now. Instead, he was numb with the terrible thing that had happened, with knowing that when he had jumped into the river, he had stepped off to hell.

As daylight came over the river, Minder saw that he had floated toward the western shore, and after a time, the log lodged in the top of a tree that was almost submerged in the flood. He stayed there into the day, until men in a boat heard his calls and rescued him. They gave him a meal and clothes, because Minder had shed his waterlogged pants and wore only his shirt and drawers, and they offered him a bed. Later, they said, they'd take him across the river, where there was a hospital. But Minder wouldn't stand for that. They might ask his name, and it would go down that he had survived, and he had decided during those awful hours on the water that his name should be listed among the dead, listed with Billy Boy's. It would be better for Kate to think that the two of them had drowned together. It wouldn't do for her to know that he lived, while Billy Boy had died.

So when he was rested a little, Minder taken out. He went west, walked most of the way, stopping here and there to work for a little food or a few coins. It took him a long time, more than a year, to reach Colorado, where he went to the gold fields, and after a time he owned a piece of a gold mine. He married then. His wife was a good woman, and he loved her. They had one child, a daughter, whom Minder named Katherine.

He never again wrote to Kate, didn't know how she had taken Billy Boy's death—and his, of course. But once, after he had commenced to be prosperous, he went back to Fort Madison. It was a long time after the war. Minder was old then, although not as old as he was now. The place had changed. Fort Madison had turned into a fine town, and he didn't recognize it. He found a hotel, wrote his name, "M. Evans," in the register. The clerk read it and said, "You're not any relation to Minder Evans, I don't suppose."

Minder jerked up his head at that. "What?"

"Minder Evans." The clerk pointed to a pile of books on the counter with a sign on top that read 25 CENTS. Minder picked up one and read the title: *The Civil War Letters and Drawings of Private Minder Evans, a Civil War Hero.*

Minder placed a two-bit piece on the counter and took a copy of the book up to his room and sat down in a chair by the window and read the dedication: "This book is published in memory of two noble soldiers, Pvt. Minder Evans and Pvt. William E. Forsythe by the fiancée of one and the sister of the other. After fighting heroically in the war to preserve the Union and surviving the indignities of Andersonville, these two brave soldiers died in the waters of the Mississippi in the tragic explosion of the great *Sultana* steamship. May they rest in peace. Katherine Elizabeth Forsythe." The book was filled with Minder's letters and drawings. Kate had saved every one of them. On the cover was a photograph taken of the men on board the *Sultana*. Kate had circled two of them, identifying them as Minder and Billy Boy, but she was wrong. The two were indistinguishable in the photograph, hidden behind other soldiers.

For a long time after he finished reading his long-ago letters in the book, Minder sat and stared out the window at the Mississippi, and then he went downstairs and asked the desk clerk what had happened to Katherine Forsythe, the woman who had compiled the book.

"Miss Forsythe's an old maid that runs a stationery store over on Avenue G, sells paper and books and whatnot. She's a little daft, and age has come upon her." The clerk chuckled. "Every year, she reads one of them Minder Evans letters at the Fourth of July ceremony. Kind of sad, isn't it? You'd think she'd get over it, but those women never do."

"Kind of sad," Minder agreed.

Minder did not intend to speak to her, although he thought it would do no harm to go by the store, look through the window, just peer in out of curiosity. But he could not keep from going inside, where an old woman in black, her hair pulled straight back, sharpening her features, looked up. "Are you Katherine Forsythe, the one who wrote the book?" Minder asked.

She nodded, and Minder thought the clerk was right: She looked older than she should have. "You were in the war," she said. It was a statement, not a question.

"I was."

"My Minder Evans was from Iowa. Were you?"

"Oh, no," he said quickly.

She waited, and Minder wondered if every old soldier who read the book sought her out. She looked as if she didn't mind, that she spent her days in the past. "Did they recover the bodies, the ones of Minder Evans and Billy—William Forsythe?"

"No. There were so many who just sank, young ones like Minder and my brother, who died short of promise. They never surfaced. I believe those two had rather die together than one of them survive." She said the words as if she repeated them often.

"I'm sorry."

She nodded and waited. Minder thought she might recognize him, half-hoped that she would, but she didn't. After all, they had met only once, and they had been much younger then. He had a beard now, and his hair was white. "I'm in need of some reading material," he said, mindful that she must make a poor living peddling books and paper and ink. He went to the shelves and selected half a dozen volumes, the big ones, the most costly, with gold on the covers. He bought writing paper and ink and pens, and when he was finished, he had spent almost thirty-five dollars.

After Minder left, it came into his remembrance that he had sent her a gold cross once, not telling her he had ripped it off a dead Confederate, and she had promised not to take it off until he came home. He had not looked to see if she wore it still, but it didn't matter. Nor did it matter that he still did not know which sister she was.

The burial ground was deserted now. The widow McCauley was gone, and no one else had come to visit those lonely graves. Minder put away his Bible, the tiny one that Kate had given him and that had survived the Mississippi in the pocket of his shirt. He trudged out of the graveyard into town, raising his hat to a woman who passed him and greeting another with "Good evening." He nodded at one or two men but ignored the Negro who came out of the mercantile. Minder knew who the black man was. He worked at the Fourth of July in the mill, but he'd never have gotten a job there if Minder still owned a piece of the mine. Minder disliked Negroes, disliked them as much as he ever had the Confederates. He hadn't cared about them when he joined up, and over the years, he'd come to blame them for the war. He knew it didn't make sense, but he blamed them anyway. If they hadn't come to the United States as slaves, if they'd stayed back in Africa, there never would have been a war. Billy Boy would be alive, and he'd have married Kate. Over the years, Minder had come to blame the black people for the tragedy of his life.

The Negro had a daughter in the school. Minder thought she shouldn't be there, learning with white people. The girl had come home from school with Emmett once, and Minder had told her to go home, that she wasn't welcome. When the boy asked why, Minder replied roughly, "Black people aren't good enough to mix with us. Don't you know that? Where's your learning gone to?"

He thought about Emmett now and hurried on. Because of the snow, he had spent more time than usual tending the graves. He could see the vast snow-covered slope gleaming beneath the Fourth of July Mine and hear the school bell ringing. He wondered what his grandson would have to tell him about the day, and suddenly, the gloom of the cemetery left Minder, and he rushed on, to be at home when the boy arrived.

CHAPTER SIX

The room was cold when Essie Snowball woke up, and under the sleep-warm quilts, she stretched, arching her back and thrusting out her arms and long legs, just like the lion she'd seen once, stretching in the barred orange-and-gold railroad car in Denver. She thought about the lion sometimes, wondering if he was still caged up, but then, wasn't everybody? Not that Essie minded. There wasn't much wrong with being fed and pampered and admired. Better than working in a factory, much better. In fact, Essie almost enjoyed it. She had it pretty good. She stretched again, thinking how quiet and peaceful the house was, although it was already noon and some of the other girls would be awake by now. Maybe it was the cold that made them stay abed, the cold and the snow. But the snow made things seem clean and pure to Essie. She laughed at the idea of a hookhouse being clean and pure.

Essie yawned and stepped out of bed onto the cold linoleum floor, which was worn in a pattern from the door to the bed to the washbasin. She wrapped the quilt around her. It was her favorite quilt, made in a Snowball pattern. The other girls thought she was silly, piecing quilts in her off-hours, but more than one of the hookers had asked to borrow a covering when the temperature fell to twenty degrees below zero. Essie thought she might be the only hooker in Colorado, maybe the entire West, who had a sewing machine in her room, covered with a lace tablecloth, of course, for what man wanted to go to bed with a whore when a sewing machine just like his wife's or his mother's was sitting in plain sight?

Sewing pleasured Essie. After all, she'd been a dressmaker since she was a girl, and she felt joy in taking scraps of material and turning them into a thing of beauty. The sewing was profitable, too, since she made dresses for the other girls, shifts that were easy to put on and take off. The two dollars she charged for each dress went into the bank. She might be the only whore in Colorado who had a bank account, too. The other girls frittered away their pay on ribbons and perfume and cheap silk bedspreads that ripped when a man caught them in his dirty boots.

"You're queer," Miss Fanny, the madam at the Pines, told her once as she watched Essie write down a sum in her bankbook. "I never knowed a whore to be so saving. It goes against their nature." But Essie had a reason to be saving.

She went to the window now and looked out through the frost-etched glass at the vast white. Essie had never known there could be so much snow in a place, had been awed by it when she first came to Swandyke. She'd loved it, however, the white that fell as thick as the cotton batting in her quilts, covering the old sheds and ramshackled buildings and rusted-out machinery that littered the old mining town. It wasn't like the snow she'd grown up with, which turned black the day after it fell as it mixed with the ashes and the dirt under the wheels of freight wagons and push-carts. Even the cold felt good, so different from the streets of the Lower East Side of New York, which in winter made you shiver with the dampness that went into your bones, and in summer steamed and smelled of rotted food and horse droppings, unwashed bodies and fetid privies.

The snow was what had given Essie the idea for her name. All the girls changed their names, some calling themselves for film stars or heroines in the romantic novels that they read in the afternoons as they smoked and nibbled on chocolate drops, waiting for the hookhouse to open. Essie considered the names Mae Marsh and Gloria Swanson, because both of those actresses had dark hair and big black eyes like Essie's. But she didn't like pretending to be someone else, so after consideration, she picked Essie Snowball.

"Why not just Essie Snow?" Miss Fanny had asked her.

At first, Miss Fanny had called the new hooker "Frenchy." That was because when Essie went to her for a job, Miss Fanny asked if Essie had ever worked as a crib girl. The crib girls were the lowest form of prostitutes, often diseased and addicted to opiates. *"Oy veh!"* Essie muttered, and Miss Fanny asked what language that was. "French," Essie replied quickly, because she did not know if Miss Fanny hired Jewish girls. And so the word went about that Miss Fanny had hired a French whore.

But Essie had liked Essie Snowball. Perhaps it was because it was derived from her real name, Esther Schnable, although nobody knew that. She'd been real particular about not telling her born name, because someone might connect it with Sophie. It wouldn't do for anyone to know that Sophie Schnable was Essie Snowball's daughter. Only the woman who tended Sophie knew who the girl's mother was, although now that Sophie was six, it was only a matter of time before the girl herself figured it out. That was why Essie was putting aside money. In another year, she'd have enough to open up as a dressmaker in Denver, have enough to live on until the word got out that she could make a dress better than any of the seamstresses at Daniels & Fisher, and at half the price.

Essie dreamed of that day, but until then, Sophie was well cared for by Martha Perce. Martha gave it out that Sophie was her niece, that she was raising her up until her mother, a tubercular, recovered. That Martha was bringing up Sophie was a stroke of luck. Martha had been a confidence woman in Denver, living in the same hotel as Essie, and she'd made a mint of money bilking a banker. She'd thought the man would be too ashamed to admit he'd been taken by a woman he'd tried to seduce, but to Martha's surprise, he'd gone to the police. "I got to get out of the business, or they'll settle my hash mighty quick," Martha told Essie when she came to say good-bye. Martha had packed her bag and was out the door when the thought occurred to her. "Say, why'n't you and Sophie come along? You got nothing here, either, and they won't be on the lookout for two women and a kid."

So as Essie had no reason to stay, no place else to go, and owed the landlord for a week, she jumped the rent and followed Martha to Swandyke, setting herself up at the Pines and making enough to pay for Sophie's keep. "Money I pay. It's only right," she told Martha. The woman had grown bored after a while, with only Sophie to tend, and so she had opened a restaurant, the Dinner Bell. Sophie was big enough to help now, to put out the forks and spoons and dry the dishes. Lately, however, Martha had gotten tired of running a restaurant and fretted about staying in Swandyke. Essie knew it wouldn't be long before Martha herself left. Then Essie and Sophie would have to move to Denver.

On Sundays, when both the hookhouse and the restaurant were closed, Essie visited her daughter, who'd been told that Essie was a friend of her mother. When it was cold, the three met in the shuttered restaurant, but when the weather was nice, they picnicked in a remote spot in the mountains. Those were Essie's happiest times, when Sophie toddled among the wildflowers, picking off the blooms and dropping them into Essie's lap. Essie gave cunning little dresses to her daughter, made on her own fingers, and more than one mother had wondered how Martha's girl could be so finely dressed. In fact, the wife of the Fourth of July superintendent had asked the name of Sophie's dressmaker.

"I wouldn't know, lady," Martha had replied. "Sophie's mama sends her clothes to me by postal." When Martha told Essie the story, the two had laughed at the stuck-up woman's interest.

"Why'n't you tell her to give a look at the Pines? Why'n't you?" Essie asked, and they laughed again.

At the window, Essie stared through the willows, which were just red sticks bare of leaves, looking down the trail the children took to school. Sometimes she caught a glimpse of Sophie, who was in first grade, as the little girl trudged along with her speller. Essie knew it was a speller, because she gave the words to Sophie when they met—*cat, hat, rat*. The girl almost always got them right, because she was bright. But then, her father had been bright—not that it had taken much intelligence to lure Essie away from the life on Orchard Street.

There were no children on the trail now. The school day

was only halfway over. Essie knew that because the noon whistle had awakened her.

She yawned and scratched her stomach, then pulled her hand back, because she was sore from the beating she'd taken the night before. For no reason, that man had punched her in the stomach. She'd screamed, and he'd hit her a second time, and then pulled back his arm to fist her again, but the scream had brought Miss Fanny and the other girls. They hustled him out of the hookhouse and told him never to come back. Essie ruminated over the fact that none of the johns had come to her rescue, only the women, but she wasn't surprised. She didn't expect much from men.

The beating had come as a shock, however, because it was rare. Essie felt safe in the whorehouse, safer than she'd been in the days she'd worked over the sewing machine in the dress factory. The man who owned the place would lean against the girls as they worked, putting his hands on their breasts, and his sons would lie in wait for the women when they went to the bathroom. More than one girl had wet herself as she sat at her machine, waiting for the men to get bored with staring at the employees and go back to their offices. Essie knew of one seamstress who gave in, and months later, a different girl was sitting at her sewing machine. It was told around the factory that the first one had fallen into the river and drowned.

The son with the hair in his nose and ears had come

after Essie, all honey-mouthed, with a pomp of manner. She tried to ignore him, but he wouldn't leave her alone. So when he slipped his fingers into her shirtwaist and tugged at her breast, she grabbed his hand, white and slippery as lard, told him to go shave the hair in his nose, and laughed at him, laughed so hard and so loud that the other girls looked up from their machines. When they saw the man, his face flushed and perspiring, trying to disentangle his hand from Essie's blouse, they laughed, too.

"Your ears you should shave, too," another girl called, and the man glanced around to see who had spoken, but all the seamstresses were bent over their machines.

Of course, others had been let go for less, and there were bets about how long Essie would keep her job, but it didn't matter, because she left of her own volition not long afterward.

Essie massaged her neck, which was sore, too. She wondered what had gotten into the man who'd hit her, because most of the johns were polite. They were miners and laborers from the gold dredge, docile, well-mannered unless they were liquored up. They came for the intended purpose, but some just wanted to talk, to be with a woman for a time, pretend she was a sweetheart. They were lonely, lonelier even than the hookers. Essie talked to them about their growing-up times, their dreams, their miseries. Hooking wasn't a bad life. In fact, it was a pretty good life. And she had a room all to herself! There'd been a time, back when she slept with eight people in a three-room tenement, that she'd never even dreamed of such a luxury.

Of course, Essie had her regulars, and they brought her presents—cigarettes and chewing gum, bracelets and silk stockings. And they were so respectful—well, most of them anyway. She liked that about the clientele at the Pines. They made you feel you were doing them a favor. And in return, Essie made them feel they were her special customers. "This hour, I have been in heaven," she would tell them.

Dropping the curtain, Essie turned and let the quilt slip onto the floor, and then she made up the bed. The sheets were dingy, but they were almost clean. Miss Fanny didn't like to change them more than once a week unless it was absolutely necessary. Essie folded the quilt and set it at the end of the bed. It wouldn't do to have some impatient man stomp it in his hurry. She opened the window a little to let out the stale air, then shined up the room, dusted the chipped enamel bed, the dresser. She straightened the calendar and the picture of a bowl of fruit, and set the washbasin and pitcher and dirty towel beside the door. Just the week before, she'd taken down the ruffles that she had pinned over the door and on the cord of the single lightbulb that hung in the center of the room, washed and ironed them, and now the ruffles hung as stiff as petticoats. She wasn't slovenly like some of the other girls. Oh no. Most men didn't notice, but some did, and they preferred Essie for that. In fact, most men preferred her. She was the most popular girl at the Pines.

"Why, you could work in any whorehouse in Colorado," a john told her by way of compliment. And Essie had taken it for one.

Of course, the remark was no surprise to Essie, who had always appealed to men. She was something of a beauty, with her long neck and long fingers, and exotic-looking, a little like Theda Bara, who Essie thought was also Jewish. But it wasn't just Essie's looks. Nor was it her figure, which was still young and ripe, although she was closer to thirty than she was to twenty. No, it was the air of happiness that surrounded her. Essie's smile could make the sun shine, and when she laughed, she made a sound like tinkling bells. Her happiness felt like good fortune, and it made a man glad to be with her. Why, if you hadn't known better—and none of the men had—you'd have thought she'd been raised up without a care in the world. "Essie, I bet you never knowed a bad day in your life, not even one," a john had told her.

"Why, aren't you just right! Aren't you!"

But he was wrong. I should live so lucky, Essie thought.

The first memory Esther Schnable had was of her mother, Emma, lying on the table moaning. The neighbor women were crowded into the kitchen, watchful, nervous, critical, as the midwife fussed and coaxed the woman. Esther's mother wouldn't have a doctor. It wasn't proper for a man to see her like that, and besides, a doctor charged ten dollars. If she was lucky, the midwife would ask only two dollars, maybe one, and she'd clean up the baby and check in later to see how the mother was doing. All the women felt that way.

Emma sucked in her breath and twisted her face in pain, raising her back a little, then relaxing as the spasm passed, and the women clucked and smiled and recalled their own labors.

"With Etta, a whole day it took. Pains like you never got," a woman bragged, pulling her old crocheted shawl around her, although it was hot in the kitchen.

"Such luck you have. My Isaac weighed twelve pounds, maybe thirteen. Tore up like a newspaper, that's me," a second woman said.

The others shushed them, but it did not matter, because the woman on the table cried out and didn't hear them.

Outside, Esther's father sat on the stoop with a handful of men, smoking, coughing, because Abraham Schnable, working in the dank basement of a factory, had begun to develop small lesions on his lungs, the mark of what was called the "tailor's disease." Over the calls of vegetable vendors and pushcart hawkers, the shrill voices of women bargaining over the price of fish and the sellers pleading poverty, he heard his wife's last scream and reacted with a combination of pride and pity—pride because of Emma's fecundity, which was really a sign of his own maleness, and pity because he loved her and was sorry for the pain he'd caused.

"Maybe you get a boy this time, eh, Abe?" One of the men poked Esther's father in the side with his elbow.

"One that's goinna live," someone added. Of the six children Emma had already borne—all girls—only Esther and her sister Rachel, nearly three years older, were alive.

Now the two little girls sat forgotten in a corner of the front room. Rachel shivered and cried softly, and it was the younger girl who was the strength for both of them. "What if something happens to Mama?" Rachel whispered.

"It won't," Esther replied. She didn't know of the two babies before her who were born dead or recall the two others born after who'd lived such a short time, didn't understand death the way Rachel did. Besides, even at that age, Esther was an optimist, with a sunny disposition that charmed both family and neighbors. She lowered her voice, as if Rachel didn't know what was happening, and confided, "Mama's going to bring us a baby. It's going to be a brother."

"Oh, so now you're a prophet," Rachel said.

But Esther was right. More screams, more moans, and they heard the midwife announce, "A boy, Mrs. Schnable! Such a boy!" And the neighbor women cooed and laughed in their relief, and one went downstairs to tell Abe.

The father burst through the door of the dingy apartment and looked at the boy, examined the raw little thing with his eyes pinched shut and his hands and feet stretching in all directions and said, "My Jakob. My boy." Then he went to his wife and patted her hand and told her she'd given him a son, as if she hadn't known. He called the two little girls then and said, "Your brother. Come. Him you greet."

Esther rushed to look at the little bundle, but Rachel held back and muttered, "A boy. Now he won't want us. We aren't his *kindela* no more."

In 1906, at age thirteen, Esther got a job in the dress factory. Rachel had gone to work at the same age, when the father announced, "Learning for a girl, who cares? We got to buy glasses for Jakob, got to buy him clothes so the kids don't make fun of him."

"Nobody makes fun of him, Papa," Rachel said.

"Mind your business," the father replied, and coughed. The consumption had taken hold now.

"Money we need," Emma, her mother, confided, and Rachel had nodded, resigned, for, like others in the neighborhood, the Schnables scrambled to make a living. Abe could work only a little now, and he spent most of his time in a chair in the front room or, in nice weather, sitting on the stoop, gossiping and reading the newspaper. Emma did custom sewing at home, and without Rachel's income, she could not have made the weekly payments on the precious sewing machine. Emma also kept the apartment clean and did the laundry and cooking for three boarders. She, Abe, and Jakob slept in the bedroom, the girls in the kitchen, the boarders in the front room.

So Rachel went off to the factory, and in a few years, Esther followed. Esther didn't mind quitting school as much as Rachel had, because this younger sister was not much for books and learning. She liked the idea of earning money and didn't brood over her life the way Rachel did. Esther believed there were good things in store for her, although she couldn't have said why. If she'd thought about it, she would have understood that a Jewish girl born to immigrant parents on the Lower East Side of New York City didn't have many opportunities. But part of Esther's optimism was that she was caught up more in dreams than in reality.

Once, she and Rachel walked uptown, walked up Fifth Avenue all the way to Central Park. It was the first time either of them had left the neighborhood, and they were awestruck at the sights. They went into a department store and watched as shoppers stepped onto a staircase that actually moved, carrying them to the floor above. They stared for a long time before Esther dared Rachel to ride it.

"We go up. How do we go down?"

"There's got to be a down way. And if there isn't"—she shrugged—"we'll stay in the store forever. Us. That's something, eh?"

So they stepped gingerly onto the escalator, which swept them to the second floor, and there they found a second escalator and went on up to another floor. But a man caught them, took in their shabby clothes, asked what they were doing in the place, and told them to go back where they'd come from. Rachel was mortified, but Esther only vowed to make herself a fine dress, a black skirt with a white waist, and return.

Farther up Fifth Avenue, they stopped to gawk at a stone mansion where a family was gathered around a great table in the dining room, sitting under a chandelier that glittered like a starry night. "We should only live so good!" Esther exclaimed.

"Oh, and why should we? We're poor Jews from Orchard Street. Us, we'll never be anything," her sister replied.

Rachel went home morose, bitter about their state, but Esther viewed poverty only as a temporary condition. She saw no reason why she, too, shouldn't live in a stone house with electricity and servants. She did not know how she would manage these things, only trusted that they would happen.

At work, she told the other girls about the houses and carriages she had seen on Fifth Avenue and the people, dressed in rich silks and heavy velvets and furs, even the children. "A fur coat she had, all white like snow falling, and her not any older than Jakob," she said, and the others shook their heads in amazement. "Me, I'm going to have a white fur coat, and it's not going to be rabbit, either. And a chandelier like stars. I'll live in a house with a chandelier."

The others laughed at such a preposterous idea, and Rachel, listening, turned red with shame, for what hope did

Esther have of leaving Orchard Street, or Lewis, or Hester? "You make a fool of us all," she said. But then, thinking it over, Rachel told Esther that maybe she was on to something. "If we ever get out of here, it'll be you. Papa isn't going to amount to anything, and Jakob, what does he care about us? He can be a doctor, and you and me he'd let live in the tenement." And so the older sister pinned her hopes on the younger one. The only way out of the Lower East Side that she could think of was for a girl to marry well, Rachel told her sister, and why shouldn't Esther make a good match? After all, she was a beauty, with her dark hair and smoldering eyes, long neck and long fingers.

Rachel herself wasn't likely to marry well. She was short and broad, with a face as plain as a loaf of bread, and indeed, her parents had already picked out her husband. This happened when Rachel was nineteen, and she was excited. She hadn't met the man yet, although she'd seen him, a squat fellow with close-set eyes and hair covering the backs of his hands. Benjamin was a butcher, the son of a butcher, a good catch. "You'll never go hungry," the marriage broker said, and the parents laughed, but nonetheless, they found that a compelling argument. Of course, Rachel had no feelings for the man yet, but what girl did when she married? Love came later, after the wedding, after the children. That was the way it was. Marrying for love was a sure sign of trouble ahead.

Esther thought Rachel's intended was nice enough but dull, but then, so was her sister, which made them a good match. Benjamin visited Rachel, although the two were never left alone, because the girls were kept strict. The father and mother sat in the room with the young couple, Abe reading the newspaper and Emma sewing, Rachel shy, and the butcher tongue-tied and embarrassed.

"Eh, you see here the newspaper tells us they found the man what robbed the shoe store over on Columbia Street?" Abe remarked. "What you think of that?"

Benjamin only flushed and made darting gestures with his arms, and Rachel came to his rescue. "God should strike him dead for stealing from a poor man," she said, and Benjamin nodded emphatically.

The three women made Rachel's wedding dress from white silk, with a bit of lace around the neck. Emma, who collected her daughters' unopened pay envelopes every week, handing over only a dollar to each for expenses, was extravagant, giving Rachel enough to buy a pearl necklace, and for Esther, pearl earrings. "Where do we buy such fine pearls?" Rachel asked. She had never purchased a piece of jewelry, never owned so much as a paste brooch, in fact.

"Not from a pushcart," Esther replied. "We go to a jewelry store. They got different, better." And so the two girls, neither knowing a pearl from a quartz pebble, went into a store, where they bargained the clerk down from ten dollars to eight for the necklace, and he threw in the earrings. "A bargain. Do I know a pearl when I see it?" Esther asked, but in fact, they could have bought the pearls from a pushcart for half that, and as for being real pearls, it was best that Esther really didn't know a pearl when she saw it.

The wedding was held in the tenement, which was filled with relatives and neighbors, and after the ceremony, the guests ate cake and drank wine while a photographer took a picture of the newlyweds, standing stiff and solemn, a little apart from each other. Rachel looked scared, and indeed she was, for neither girl knew what would happen to the bride on her wedding night. Still, Rachel was happy, because she was anxious to leave the crowded tenement for her own home. And it was the first time since Jakob was born that Rachel was the center of attention. But she would miss Esther, her sister knew as she passed the cake, pressing it on the guests, for it would be unthinkable that any would be left. As Esther neared Rachel, her sister took her hand and whispered, "Tonight . . ." but she could not say more.

"You'll be all right. Have little fear."

Rachel nodded. "I will tell you. I will tell you everything then. You should not be an ignorant bride like me."

"Everything?" Esther giggled, and her sister turned crimson.

After the party was over, the wine drunk, the cake eaten, the presents opened and admired, Rachel and Benjamin left. The men gave each other knowing winks, but the women held back. "He's a kind man, her Benjamin," one whispered to Emma, who nodded and replied, "Esther, I hope she is so lucky."

In fact, Rachel did not tell Esther everything. When Esther pressed her, Rachel grew red, and her hands perspired, and she turned away, mumbling, "It is not such a big deal. Nothing to fear. Not such a big deal at all. One day you will know."

Although Rachel was married and lived a few streets away, life for her was not so different from the way it had been before her marriage. She had the care of her own tenement apartment, and she went to work in the dress factory every day, sitting beside her sister. At noon, she gossiped with the other girls, as she always had. And at night, when her husband was working or out smoking and drinking with his friends, Rachel and Esther went out themselves, to the candy store or the picture show or sometimes just to walk the crowded streets. When there was a cost to their outing, Rachel paid for the two of them, for, like any wife, she had charge of her own family's funds.

Sometimes the sisters walked past a dance hall, stopping to listen to the ragtime music. They peered in at the couples holding each other close. "Benjamin should take you dancing," Esther said once.

"Benny dance? I should live so long!" Rachel replied, and sighed, for while she had never danced, she loved the music.

"Then let's go inside by ourselves, you and me," Esther said, and, struck with the idea, grinned. "Let's do it right now."

"I couldn't. What if Benny finds out?"

"What? Benny doesn't have a good time when he wants to? All we'll do is pay a dime to listen to the music. It will do the heart good."

"No, I couldn't," Rachel repeated.

"Then stay. I'm going in."

"By yourself?"

"Unless I find somebody to pay my way."

"Esther!"

"It isn't my fault if my sister won't come along to be my chaperone."

Well, if Esther put it that way, Rachel replied, and she took two coins from her pocketbook, and the sisters went inside.

The place was dingy, and it smelled of cigar smoke, which turned the air a bluish gray. The room was close and stank of sweating bodies, too. But to the two sisters, who had never been inside such an establishment, the dance hall was exotic, a bit wicked. They clutched each other and stood at the rear of the hall, watching the dancers as they leaned toward each other. Rachel looked shocked, but Esther only smiled, and before long, a man came up and bowed a little and asked if she would like to dance.

"No," Rachel told him.

"You I didn't ask," the man said, and held out his hand to Esther.

"I don't know how," Esther admitted.

"I'll teach you."

Esther looked at her sister, who frowned and shook her head, then looked resigned and waved her off. "Dance. Dance. Who's to stop you?" And so Esther took the man's arm and the two moved onto the dance floor.

She had not danced before, true, but Esther was light on her feet, and before the music ended, she had picked up the steps. And when she returned to her place beside Rachel, she was invited to dance by another man. And so the evening went. Even Rachel was asked out onto the dance floor, but each time, she replied that she was a married woman. The men did not understand that, for what did marriage have to do with a spin around the room? But Rachel stayed where she was, watching Esther, a chaperone.

When they made ready to leave—Esther was expected home at a certain hour, and Benjamin would be anxious if he returned to the tenement and found his wife was away—a man invited them to go to a saloon for a glass of beer, which horrified both of the woman.

"No," Rachel cried.

Then he would see them home, the man said.

"Don't take the trouble," Esther told him, and both women hurried away.

"God should strike us dead if anyone finds out about this," Rachel said.

Esther was not as concerned. "What harm did we do?

We had a good time, didn't we? What do the women have but work, work, work? Why shouldn't we have the good time, too?"

"You would go back?" Rachel asked.

Esther shrugged. "I didn't say so." But she knew she would. She had never had such a fine time in her life. "Who knows. Maybe I could meet a husband there."

"In the dance hall?"

"Better than Mama marrying me off to a butcher." When she realized what she'd said, Esther grabbed her sister's hand and apologized. "I didn't mean . . ."

But Rachel shrugged. "A butcher is fine for me. I got no complaint. But you, you can do better." She thought a minute. "Besides, you dance like an angel. Maybe a big theater man will see you. Maybe you don't have to go to the matchmaker for a husband." She struggled with herself and added, "So what harm to go back?"

And the sisters did, maybe once every week or two, and Esther remembered what her sister had said about meeting someone from a theater who would hire her. Perhaps that was the way she could get a house with a chandelier.

Sometimes they encountered other girls from the factory at the dance hall. At first, the two were afraid that their friends would tell on them, but then they realized that the others had sneaked out, too, and so they felt safe. As they sat on the fire escape at lunchtime, the girls compared their dancing and their dance partners. They giggled over who had the most dances, who the handsomest partner.

In time, Rachel, who became pregnant not long after the wedding, began to show, and she refused to go to the dance hall, for fear of looking ridiculous. Esther brooded about missing the fun, because dancing had become important to her—not only the feeling of flying through the air like a feather but the thought of meeting the handsome young men who sought her out, who admired her. "I could go alone," she told Rachel.

"Mama would never let you out of the house for such goings-on."

"No kidding." Esther thought a moment. "So I'll tell her I'm with you. It's no different from how it was before. There is nothing to be ashamed of."

"Who will look out for you?"

"Me. I'll look out for myself."

"I think you are not so good at that," said Rachel, because Esther could not always be trusted to know what was best for her. But Rachel agreed Esther would not be young for long. Besides, Rachel's pregnancy shouldn't spoil Esther's fun, her sister said, and so she agreed to cover for Esther.

Now, Esther went to the dance halls by herself or with a friend from the factory. She was known as a good dancer, and, pretty as she was, she had no trouble attracting partners.

More than one suggested something improper, but Esther had learned a little more about men, and she laughed them off. She did not laugh off Max Dora, however, but then, he never suggested anything improper.

Esther had seen Max before, sized him up and decided he was a swell. He wore the best clothes, not something purchased off a pushcart. His black hair was glossy, combed straight back, and although he was small, he had an air of confidence that made him seem larger than other men. One night, he asked Esther to dance, and she did not know she could ever be so light in a man's arms. They twirled and whirled, for Max was a virtuoso on the dance floor, and others stopped dancing to watch them.

After that, Esther looked for Max whenever she went out, searching for him with veiled eyes, pretending to be surprised when he came up beside her and took her hand. Sometimes she hummed the song, and Max told her that her voice was as sweet as her feet. Once when they started for the dance floor, Max touched Esther's arm and suggested that they talk instead. "I would like to get to know you a little," he said, and so they sat for an hour and then another, telling each other about themselves.

Max, as it turned out, was not a swell. In fact, he was not so different from Esther. Born in the tenements, like her, he, too, longed to get away. His chances of rising in the world were better than Esther's, since he was a man. Moreover, he had worked in one vaudeville show and been promised a job in another. Who knew how high he might rise. "You should come and see me," he said.

Esther laughed. "I should fly to the moon."

"Maybe you could be a dancer, too. I could put in a word. Perhaps they need a girl."

Esther's eyes glowed, but she shook her head. Bad enough she should sneak into a dance hall. She and her parents would quarrel to death if she went to work as a dancer. "Don't take the trouble," she replied.

She didn't tell Rachel about Max for a long time, afraid her sister would disapprove. But the bright look in Esther's eyes was obvious to Rachel, who knew it did not come from dancing alone. "I think you're in love," Rachel told her sister one day.

Esther didn't deny it. "So what does it matter? I don't even see him much now, because he's in a vaudeville show," Esther said. She added self-consciously, "He says maybe he can get me a job as a dancer. Think, Rachel, a dancer."

"Well?"

"You know what Mama would do."

Rachel shrugged. "You want to spend your life here, like me?" Rachel stretched out her arm to indicate the dirty dishes in the basin and the diapers hanging on a line across the room. "You should try for the job. Where's the harm?"

So Max set up an audition, and one morning, Esther got up from her sewing machine at the factory and announced, "I don't feel so good. I'm going home," and she went uptown and applied for the job. She didn't get it, and she was disappointed, but she was relieved, too. As time went by, however, she began to think she had lost out on a great opportunity, so when a dancer had a spat with the manager and was fired and Esther was offered the position, she accepted.

Now it remained to tell her parents, and Esther almost shook with fear that they would refuse to let her work in the show. She took Rachel with her for support, although Rachel was more timid than Esther. Neither girl had ever stood up to Emma or Abe.

The announcement took the parents by surprise, and at first, they said nothing.

Esther took that as a good sign and explained, "I'll make more money than at the factory—twice, maybe more."

"A dancer," Emma said at last, looking up from her sewing.

"I'm good. Everybody says so."

"How does everybody know?" her father demanded.

"When I dance, I am happy," Esther said, but her parents did not care about that kind of happiness.

"Happiness comes from a husband and children," her mother replied, her eyes returning to her sewing and taking half a dozen tiny stitches with her needle.

"It's Esther's chance to get away from here," Rachel put in.

"And what's so terrible here?" Emma pressed her lips together but did not look up. "Maybe Esther should count her blessings. Maybe it's time to find her a husband, before she disgraces herself."

"I won't marry somebody you choose. I'll pick my own husband, and I'll get married when I want to," Esther retorted.

Emma was shocked and set aside the needlework. "Such fresh remarks! To me, you don't talk like that."

Abe added, "In this house, you do what you're told. If Mama says you need a husband, you need a husband. Look at your sister. So much happiness she has. Tomorrow, we look for a husband for you. We talk to the matchmaker. Dancing! Such shame you will bring on us." He sniffed and returned to his newspaper.

The mother, too, went back to her work, the conversation ended, and Esther walked her sister down the stairs. "You should be glad they didn't ask where you learned to dance." Rachel sighed. "Maybe they will find you a good husband, better than Benny, not that he is so bad, of course. You are pretty."

"Who will ever know?" Esther replied. She said no more to her parents and spent the bitter hours of the night examining her life, her future. There was nothing for her. Maybe it was best they find a husband for her and get it over with. She did not feel so optimistic now.

Esther did not see Max for several nights, because her parents were watchful. Then Rachel called at the apartment and asked if Esther would go home with her and help cut out a shirt for Benny. So Esther was allowed to go to her sister's house. But it was only a ruse, and instead, Esther went to find Max.

"They put a stone upon my heart," she told him. "If I work as a dancer, they will throw me out of the house. They even said they will find a husband for me."

Although it was cold, with rain beginning to fall on the pavement, the two sat on the stoop of a tenement a few doors from the dance hall. Max took Esther's hand, removed her mitten, and squeezed her fingers softly. "Such a pity. You could be a Ziegfeld Girl one day. You're that good."

The compliments did not make her feel better.

"Maybe a star even."

"Go on!" Esther said, shivering a little, either from the cold or the remark—she wasn't sure which.

"I mean it." He thought a moment. "Maybe I could talk to them."

Esther shook her head. "Papa would throw you out."

"I'll dodge him."

Esther laughed despite herself, and Max put his arm around her. He had never done that before, not when they weren't dancing, and she wondered if it was a gesture of sympathy or something more.

"What would it hurt? He already said no. He can't do more than say it again," Max told her. Esther shrugged, and encouraged, he added, "Besides, I can't go to the dance hall if I work nights. There's no other way to see you." Suddenly, he leaned down and kissed her on the lips. When he drew back, she looked at him, startled. Such a thing to happen on a night that had started out in sadness! "I'll talk to them now. Tonight. What do you say?"

So they walked through the cold, Esther with a shawl wrapped around her, Max pulling the flaps of his cap over his ears, because it was already that cold. Sleet fell now, landing on the rooftops and dripping off onto the people who hurried along the streets. They reached Esther's building and climbed the stairs to the third floor. Esther was aware of the smells that assaulted them, of cooked cabbage and dirty toilets, and she wondered if Max knew how very poor she was. But Max did not seem to notice.

When they reached the apartment, the two paused a moment to catch their breath. Then Esther knocked, because her mother kept the key. After a moment, Emma opened the door, glancing uncertainly from Esther to Max. She stood aside and let them enter. "Abe," she called into the front room, where her husband was reading with his son.

Abe looked up and frowned. "What is this?"

Max did not reply. Instead, he looked around the room and said, "A fine place you have here."

Esther's parents were not to be distracted, however, and Emma asked, "Who is this you bring with you, Esther?"

"This is Max. Max Dora," Esther said, and she wondered then if she had made a mistake. Her parents could do more than say no. They could lock her in the apartment until a marriage had been arranged.

"I'm Max," he repeated. "I'm the assistant manager of a vaudeville theater, and I came to say let Esther be a performer."

Max had never told her he had such a position, and Esther wondered if he was lying.

Abe rose, his face twisted in anger. "What fresh grief is this? A performer! Our daughter does not make herself into a whore for men to look at. Get out." He pointed at the door.

"Go," Esther whispered. "It's no good. You are making it worse for me."

Max did not go, however. Instead, he said, "A dancer is not a whore, Mr. Schnable. Esther is an artist. She could make good money for you, twice as much as she does at the factory. Three times."

Abe dropped the book he had been holding and started toward the kitchen. "Such lies! You are a mutt. I curse you! God alone knows what will happen to you if you don't get out of my sight." He coughed and wheezed, because the tailor's disease had a strong hold on him and had turned him into a thin, gray old man. Still, Esther knew that would not stop him from going after Max.

"Go. Go," she repeated, making shoving motions with her hands.

Max opened his mouth to speak but then thought better

of it and walked out the door. The family stood there, listening to his footsteps grow faint, and then there was the sound of the outside door slamming. Esther longed to run to the window for a last glimpse of him, because she knew she would never see him again. But she was rooted to the floor.

Abe walked slowly into the kitchen and raised his hand, and Esther believed he would hit her. Instead, he muttered, "A mutt, a bum," and lowered his hand as he went into the bedroom. Emma followed and then Jakob, who shut the door.

Esther remained in the kitchen, staring at the closed bedroom door, and then she whirled around and rushed down the stairs. If she was forbidden to see Max again, she at least would tell him good-bye. She went out into the rain, but the street was deserted. "Max! Max! Are you there?" she called, and in a moment, he emerged from a doorway.

"I'd hoped you would come, so I waited," he said.

"I am saying good-bye."

"No. You are coming with me." He took her hand. "I have a room by myself."

"Oh, I couldn't!" As much as she wanted the future she had glimpsed, Esther would not disgrace herself, or her family, by doing such a thing.

"Don't you see? We could be a team," he said. "I've given it thought. A dance team. Everybody loves a dance team. I'll teach you all the steps. We'll call ourselves Max and Esther."

But Esther shook her head. She felt as if she were be-tween two fires—her family and Max—but she would not let herself be lured into sin.

"Then how about the Dancing Doras?"

Esther stared at him, then lowered her eyes in shame and said, "You should not joke."

"Who says I'm joking? Your folks want you to marry. So what's wrong with me for a husband?"

"You're asking me that, to marry you?" Esther touched her ears, as if she could not believe what she'd heard.

Max nodded.

"They wouldn't let me."

"Then we won't ask them. We'll marry on our own. Now. Tonight, if you like. Have no fear of me. I want to be your husband." Max grabbed her arms and pulled her to him and kissed her hard. "You know you drive me crazy."

"You're not joking?"

"Esther, look at me. I am serious. Don't you want to be my wife?"

"I do, Max. Oh, I do. God alone knows how much." She looked up at the window of the apartment, which was dark, and turned her back on it, and hand in hand, she and Max Dora hurried away.

They were married, but there was no one, not even Rachel, to stand up with them, and Esther never went back to her parents' tenement. They disowned her. Rachel tried to intervene, telling them that Esther cried over the estrangement, missed them, missed Jakob. But her father retorted, "She brought shame on us. We should be pitied, not her. Let none call her unfortunate." Emma was more forgiving, but she would not go against her husband.

And so Esther began her new life, and despite her parents' decision to have nothing to do with her, she began it in great happiness, because she and Max danced in the show every night and then went home to a little apartment, where Esther kept house. She did not for one minute regret her impulsive marriage. When the theater closed, the two found another job together, although it did not pay as much. As it turned out, there were already too many dancing couples, some better than the Dancing Doras. So while they got work, they did not become stars. Sometimes they worked together, other times separately. It went on like that for a year or more, with Esther doing dressmaking on the side to earn a little extra money. She was disappointed that they did not have success right away, but she was cheerful and hopeful and never doubted that at least Max would find stardom. It would take time, but one day they would have the good life.

After a while, Max announced they should go to Chicago. There were great opportunities in Chicago and not so much competition. So they rode the train to Chicago and made the rounds of the theaters, and because they were young and attractive and fresh faces, they were employed, and they thought this was their great opportunity. They would become successful in Chicago and then return to New York.

But after a time, Chicago was a bust, and so was Kansas City, and finally "The Dancing Doras, Straight from New York's Broadway" landed in Denver. They made the rounds of Curtis Street, Denver's Great White Way of vaudeville theaters and movie palaces, so called because of the many lights. Curtis Street was not like Broadway, but Esther thought that diamonds could not be prettier than the electric lights on the theaters, and she believed that she and Max would at last reach stardom in that place.

"They are greenhorns here. They know nothing about theater. A dancing bear could get a job in Denver," Max told her. But in fact, bears were a greater attraction than dancers straight from New York's Broadway, and they discovered the jobs were even more difficult to find than before. Max worked now and then as a dancer, but more often, he found other employment—shoveling snow and working in a stable. There were even fewer jobs of any kind for women, because Denver had no manufacturing, so Esther turned to dressmaking again and convinced Max to buy a sewing machine.

Their story and where it had led was not so unusual. Unable to find the work he wanted, Max became morose. He did not blame Esther, not to her face at any rate, but she began to believe that he was sorry he had left New York, maybe sorry he had married her. Sometimes he went out at night and did not come home until morning and would not tell her where he had been. And while she was naturally cheerful, Esther, cut off from her family, with no friends, began to feel uneasy. Eventually, she began to wonder if Max would leave her.

One afternoon, Max burst into their room with the news that there was a great part available—the lead—in a new show on Curtis Street, and he was being considered. He grabbed Esther and danced with her around the room. Her good spirits were restored. Such happiness she had not known since they arrived in Denver. Each day after that, Max was giddy with the belief he would be chosen for the part. He brought Esther presents—a hair ribbon, a sack of chocolate candy. He even brought home the producer to meet her, in hopes there might be a part for Esther.

A few days later, the producer stopped by alone. Esther invited him in, offered tea, because the couple did not keep wine in the room. The man asked where she had danced before, what steps she knew, and she insisted she could learn anything. After he left, she thought it odd that he had not asked after Max, and she decided not to tell her husband about the visit. And then the man came a second time, a bottle of wine in his hand. She opened it and poured him a glass but did not take one herself.

He asked if she would wear a skimpy costume in the show, something that was short and cut low in front. Maybe she could try it on for him. Esther, confused, said she would have to ask her husband, and then she inquired if Max had been offered the part. "We'll see," the man said, and moved over beside her and patted her hand. Esther was uncomfortable then and stood up, walking back and forth across the room.

"Don't be nervous," the man said. "This is how it's done; you know that. I give your husband a job. You show me you're grateful."

Esther told him he should leave, and he laughed at her and went out. She forgot about the bottle, and Max saw it when he returned and asked where it had come from. So Esther told him

"I think he wanted me to . . . you know."

She thought Max would be furious, but instead he shrugged and said, "That's the way of it. The job, it's just what I need."

"The way of it! For you to get hired in this show, you advise me to disgrace myself with the man? Adultery it is, a sin."

"Isn't it also a sin to go hungry, to shovel horse droppings in a stable when I could be dancing? God intended me to be a dancer."

"Don't talk rubbish."

"Rubbish, is it? This man, it's only a little thing. It's not adultery if your husband says it's all right."

"You don't mean that!"

"You'd rather your husband was a mutt?" Max walked

out on her that night. Later, the man came back—Esther knew in her heart that Max had sent him to her—and she did what he wanted. Afterward, she scrubbed with soap and water and then vinegar to rid herself of his stink. When Max returned, he presented her with a tiny bouquet of violets and a pot of rouge, and because her husband was so grateful and believed that his future was secured, she did not tell him how cheap she felt. She put the incident behind her and believed in the future.

The show did not open, however, leaving Max with his odd jobs, and Esther thought with irony that she had sinned for nothing. But the episode introduced her to a new way of life, because after that, Max began bringing men to the room, and when Esther protested, he cuffed her, once blackened her eye. He said being with the men was only for a time, until something broke for him. But he no longer looked for work in the theaters, and he began hanging out in the saloons instead, and it wasn't long before Esther supported both of them with her dressmaking and the encounters with men. She did not know how much Max charged them, because he found the men and brought them to the room and waited outside in case there was trouble.

To her surprise, Esther found that with time, she did not resent the men so much. That work, if one could call it that, was not so difficult—easier than bending over a sewing machine—and the men were nice. Some came back and brought her little presents, such as perfume and jewelry, both cheap. A few of the men talked to her when it was over, and she realized then that not all of them came to her only for the sex. Some just wanted to be with a woman. So she fixed them tea or gave them wine, and when she had it, cake, just the way her parents entertained their guests.

And then one day, a man told her, "I like you ever so much better than Evelyn. I suppose everyone does. That's why he charges more for you."

The man expected her to know who Evelyn was, so Esther pretended and said, "Evelyn, what's so bad about her?"

"You don't mind, then?"

"Why should I?"

"Oh, I'd think you'd be mad, him being your husband and her just being another whore. She's pretty enough, but with her, it's hurry, hurry, and get out. 'Minutes is money,' she says. Never a word to spare or a cup of water to drink."

Esther did not hear any more of what the man said, and after he left, she sat in the chair brooding. She was there when Max came in, and he frowned. "What ails you? Are you sick?"

Esther looked up and stared at Max for a long time. "You eat my heart out."

He frowned and came close to her. "What do you mean?"

"I mean Evelyn."

Max was startled and went to the window, where he stood looking out, his back to her. "What do you know about Evelyn?"

"I know everything. Do you think I am so stupid? You have two whores. Maybe more."

"Well, what of it?"

"You say that to me, your wife?"

"Are you?" He snickered as he turned around to face Esther.

"Of course I am. I have the paper."

"So does the other one, the woman I married before you. She lives in Baltimore now. I never got a divorce. If you're not stupid, you should have known."

Esther thought of many things to say then, but in her heart, she knew Max spoke the truth, and as she was not used to arguing, she saw no reason to continue the conversation. She knew, too, that what she did with the men was not just a temporary thing to help Max. She was a whore, and her bigamist husband was a pimp. Oh yes, they both knew those names now. But she knew something that Max did not—that she was pregnant. The child was his. She was sure of that, because she had been pregnant when he brought the first man to her. But she would not tell Max. She did not want such a man to be the father of her child. She would not even give the child his name. Instead, she ordered him to leave.

"Is it such a bad life?" he asked. "You don't have to go out on the street. I protect you. You have it better than most. What does it matter if there are others?"

"I will manage," she said. "I have my sewing machine."

But in fact, hooking was more lucrative, and the men came back to her, and so she earned her living as she had before, keeping the money now instead of giving it to Max. She worked almost until the baby was born, because there were men who sought out hookers in advanced pregnancy.

After Sophie came, Esther sent a letter to her parents, asking if they had forgiven her and would let her return. "I write this letter with my heart's blood," she told them, explaining that Max was gone and that she had a baby girl. "I am an *agunah*, the most dreaded word in the Yiddish language, a deserted wife." But she never heard from them, and after a time, she was almost glad, because she liked the West and its sunshine and fresh air, so different from what she had known as a girl. And she did not want to bring up Sophie in a tenement.

Esther turned again to dressmaking, but she did not have enough clients to support herself, nor enough money to wait until she built up her business, so she had no choice but to leave the baby in the care of a woman and go to work in a house on Market Street. Then the war came, and the police closed down the brothels, scattering the girls, and she had to set up in a room across the hall from Martha, the confidence woman. The two became friends, Martha often caring for Sophie, whom she treated as her own, when Esther was busy. So it seemed a natural thing, the three of them moving to Swandyke, where Esther, now Essie Snowball, got a job at the Pines, and Martha went to housekeeping with Sophie. In Swandyke, Essie Snowball decided that life as a hooker was not so bad, not so bad at all.

Essie spent the early afternoon at her sewing machine, making a white dress for Sophie. The dress was a bit of foolishness, and Essie had no idea where the girl would wear it. Perhaps to church, because Martha talked about sending Sophie to Sunday school. Essie said nothing about it. She was conflicted. She herself was not religious, but she thought it might be a sin to raise a child of Jewish parents as a Christian. She had not told Martha that, because, like the women at the Pines, Martha did not know Essie's religion. Perhaps it would do no harm if the girl went to the Protestant church. Maybe it was better that Sophie have some religion, and there was no Jewish congregation in Swandyke.

Essie finished the dress and held it up against the window, thinking the little garment was as white and pure as the snow outside. She hid the dress in her trunk, because she did not want anyone to come across it and ask questions. Then she went into the kitchen, where the other girls were eating eggs and drinking coffee.

In a few minutes, the school bell rang, and one of the girls sighed, because soon the men would start to arrive. "Damn bell," she said.

"Damn brats," another said. The boys from school sometimes veered off the trail and approached the whorehouse, throwing snowballs or running sticks across the wooden fence.

"Watch what you say. Ain't long before some of them boys'll come here as customers."

"And some of the girls will be asking for jobs."

Essie turned and stared at the hookers who'd said that, thinking again it was time to take Sophie away from Swandyke. She knew that some of her customers had children who went to school with Sophie. Minder Evans was one, that strange old man who liked to sit in her room and talk to her. Once, he'd asked if he could call her Kate, and she hadn't minded. And there was the black man she'd seen staring at the hookhouse. He had a daughter. Of course, he'd never come to the door, perhaps because he knew Miss Fanny didn't allow Negroes. Essie wouldn't have cared, because he was a nice man who always touched his cap when he passed her, even in the middle of town, where most men ignored the hookers.

She turned again and stared through the filmy curtain that hung in the window. Sometimes Essie could make out Sophie as the girl trudged along the trail. She could see better if she pushed aside the curtain, but Sophie might look up and recognize her from the Sunday visits, and that would not do. A group of children, the little ones, maybe ten of them, appeared in the distance, pushing their way through the snowdrifts ahead of the others, and Essie thought Sophie might be one of them. She watched as they passed the turnoff to the hookhouse and started across the road below the Fourth of July Mine. Essie watched the dark little figures against that vast field of white that was gleaming like quartz in all its beautifulness.

CHAPTER SEVEN

Squinting into the sunlight glaring off the vast snow-field beyond the window, Grace Foote watched a cornice of snow break off and drop onto the slope beneath it. The snow puckered and began sliding, was funneled into a chute that was formed by a rocky outcrop. Coming out the bottom of the chute, the snow slid a hundred feet farther, until it reached a ridge, and then with a loud *woompf* that Grace could hear through the glass, the harder top slab of snow collapsed onto a layer of sugarlike crystals beneath it that rolled and slid like marbles. That vast snowfield beneath the Fourth of July Mine, five hundred feet high and a thousand feet wide, split in half, east to west, cut by a ragged horizontal line that was like a tear in a white silk gown.

As the snowpack crumpled, releasing the upper layer of

soft, wet snow, the face of the mountain began sliding with a terrible hissing, scraping sound. For a few seconds, the edge of the avalanche moved slowly down that slope. Then the slide gained momentum, crashing downward with a roar like a giant waterfall, gathering rocks and stubs of trees that had pushed up through the toxic yellow waste beneath the snow and the remains of buildings and machinery, taking everything in its way, tumbling and smashing the debris like ore in a stamp mill.

Grace stared as if she were looking at a painting that had suddenly come alive, fascinated at the power and majesty and raw beauty of the avalanche. And then she realized what was happening, what that premonition she'd felt was about. Her eyes swept down the mountain ahead of the snowslide to the children walking along the road that led from the school on the west of the slope to the town on the east. They had stopped to look up at the mountain of snow bearing down on them.

For no reason that she could recall later, Grace counted the children in the slide's path—seven, eight, nine. Sensing the danger, one or two of the little ones bolted down the road, as if they could outrun the mass of white. Grace's throat tightened as she thought that Schuyler might be among the children, and she searched frantically for the little figure. "Run!" she whispered, although she was inside the house, alone, the doors closed. "Run!" But she knew there was no way the children could escape the slide that rushed toward them at the speed of a freight train. She stood frozen at the window as the mass of snow reached the children, saw a black shape tossed into the air, but she could not tell through the veil of white mist whether it was a child or a tree. From the time the cornice broke off until the slide ended in the gully below the road and started up Turnbull Mountain, no more than thirty seconds had elapsed.

Not waiting for the snow in the air to settle, Grace rushed to the telephone and dialed the operator. "There's an avalanche below the Fourth of July," she said.

"Well, I thought I heard something," the woman replied in a gossipy voice. "I'm not surprised. The snow—"

Grace cut her off. "There are children caught in it. At the bottom, on the road. Notify . . . well, notify whoever you're supposed to." She hung up before the operator could reply and picked up a second phone, one with a direct line to the mine office, and when it was answered, she didn't waste time asking for her husband. "This is Grace Foote. There's been an avalanche."

"We know. We'll get someone to clear the road."

"You don't understand. There are children—"

"Day of judgment—children! On the road? Are they all right?"

"I don't think so. I think the slide caught them, maybe nine of them." She took a breath and added, "Tell my husband that our son may be among them."

"Oh, Mrs. Foote . . ."

"Now! Do it now!"

Grace hung up the phone and grabbed her coat, slid her feet into heavy boots, and rushed outside, where white flakes hung in the air, scattering the light so that the snow left behind in the slide's wake sparkled as if it had been sprinkled with diamonds. A fire alarm split the air as she grabbed two shovels propped beside the porch and started down the mine road toward the slide, but a group of men passed her, running, and one said, "We'll take them shovels, Mrs. Foote."

"There are children—" she began, but the man cut her off, saying he knew, and the two men rushed on.

Grace looked around for something else she could use to dig—a spade, a pick—but all she could find was a washtub in a yard, an old and battered tub, and when she went to it, she saw that its bottom was rusted through. Well, it would have to do. She picked it up and dragged it along the street toward the slide, hurrying, for it was in her mind that she had to dig out the children herself, that she was the only one who knew where they were.

When she reached the place where the snow had closed off the road to the schoolhouse, however, she found others there, already digging in the snow, the men with shovels, the women with basins and dishpans and even their hands, and more rescuers coming. Grace looked down at the tub and realized she could not dig with it, so she left it beside the road and went to stand with a group of women gathering at the eastern edge of the slide.

"There's one's okay. We heard it cry. It must not be all the way buried if we heard it cry," a woman told her, taking Grace's fingers. It was a familiarity that would not have pleased her in the past, but Grace was grateful for it and squeezed the woman's hand. They were all the same here, mothers hoping that the wail they heard came from their own child. "Please let it be Schuyler," Grace prayed. "He's such a little boy, only seven. He hasn't had a chance yet." She realized the other mothers must be saying the same prayer.

Grace wondered then if she had overlooked something that portended the avalanche, some omen, some sign she had ignored. Was the disaster her fault? Had she caused it by violating some superstition? And then she pushed the thought from her mind. Fool, she told herself. You are a self-deluded fool. Forget that rubbish. Forget about yourself. This is no preordained event. Nothing is preordained. It is a random act of nature. Pull yourself out of your self-pity. This is what matters—Schuyler, these people, not you. She called to the men who were digging. "I saw the children, nine of them, I think. They were there in the middle. Some were just starting down the road, on the west side. None on the east."

The men spread out in their digging then, a few looking

up the slope toward the Fourth of July, because it was possible that a second avalanche could come down on them.

Hurrying down the street to his house, the old Civil War veteran Minder Evans heard the sound and knew it was an avalanche. He couldn't see the slope below the mine, but he was aware that the mountainside was where the avalanche would be, that vast open space where years of hydraulic mining had cleared the area of trees. As he'd walked Emmett to school that morning, he'd looked up at the crust of snow at the top, the long cornice of white that could break off and trigger a snowslide. He'd lived in these hills a long time, some fifty years, and he'd seen the power and destruction an avalanche brought.

Then he heard the siren, loud and piercing, like the wail of a freight train that would not give up. Minder would help. That was what you did in a mining town. He was an old man, but he would do his part, because in an avalanche, every worker was needed. Anyone who was pushed under in the slide would live only a few minutes—five, maybe ten, fifteen at the most—and then he'd suffocate in the wet snow, heavier than the muck in a mine. A man could dig a prospect hole in that land of decomposed granite faster than he could dig through a snowslide.

The old man stopped first at his house and took the

shovel off the porch, and as he did so, he was struck suddenly by the thought that the grade school had already let out—he'd heard the bell himself as he was coming back from the burial ground—and that children walked home along the road at the bottom of the Fourth of July Mine. Children like his grandson, Emmett, and maybe Emmett himself. The boy was always one of the first to leave the schoolhouse, anxious to see Minder, to tell about his day, that poor boy whose mother was dead and his father gone. That was why Minder rushed home each afternoon when he heard the bell, to be there when Emmett arrived.

The shovel in his hands, Minder made his way toward the avalanche. There were others hurrying along the paths that had been carved out in the snow, but the old man outran them. Emmett had to be safe. God, that angry God whom Minder had rejected wouldn't take the boy from him, would he? Minder had lost everyone else. Couldn't he be spared this one small soul? Or was it some final retribution? Would Minder be left with nothing? Wasn't it enough that he had been weighted down with guilt all these years? Was he being punished again for what had happened so long ago when the *Sultana* exploded? Minder thought that maybe he alone wasn't being punished but that Emmett, too, must suffer for Minder's weakness, just the way his friend Billy Boy had. Billy Boy had told him once about the sins of the fathers being passed down from one generation to the other one. It was in the Bible, Billy Boy had said. So even Minder's own death would not end the terrible chain of events he had set in motion.

He reached the snowfield and began to dig. Mrs. Foote, the wife of the manager of the Fourth of July, had seen the slide, had told them where the children were. That was a help, although the little bodies could be anywhere, flung a hundred feet away by the force of the snow. It was hard to see with the fog of snow crystals glistening in the air. But the men had found one of the children—found it alive. Minder heard the cry and rushed over, but the wail was not Emmett's. He would have recognized Emmett's cry. Still, finding the child was a hopeful sign. Maybe others were alive, too. Maybe Emmett. So the old man began to dig a little farther away, began digging as if his life depended on it. And it did.

Washing dishes, Lucy Bibb did not hear the slide, did not know that half the mountain had slid down into the gulch. But she felt it. As she wrung out the washrag, she felt the skin on the back of her neck prickle and her hands itch, and there was a chill, as if the door had blown open. But it hadn't. When she looked out the window, she saw the queer wintry light, and at first, she thought the cloudy air meant that snow was about to fall. But when she opened the door to throw out the dishwater, she heard the siren and thought perhaps it was a fire, that smoke had clouded the air. A fire was a terrible thing in a mining town in winter. Not only were the buildings old and dry and close together, but the water in the fire hoses froze. A fire could take the entire town. She stepped outdoors to see if she could tell where it was. But the moment she was outside, Lucy saw the snow suspended in the air, and she knew that there had been a snowslide, and a big one.

She heard the sound of boots in the snow behind her and yelled, "What happened?"

"The Fourth of July broke loose," a man replied, rushing past. "Somebody says there's kids. . . ."

"Kids?" Lucy called after him. "Whose kids?"

"Lady, I don't know. I got to get there." And he rushed past her in the snow.

"Bless God!" Without stopping to take off her apron or put on her coat or her rubber shoes, Lucy started after him, the dishpan in her hands, sloshing water onto her starched apron. She had forgotten to empty the basin. Others joined her, pouring out of houses and stores, carrying shovels and spades and picks, whatever they could put their hands on. But no one ran faster than Lucy. She reached the huge bank of snow left by the avalanche and asked a man who was digging, "What children?"

"Nobody knows. They say there's nine."

"Nine?" Charlie and Rosemary could be among them, she thought, a sense of terror coming over her. They would have hurried out of school that afternoon to see the new puppy that Henry had brought them only the day before. They would have rushed out on a tear, maybe the first ones to leave the school. Lucy stared at the wall of snow that filled the road, then found an empty place and began digging, forcing her dishpan into the heavy snow. She made little headway, since the snow was compacted, but she would not stop. She would dig all the way to hell if she had to.

In a minute, a man took the pan from her hands and said, "Mrs. Bibb, you stand over there with the women, please."

"No. There are children buried, maybe my children."

"You're in the way," he told her roughly. "We got shovels; we got machinery coming—plows, diggers." He added, "Please." The man took the dishpan out of her hands and flung it away.

And so Lucy joined the group of women who were standing together, forlorn, a little out of the way. There were perhaps thirty of them by then, gathered in clusters, holding hands, more arriving. Some cried. Others prayed. One woman shouted curses. An immigrant girl with a thick woolen scarf tied around her head muttered something in a foreign language to the woman beside her, the manager's wife. Mrs. Foote replied in the same language and put her arm around the woman, who'd begun shaking and speaking incoherently. Even those who didn't understand the language knew that the young woman was babbling.

Lucy backed into the crowd, aware now that her shoes were soaked and her feet cold. She began to shiver and thought she should wrap her apron around her shoulders, but it was wet from the dishwater. Just then, someone moved next to her and opened her cloak and wrapped it around the two of them. "Thanks," Lucy muttered, turning to look at the woman, and she saw with a start that she was her sister. Lucy had not been that close to Dolly since they were girls, had not spoken more than a dozen words to her since Dolly married Ted.

Dolly did not greet her. Instead, she seemed to feel it was natural that the two sisters should stand together in a time of trial. "There's one that's all right," Dolly said. "We heard it cry. Maybe it's one of ours."

"Pray God!" Lucy replied. "Pray God, Doll."

"They got a hundred or two men digging. They'll find them," Dolly said.

"They've got to," Lucy replied. And the two sisters put their arms around each other and held tight.

Joe Cobb did not hear the slide, did not know that there had been an avalanche until he heard the machinery in the mill go silent. That happened only for a reason, maybe an accident. He hoped not. He hoped that it had been only a breakdown, because he'd seen mill accidents, and they were terrible things. A man would reach into the machinery and catch his jacket, and before he could cry out, his arm had been pulled from its socket. A worker could crush a hand or foot. Or he could shove a pole into the chute to push aside a rock that had caused a jam-up and get himself buried under a ton of ore. Mining and milling were dangerous work. Joe thought the mountains took their revenge on the men who ripped up the earth to follow the slender veins of gold, then crushed the rock to get it out. No, he hoped it hadn't been an accident.

He heard a commotion near the door of the mill, heard men yelling. "We'll all of us go. There's kids down there," someone shouted, a voice of authority, and the men picked up shovels and picks. Another voice called, "Get the plow. Get anything that'll move snow."

Caught up in the excitement now, Joe hurried to the front of the mill and asked what had happened. "A slide," someone told him. "Below the mine, where it's bare. Took the whole face off the mountain. It ran all the way across the road. The manager's wife saw it and called up to the office. Didn't take half a minute."

"A slide?" Joe said. "Hell's fire! Is that enough reason to shut down the whole mill? Last winter when it ran, they just plowed a road through it."

"That was only a little slide. This time it's took the whole mountain, maybe a thousand feet wide."

Another man handed Joe a shovel. "You don't understand. The school's on the other side of the slide. Nothing over there but the school and the hookhouse. There's kids down there. The school's just let out. Them kids was coming along the road when it happened. Mr. Foote's wife saw them."

Joe stiffened. "Kids? Whose kids?"

"How the hell would I know?"

"I got a little girl, Jane. She goes to the school."

"I'm hoping she's all right, Cobb," the man said, touching Joe's arm in a gesture of sympathy the mine workers did not often express. "Now, let's us git."

Joe shoved the man aside and ran out the door of the mill ahead of him. As he emerged, he stopped for a fraction of a second to take in the vast slope of white in front of him and the frenzy of figures at the bottom, already digging in the snow. Jane might be there. She always hurried away as soon as school was out, because Mrs. McCauley took her cookies out of the oven when she heard the bell.

At the west edge of the slide, Essie Snowball and two of the prostitutes were eating an early dinner before the hookhouse opened when they heard the snow crash down the slope, heard a roar louder than a steam engine and looked at one another and frowned.

"Avalanche," said Margery, one of the girls.

"I guess that means we'll be playing solitaire tonight," complained her friend Thelma. "Those boys will be working all night, and even if they ain't, they'll be too tired to come here. No use bothering to get dressed." She yawned. "I sure wish I was in California, where they don't have to live with snow. Might be I'll go there." She said that every winter.

"Maybe we can make fudge," Margery said. "You think Miss Fanny will let us make fudge, Essie? You'll ask her, won't you? She likes you best."

But Essie was not listening. She stared out at the snow swirling around the hookhouse, snow thick as a snowstorm, because the hookhouse wasn't more than two hundred feet from the edge of the slide. She watched as the snow began to settle and the noise of the avalanche died down. And then she heard something else. Children who were stopped on the road to the west of the snowfield had begun to wail, pitiful long screams that pierced the wintry air all the way to the hookhouse.

"There's kids out there. There's kids caught in the slide," Essie yelled, turning around and grabbing a coat and rubber shoes. "Maybe Sophie's been taken."

By now, all five girls were in the kitchen, and Miss Fanny, too. "We got to help," Essie said. "Me, I'm going out."

"What do you care?" Thelma asked.

"It might be Sophie in there. What if it's Sophie?"

The girls looked at one another, not understanding. "Who's Sophie?" one asked, but nobody knew the name.

"Those kids can come here if they don't want to go all the way back to the school," Miss Fanny said.

"To the hookhouse?" asked a new girl. "Their mothers'll skin us alive, if they don't drive us out of town first."

"This is a mining town. Don't matter a tidbit who you are when there's trouble. We all work together. You go with Essie and tell those kids to come on in here and get warm. Essie . . ."

But Essie was already running down the path toward the slide, screaming, "Sophie! Sophie!"

The rescuers worked frantically to release the small figure whose head was above the snow. The child's wail had turned into a whimper as the men dug out arms and torso and then legs. "You okay?" a man asked, but the little one just stared at him.

"Who is it?" one of the men asked, but the others shook their heads. "Whose kid is it?"

"You know where the others are, how many got caught?" a man asked the child.

"No, 'course he doesn't," another replied. "How would he know? You wouldn't yourself if you got caught in a slide."

"I see another arm," a worker cried suddenly, and the rescuers turned to dig out the second little one.

A man picked up the first child and walked carefully through the packed snow to where the women were waiting. "I got a boy here," he said.

Some of the women, the mothers of girls, groaned. The

others rushed to the man, calling, "Who is he?" and "Is it my boy? Is it Bill?"

And then the boy called out, "Mother," and most of the women stepped back, some crying out in grief as they knew the child was not theirs.

"Mother," he yelled again, and Grace gasped, almost sinking down into the snow in her relief.

Instead, she cried, "Schuyler?" She rushed to the little boy and took him into her arms. "Are you all right? Are you hurt?" She covered his big ears with her hands to warm them, thinking as she had so many times how much he looked like his father. The boy's face was scratched, his cap gone, and he wore only one boot.

"There was so much snow," he whimpered. "It rolled me over and over like a snowball. I thought I was going to get buried." He put his face against his mother and cried.

The other mothers stepped back a little to leave the two alone. They could have been resentful that the first child rescued was the son of the mine manager and his wife, the woman from outside with all her entitles, who thought she was too good to mix with the townspeople. They might have asked why she was so lucky, might have hoped her child would be the last to be found. That would take her down a buttonhole lower. But they didn't. Instead, they were glad for her, glad that one child was safe. It didn't matter whose child he was. Besides, if one victim was rescued, others might be, too.

"Come on, Schuyler, we'll go home. We'll fix cocoa. . . ." Grace glanced at the faces around her, the faces of women crazed with worry over their children, and realized how blessed she was. Compared to these women, she had always been blessed. She bit her lip, and then she said in a loud voice, "We'll fix lots of cocoa, for anyone who wants it. And coffee—gallons of coffee. People will need it. And we'll open up the house." She raised her voice. "The children will be cold and in shock and maybe hurt. Bring them up to the mine manager's house. The doctor can tend to them all in one place. It's close by. We have plenty of room. Please."

She started for the house, and as she did so, one of the women broke away from the crowd and hurried after her. "Like Mrs. Foote says, you bring 'em on up to the manager's house," Mittie McCauley called, and because Mittie had been in Swandyke since the beginning and was much admired, the women nodded and knew they'd be welcome. Mittie caught up with Grace and said, "I expect you can use some help with the coffee, Mrs. Foote." She paused, remembering a conversation of sometime past. "And the beds. I don't suppose you keep your beds turned down."

The crowd of women forgot about Grace then, because one of the workmen called to them, "We found another'n, and it's alive."

The women moved forward as close to the digging as

they could get and asked one another, "Do you know who it is?" They watched anxiously as the men dug around the child to loosen the arms and then the legs.

"Alive!" a workman called. "A girl." He pulled the child out of the snow and picked her up in his arms.

Lucy saw the green coat and clutched Dolly. "It's Rosemary," she said, tears running down her face. "Oh, Doll, is she all right?" The little girl gave a cry, and Lucy said, "She's safe," and lifted the hem of her damp apron to wipe her eyes.

"Safe!" Dolly said.

Lucy pushed her way out of the crowd of women and reached for her daughter, whose blond hair and chubby cheeks made her look so much like Dolly, taking her into her arms and holding her tight. Rosemary's eye was black, and there was a long gash on her arm. She was barefoot, with most of her clothes torn away, and she shivered so. Lucy had no coat, so Dolly removed her cloak and wrapped it around the girl, but the little one was still cold. "Take her to the manager's house," Dolly said. "She'll get pneumonia. I'll watch for your Charlie."

"Jack and Carrie and Lucia, too. I hope your three . . ." Lucy began, but they both knew what Lucy hoped, so she did not need to say it. "I'll warm her up and be back." Then she touched her sister's arm, and when Dolly turned her gaze away from where the men were digging to look at her sister, Lucy said, "They'll find them, Doll. They don't know where they everyone are, but they'll find them." Lucy told herself that that had been a stupid thing to say. Of course the children would be found. But would they be found in time?

Dolly seemed to know that her sister meant well, and she smiled a little, motioning for Lucy to hurry. So Lucy carried her daughter the few hundred yards to the Foote house and went in through the back door. People always entered through the back door in Swandyke. Even in that time of great trouble, Lucy didn't think to use the front door.

"Fetch her here," Mittie McCauley said, indicating one of the straight chairs that the old woman had already drawn up to the stove in the kitchen. Lucy set down her daughter and wrapped a blanket around her. Grace and Mittie had already piled blankets on the table and were filling kettles with water and setting them on the cookstove.

"This is my daughter. She's got a bad cut on her arm. The doctor ought to check her out. I've got a boy, Charlie—" Lucy said.

"You go on back. The doctor's in the other room. We'll see to your girl," Grace said, interrupting Lucy, then turned to the child, recognizing her because she was one of her son's playmates. "Rosemary, isn't it? I remember your name because no other little girl in Swandyke has such pretty golden curls. We'll feed you on cookies while Doc takes a look at you." She brushed Rosemary's hair out of her face and told her son to pass the plate, then find a shirt and over-alls for Rosemary to wear. The little girl reached out with a cold hand and took two of the confections that Grace had baked that morning.

They did not look like cookies, but more like small cakes, Lucy thought. Maybe they were what passed for cookies with rich folks. Lucy's heart swelled as she watched her daughter taste the treat. "Her choice food is cookies," she said, barely able to get out the words because her heart was constricted. "I hate to leave her."

"She's fine with us," Mittie said.

"I'll be right back. I'll just fetch Charlie."

Mittie stopped her. "Your feet are wet. You'll catch your death. Take these." She sat down in a chair and removed her rubber shoes, handing them to Lucy. "And my coat, too."

Lucy put on the shoes and coat and hurried back to the group of women. When she reached them, she saw that Doll had her arms around a little boy, who shook with cold. "They found your Charlie," she said. "He's safe, Lucy. Both of yours are safe."

"Yours, Doll?" Lucy asked, hugging her son. "What news of yours?"

Doll shook her head, biting back tears. She might have thought it unfair, might have been a little jealous that Lucy's two children were all right when her own three had not been found. But she was not. She joyed for her sister.

Just then, Henry Bibb, who had been working underground at the mine, came up beside his wife. He saw Charlie and smiled, then he turned to Lucy, but before he could ask, she said, "Rosemary's at the manager's house. She'll be fine. You take Charlie up there. I'll stay with my sister. Dolly needs me."

Henry stared at Dolly, just then recognizing her. He had never seen his wife and her sister standing close together, but he did not comment on it. Instead, he asked, "Her children? Are they all right, Mother?"

Lucy shrugged.

"We will pray for you, Sister Dolly," he said.

Then it was Lucy's turn to stare. She'd never heard her husband utter Dolly's name.

On the far side of the slide, the children were gathered in a group, frightened and whimpering, while two of the teachers tried to calm them.

"There's no need to worry. The men will dig out your little friends in no time. They won't have a scratch on them," said the young teacher, who had been employed at the Swandyke school only since the fall.

The other teacher, the older one, who had been there for a long time, shushed her. "The children know better than that. They've lived here all their lives, and they know what an avalanche does. That's no way to comfort them." She raised her voice. "The men are digging as fast as they can.

Let's all go back to the schoolhouse. Your fathers will come for you when the road's clear."

She was herding the little ones toward the school when Essie reached the road, calling for Sophie. If the teachers—or the students, for that matter—thought it odd that a hooker was looking for one of the schoolchildren, they didn't say anything. "Sophie?" asked Essie, breathless, as she reached the children. "Where's my Sophie? Is she here?"

The teachers looked around but did not see Sophie, and then a girl spoke up, "She's up ahead. She went with Rosemary to see the puppy. They were in a hurry."

Essie looked at the older teacher, who gestured with her head at the tons of snow now resting at the bottom of the slide. "I'm afraid . . ."

Essie put her hands over her face.

"But the men are digging," the teacher added. "There's a good chance—" She stopped and then said brightly, "Would you help us? We need someone to take a list of the missing children to the families on the other side." She corrected herself. "We need to tell them the names of the children who are safe. We'll go back to the schoolhouse and—"

"Take them to the Pines," Essie said. "It would possibly be good for them to go there. Miss Fanny's got hot food. And beds she has."

Another time, the teacher might have chuckled at the remark about beds at the hookhouse, but young children had been caught and perhaps killed in the avalanche, and it was no time for jesting.

Essie led the way back down the trail, and while the hookers petted and fussed over the little ones, feeding them bits of cake from their own dinner, Essie, together with the teachers, made out a list of the children who were safe on the west side of the slide. Then she wrote a second list, a harder list, of the students who were missing. One of the teachers offered to take it to the families, but Essie insisted she would do it. "I will wait with the other mothers," she said.

The young teacher looked at her sharply, but the other one said, "Good luck to you, miss."

"*Mrs.* I am," Essie replied. "Mrs. Esther Schnable. Sophie Schnable's mother." Clutching her lists, she went back up the trail, and stepping like a bird on sore claws, she crept across the snow, past a child's boot, a plaid scarf, an arithmetic book. "Sophie," she called out softly, but she heard no answer, and the men digging in the hard snow ignored her. She picked up a cap lying on the ground, but it belonged to a boy.

Finally, one man told her kindly, "Lady, the men are tasked to do this. Best you wait with the mothers over there. We've already found three, two boys and a girl."

"Sophie?" she asked.

The man shrugged. "I don't know what they call the girl. She had on a green coat."

No, that was not Sophie. Essie went to the group of

women, standing a little apart from them, as was proper for a hooker, and then she realized that the others didn't know who she was. Besides, she had the lists, and so she spoke up. "I came from the other side of the avalanche. The children that are all right, I saw them. Here's their names. The teachers say to them, 'Stay until it's safe to cross.' We got food there and beds."

"Why, there's nothing over there but the hookhouse," said an old woman. She had no teeth, and her chin turned upward.

"Where else could they have went?" asked her friend. "You want them to stand in the cold?"

The first woman ignored her. She stared at Essie a few seconds instead, looking at the eyes that were outlined in black stuff and the thick hair piled on top of Essie's head in a fashionable way. "Why, you're nothing but—" She put her hand over her mouth.

"I'm a mother," Essie said fiercely. "I am distressed."

"Let her be," a woman said.

"The list. Who's on the list?" someone cried, and the crowd grew as still as midnight.

Essie read the names on the first list quickly, and with each name, a woman sighed or cried out or thanked God. One fell to her knees in prayer. When Essie had finished, she looked out over the crowd of women, seeing the ones with fear still on their faces. "I got another list. These here are the kids that started across the road."

"The ones caught in the slide," a mother whispered.

"Hush, let her read."

Essie started on the second list. "Rosemary and Charlie Bibb."

"Found!" someone called. "They've already been found."

Essie's spirits rose at that, for if two had been found alive, maybe Sophie was all right. She read the next name on the list, Jane Cobb, hoping someone would cry out that Jane had been saved.

But there was silence, until a woman muttered, "That's the Negro girl. I reckon she's still buried."

"Schuyler Foote," Essie read.

"He's safe, too."

"Jack, Carrie, and Lucia Turpin." Essie paused, because no one spoke up. Then she saw a woman with long yellow curls, tears running down her face, and knew she was the mother of the three.

"Emmett Carter."

Again there was silence, until someone muttered, "He's Minder Evans's grandson. Minder's digging out there. I'll go tell him."

"Sophie Schnable." Essie's voice wavered a little. It was like a stroke of death to her to pronounce her daughter's name.

"Martha's girl," a woman said.

"My girl," Essie told her, and then she added, "That's all of them."

She stood by herself a moment, and then Lucy Bibb, standing with the woman with the yellow curls, reached out to her. "Come and keep warm with me and my sister," she said.

A long time had passed now, ten minutes, maybe fifteen, and the men dug frantically, knowing the chances were not good that a child could live even a minute or two longer buried in the snow.

"Here's a coat, a boy's coat," one of them called, and the crowd of women leaned forward as one. Knowing their children were safe on the other side of the avalanche, some of the mothers had gone home to gather food. It would be a long night, and the men would need to eat, and the women, too, because they would stand vigil as long as the men were there. They stayed because it was a town tragedy that had happened.

"Who is it?" the women asked one another.

"Jack, it must be Jack," Dolly whispered, and Lucy's heart leapt.

But it was not. The women heard one of the rescuers cry out, the long wail of an old man, and Minder Evans dropped his shovel and took the boy in his arms.

"It's Emmett Carter," Lucy said, and felt Dolly sag against her. "He's limp."

The women watched, silent now, as Minder struggled to

carry the boy. Emmett's arms were limp, broken, and his skull was crushed. A man offered his aid, but Minder told him no.

"Is he alive?" Dolly whispered, and Lucy heard the hope in her sister's voice, because if Emmett were alive after all this time, Dolly's three children might be, as well.

Lucy shook her head. "I don't know. He's not moving."

"Carry him to the Foote house. The doctor from the mine is there," someone told Minder.

The old man struggled up the path to the big house, others trying to help, but Minder wouldn't let them. He carried the boy into the kitchen, where women were already spreading food on the table—pot roast and chops, cakes and pies and plates of fudge and gingerbread, food that they had prepared for their own families' suppers. It would feed the rescuers now—and the rescued.

"The fireplace room. Take him there." Grace set down the coffeepot she was filling and followed Minder into the parlor, the very room from which she had watched the avalanche. Minder laid the boy on the davenport, and Grace covered him with a white throw as soft as duck down, which she kept on the back of the sofa. The boy was pale and white and did not stir, and he looked like death. The old man, too, looked devoid of life, his eyes black and hollow, the skin on his face and neck as gray as mine muck. He looked as old as the mountains.

"Doc?" Grace said to a man who was sitting on the floor

talking to the Bibb girl, but the doctor was already getting to his feet. He went to Emmett, took a mirror from his bag, and, kneeling down, held it to the boy's mouth. He examined Emmett's head, then listened for his breath, his heartbeat, and after a few minutes, he rose and took the old man's hands in his and shook his head.

"He must have been hit by a log or a rock. I'm sorry. He died of a concussion."

Minder slid to the floor and put his arms around the boy. "He died of cowardice, Emmett did. Cowardice. That's what."

"You mustn't say that. There was nothing cowardly about the way he died. He was caught in the slide. You can't blame him."

"I don't," Minder replied, not looking up. "I'm the coward. It's my abomination. That's why he died. Retribution for what I did." The old man began to sob, long, tearless cries that racked his body and seemed to draw the blood from his face drop by drop. "I was going to raise him till he's grown, raise him up to be righteous." His eyes grew even darker, until they were like dead coals, and he collapsed onto the body of his grandson. Grace and the doctor laid the old man on the floor. The doctor examined him and said he was all right, and Grace covered him with a blanket. "When he comes to, we'll give him something strong to drink. It will stimulate him."

"Does he want to be stimulated?" Grace asked.

The doctor smiled sadly. "We can heal the body but not the heart. That's up to him, and it's not likely he'll do it. I know Minder Evans. He's been through the war. Some of them never got over it. There's times I think I ought to let people die." He took a deep breath and stood up. "But it's against my calling. Let's move the boy's body. Is there a place we can put the dead? That's what the next ones will be."

Ted Turpin came up to his wife, who was standing among the women with her sister and the girl from the Pines. "We just got the word down at the dredge. The kids?" he asked, breathless, because he had been running.

Dolly turned her face to her husband and opened her mouth, but she was so full of misery that the words wouldn't come out.

"They haven't found them," Lucy told him.

"Luce?" Ted asked.

He had not spoken directly to his sister-in-law since that night so many years before outside of his house, and Lucy thought how much he had aged. Where once he had been slim and hard as a bone, he was fleshy. The whites of his eyes were streaked with red, and his skin was flushed, perhaps from the cold, but it might have come from being filled with drink, for he had become an imbiber. It was known that he had once passed out in a snowbank and would have frozen if someone had not found him. Ted still worked on the dredge, but he had never been promoted, and people thought of him as a man whose education got in the way of his common sense. Ted's life had not been a good one, but that was his fault, and Lucy did not waste pity on him, not for his life. But she did feel sorry for him that his children were buried in the snow. "We're waiting. Some of the children have been rescued already. There's hope."

"Yours?"

"They're safe."

"Thank God for that," he said, and Lucy thought he meant it. He glanced at the girl from the Pines, and he seemed to recognize her, making Lucy wonder if stepping was another of Ted's vices.

Lucy stared at her brother-in-law a moment, trying to remember what she had seen in this man that had made her love him so. She had spent too many years resenting him, and now she asked herself if he had been worth it. He was weak, unsure of himself, and the thought came to her of a sudden that she had married the better man. Henry Bibb was not as educated, but he was steady and was respected for his knowledge of mining, had been promoted three times since their marriage. Henry loved their children, came home in the evenings and read stories to them, selecting a book from among those that were lined up with Lucy's college texts on a shelf that he had built. He put aside five dollars each month so that Charlie could go to college, and Rosemary, too, because Henry was a man proud of his wife's education. He did not feel belittled by it. There is something lacking in Ted Turpin, but not in Henry Bibb, Lucy thought, and if her heart did not flutter at the sight of Henry as he sat in the easy chair each evening reading the newspaper and smoking his pipe, it at least was filled with affection, and with gratitude that she had married a man with such a good heart.

Then, as if her thinking had brought him to her, Henry stood by her side and put his arm around her. He was not much for such public display, and Lucy knew how deeply he must feel. "The children are eating cookies. Have they found the others, Mother?"

Lucy shook her head.

"I guess they can use another hand at the digging, since they can't use the heavy equipment yet, for fear of hitting a kid. Ted, you coming?"

Ted said he would stay with his wife, and at that, Lucy gave him a hard look, trying to determine whether he was too shaky to dig. Perhaps he had been drinking on the job. Or was he a coward, afraid of another avalanche? Lucy did not want to think so. Maybe he just felt his wife needed him by her side. Lucy hoped that was it and looked over at her sister. For the first time, she observed how Dolly was dressed—a threadbare sweater that she had worn since high school, rubber shoes held together with adhesive tape, gloves worn through at the fingertips. Lucy had not known things were that bad for Dolly. She had not cared, she reminded herself.

As Henry started for the area where the men were working, a clump of snow broke off high up and began rolling
down the mountain. Henry glanced up at it, watched as the
ball gathered speed, puckering the snow and starting a
slide. But the avalanche was small and short-lived, and
Henry went across the packed snow to where the men
were digging. He picked up the shovel that Minder Evans
had dropped and began scooping up snow. Just as he did, a
cry went up that another child had been found—no, two
children.

Dolly gripped Lucy's hand with both of hers, and Lucy
thought how odd it was that her sister turned to her for
comfort instead of to Ted. But she did not hold that notion
for long, because the men lifted the two little bodies, and
even from a distance, Lucy recognized Jack and one of his
sisters, although she did not know whether the girl was
Carrie or Lucia.

"Oh please, God," Dolly whispered. "Lucy, God, let them
be all right." Tears ran down the mother's face, smearing
the powder she used on it, and with her childish curls, the
tears gave her a grotesque look, like a carved wooden doll.
Age had not been kind to Dolly. Ted stood mute, but Dolly
held out her arms to the little ones being carried to the waiting knot of mothers. "Jack, Carrie," she said.

"Ted, you take one," Lucy ordered. "Doll can carry the
other. I'll wait here for Lucia." She swallowed as she said
the name, thinking how Doll had reached for her when she

called her third child Lucia for Lucy, but Lucy had been too hurt and angry to accept the gesture.

Ted picked up Jack, while Dolly took Carrie into her arms, both children limp and white, bruised, their clothes shredded, and together, the parents carried them to the manager's house. Henry went over to Lucy then and said quietly, "They're gone. There's no hope for them."

Lucy put her head on his shoulder and cried. "Then you have to find Lucia, Father. Dolly has to be spared one child. She's my sister. How can she live if she loses them all? How could anyone?"

"We're digging," Henry said, and went back to the workers, and just as he reached them, one called, "Here's another'n." It was not a cry of glee, for now the men knew it was unlikely they would find another child alive. The little ones had been buried too long—twenty minutes, maybe thirty now. No one could live that long covered in snow, deprived of oxygen.

Ted carried the girl to the crowd of mothers, and Lucy recognized the brown hair so like her own. "It's Lucia! Let's take her up to the Foote place." Henry stopped long enough to wrap his coat around the girl, who was neither bruised nor scratched, but only still, and then he did an odd thing. Later, Lucy asked how he'd thought to do it, but he didn't know. He put his mouth to the little girl's mouth and breathed into it. He forced another breath into her mouth, and another. The women standing at the edge of the slide exchanged looks, because they had never seen such a thing. But Lucy had such faith in her husband at that moment that she knew Lucia would be restored.

And in a minute, she was. The small chest began to move, and before long, Lucia's eyes opened. Her own eyes filled with wonder, Lucy looked at Henry with awe and whispered, "We'll take her to Dolly."

Together, they carried her up the mountain, where Lucy found her sister sitting in the manager's house on a chair by the cookstove, a blanket wrapped around her, a cup of coffee in her hands. But she was not aware of the cup, and the coffee was cold. Lucy took it from Dolly and handed it to a woman, then said, "Here is something precious for you to hold." Henry set Lucia on Dolly's lap. Dolly, too overcome to speak, simply put her arms around the girl and held her tight.

"I went to sleep in the snow, Mama," Lucia lisped.

"You it was who saved her life, Mr. Bibb," said a woman who had entered the house behind Lucy. "There wasn't a God's thing to your girl until Mr. Bibb breathed her life back in her. He brought a miracle."

"Likely there was an air pocket," Henry explained, uneasy with the praise. "I'll be getting back to the digging now. There's two more still missing."

Henry left, and Lucy sat down on the floor beside Dolly's chair. "Is there any hope for Jack and Carrie?"

Dolly looked down at her sister. "There's a preacher

in there. He said the Lord took them because they're Christians and it's best to take them when they're young, while they're saved."

"That's hogwash," Lucy said.

"I was thinking so myself," Dolly replied.

An hour passed, two, then three. The children on the west side of the avalanche were led across the snow to the crowd of mothers, who took them home. The group of waiting women thinned out then, and some of the ones who had stayed behind in support began slipping away as night came on, bringing the winter cold. In lantern light now, the men kept on digging, their figures casting eerie shadows on the snow, long, thin shadows, as though they were giants. When their hands grew too cold to hold their shovels, the men went to the manager's house, where they warmed themselves with the stews and roasts, potatoes, the pies and cakes. Grace served them on her good china plates, took the dishes out of the cupboard and used them instead of the cheap earthenware because she thought no dinner party she'd ever give was as important as the gathering in her kitchen that night. She even set the table in the dining room with sterling flatware and linen napkins, but the townspeople were more comfortable in the kitchen, standing up, the plates in their hands.

Jim Foote came into the kitchen once. He had been

directing the digging and had gone to the house for only a minute to warm his frozen hands and gulp down a cup of coffee. Grace had not known he'd entered the kitchen and looked up with surprise as she saw her husband glancing around the room, taking in the table set with food, the men standing near the stove eating, Grace filling plates. He caught her eye and nodded, smiling a little. "I'm proud of you." He mouthed the words, but Grace caught them, and for the first time in her marriage, Grace was proud of herself. In fact, she gloried in her husband's praise. It was as if the two of them were a team that day, he in charge of the rescue, she ministering to the rescuers, not Lady Bountiful, but just another woman bringing aid to her neighbors. She started across the room to go her husband, but a child touched her arm, and she looked away. When she turned to Jim again, he was gone.

Minder remained in the bedroom that served as a morgue, hoping against all hope to see a leg move, an eyelid twitch. The minister tried to say words of comfort, but nothing comforted Minder. When Dolly crept into the bedroom to see her two dead children, she asked the preacher why, but his reply felt empty. He was a newly minted minister, and his inadequacy added to her grief—and to his, too, it seemed, because it appeared that the young man had taken the tragedy as his own.

After a time, Ted and Dolly took Lucia home. Henry and Lucy and their children went home, too, but something in Lucy would not let her remain there. Her body itched and twisted and would not stay still, and after the children were in bed, she told her husband that she would return to the avalanche. "There's two not yet found and a woman there . . ." she said, but did not finish. In her mind, she saw the girl from the Pines standing in the cold and thought she should not be alone. So Lucy put on her arctics and her heavy coat and mittens and, taking a blanket with her, trudged back to the site of the avalanche, where men were yet digging. Many, exhausted from the work, had gone home, knowing there was no chance now that a child would be found alive. They would return with the daylight.

Essie Snowball stood by herself at the edge of the snow-field, near a pile of caps and mittens, shoes and schoolbooks that the men had uncovered in their digging. She had stopped shivering and stamping her feet. In fact, she was no longer aware of the cold that reached every part of her body. Martha, the woman who cared for Sophie, had stayed with her for a time, but Martha was restless and said she couldn't bear the waiting. She would be more help cooking for the rescuers. "I can outcook any woman. You don't mind, do you?" she asked, and Essie shook her head, not quite hearing.

So Essie stood there like a lone sentinel, apart from the others milling around, both men and women. Lucy went up to her and put the blanket around Essie's shoulders. She didn't ask if Sophie had been found, because if she had been, Essie would not be standing there. Nor did she offer words of comfort, because they would be as inadequate as the preacher's. Instead, she stood beside Essie and waited, as women in mining towns always waited in a tragedy. From time to time, others came up to them and asked if there was news. Like Lucy, they could not completely abandon the one woman who waited. It was the way things were done there. The grief of one was the grief of all.

Mittie McCauley carried a plate of food from the manager's house, encouraging Essie to eat. Others brought coffee, tea, even liquor, although Essie did not consume spirits. The women knew Essie was a hooker, but they did not look at her with hostility or even curiosity, but only with pity and maybe guilt that other children had survived while Essie's daughter had not. They knew that by then—and Essie did, too—there was no chance the girl would be found alive. Essie's soul was not filled with hope, but only with resignation.

"It turns the heart heavy, waiting like this, the knowing and not knowing," one woman told Lucy.

"I wouldn't be her if it turned me into gold," remarked another.

They came and went, some talking, more to steady their own nerves than Essie's, others standing silently. Essie did not respond to them, but she knew they were there and drew comfort from their presence.

Sometimes the men, too, stopped their digging and came to stand beside Essie. "We're doing our best, missus," one said, and Essie thanked him. Essie roused herself then. She took a bite of meat from the plate a woman had given her, wondered at the taste, and asked Lucy what it was.

"Pork," Lucy replied.

"I never ate a bite of pork in my life," Essie said.

"Never?" Lucy was surprised, because pork was a favorite in a mining camp.

"I'm a Jew," Essie explained. "We don't eat pork."

"Oh." Lucy did not think that was something worth remarking on. She had known Jews in college and found them no different from anyone else.

But another woman standing nearby overheard and muttered, "Oh my goodness!" And Essie knew it would not be long before the woman told it around that one of the hookers at the Pines was Jewish. But she didn't care.

The way the women waited with her reminded Essie of her childhood, when death and childbirth brought the women into the crowded apartments in the Lower East Side tenements. There had been wailing and lamenting and raging, but sometimes in the middle of grief, there had also been humor and raucousness. The mirrors had been covered, and friends had come with their cakes and condolences to sit Shiva.

It was so different here, the people standing silent, resigned, instead of screaming their loss. Still, they seemed to bind themselves to one another. She had missed that connection with women, for there weren't many deep friendships formed in a hookhouse. Essie longed to have her sister with her now, her mother, some of the old women whose keening she had once found stifling but now would have eased her pain. She was grateful for the woman who stood beside her. Essie wondered if she should ask her name.

A man came over to the women. He carried wood that he had chopped and arranged it into a sort of tepee and set it on fire. He brought more wood and stacked it, saying it wouldn't burn as well as it should because the fire was set on a base of snow. Still, if they fed it, the fire would keep going and warm them. Then someone carried old chairs from a house nearby, and the women sat down. "I know what a clerk in a store feels like, standing up all day," Lucy remarked, and Essie smiled a little. "Did you ever work in a store, Mrs. Schnable?"

"A factory. I sat."

The wind came up, and Lucy tightened her coat around her and pulled her cap down over her ears. "Your girl, Sophie, how old is she?" Lucy said *is* on purpose, instead of *was*.

"Six. She's in the first grade."

"My boy, Charlie, is eight. I think I know her. Does she have long black hair?" It was an easy guess. Most of the girls in Swandyke had long dark hair.

"Hair like a raven. And her neck and fingers, long, like mine," Essie replied.

"Pretty like you, then," Lucy said, "and smart."

"She read. Before she started school, she read. And did sums. And draws! Like an angel, she draws."

"A sower of all seeds," Lucy said, and when Essie did not understand, Lucy explained. "Many talents. She has many talents."

They talked then about their children, about school. "I didn't like it that the school was over there, on the other side of the slide," Lucy said. "We shouldn't have allowed it."

"Who knew?" Essie replied, adding that she'd been glad the school was located where it was, because she could catch a glimpse of her daughter on the road. "Was that your sister, the one whose two . . ." When Lucy said it was, Essie asked, "Ought'n you to be with her?"

"She has her husband." Lucy paused and added, "We didn't speak for the longest time. It was foolish, wasn't it?"

"Not so foolish. I haven't heard from my sister in a long time, either. Mama and Papa, they wouldn't have anything to do with me after I got married. They called my husband a bum. They were right. I wrote them about Sophie, but her they don't care about, either."

"It's their loss."

"It's my loss," Essie said fiercely. "My loss." She quieted herself, and after a time, she said, "There is no such idiot as me. I should have given up the life last year and gone to Denver. I'm good with a needle. I could be a dressmaker."

She cried, "But no, I had to have more money before I left . . ." Her voice faded out.

"You can still be a dressmaker," Lucy told her gently. "You don't have to go back to the Pines."

Essie didn't reply, and the two sat and watched the shadows on the snow.

Just before midnight, the men grew quiet and gathered in one spot. There was a hush, and the women leaned forward in their chairs, trying to hear, but the wind took away the words of the workers. Essie stood and walked slowly into the slide area, but a man held up his hand, and she stopped. "We found something," he said. "A hand, a mitten on it. Did your girl wear mittens?"

"I don't know."

The men didn't talk as they dug the body out of the snow, didn't hurry, for surely it was a body. No one had ever lived that long buried in an avalanche. And it would be the body of a girl. Only two children were unaccounted for now, and both of them were girls—Sophie Schnable and Jane Cobb. They dug deeper, and they uncovered the little white face. One of the workers went to Essie and said, "Missus . . ."

Essie looked at him a long time, and then she began to wail, a primitive keening that erupted from deep inside her, that came from her bones. She cursed the evil that robbed her of her daughter, screamed her loss, beat her breast, and tore at her hair. Not one of those standing near the avalanche had ever heard such lamenting. They were people whose grief was mostly private, who showed their sorrow inside their homes. They looked at Sophie with fear and perhaps shame that the woman's wailing was so public and uncontrolled, so animal-like.

After a time, Lucy took Essie into her arms and said, "Come, we'll take Sophie where she'll be safe." She led the way to the manager's house, where the lights were still on. A man followed them, carrying the girl.

The other little bodies had been taken to the undertaker's parlor, where an order had been sent to Denver for children's coffins, but Grace had left the bedroom as it was, the window open, so the room was as cold as the air outside. "Put her on the bed," Grace told the man, and she herself tried to straighten the broken arms and legs, but they were frozen into grotesque positions. So Grace covered the body, letting only the face show and the long black hair, and she and Lucy stood to one side while Essie knelt beside her daughter. The two observers stayed like that, shivering in the cold room, until Grace raised Essie to her feet and led her into the kitchen, where a low fire burned in the cookstove, keeping the food warm. Grace urged Essie to have a cup of tea, a plate of soup, but the mother could not swallow anything.

Essie swayed a little on her feet, her eyes heavy, her hands gripping the back of a chair, and Lucy, knowing how tired she was, suggested that she go home and sleep.

"She can stay here. We've plenty of room," Grace said.

Lucy nearly told her the woman was a hooker, because it was an unseemly thing that a girl from the Pines would sleep in the house belonging to the manager of the Fourth of July Mine. Instead, Lucy caught herself and only nodded. Grace knew the names of the children caught in the avalanche, had heard the women gossiping around the stove. She would understand what Mrs. Schnable was, would know that Essie must make a long, cold journey across the avalanche to the hookhouse. Lucy marveled at the kindness of the manager's wife, the woman who did not mix in town. But then trouble, which often brought out the worst in people, sometimes brought out their best.

"They're all accounted for now except one?" Grace asked.

"The little black girl. Jane."

"Are you going home, then, Mrs. Bibb?"

"I suppose," Lucy said. "There's no one down there to wait for her. No mother, I mean. It's odd. I never wondered where the mother was. I suppose she's dead."

"He's there? Her father?"

"He was one of the first to dig. He's never stopped. As long as he's there, the others will stay."

"Is there hope?"

Lucy shook her head. "Even with an air pocket, she couldn't last this long. They're digging for a corpse." Lucy left then, and instead of going directly home, she went by way of the avalanche, hoping that the other body had been found. But the men were still digging.

At home, she undressed in the dark so that she would not wake her husband, but as she got into bed, Henry asked, "Did they find the last ones?"

"The Schnable girl. She's dead. The other, the little Negro girl, Jane, is still buried."

Henry threw back the covers. "I'll be going, then. I best help with the digging. Joe'll want us to dig with shovels." Like the other parents, Joe had refused to let the plows and diggers from the mine onto the snowfield, for fear they would tear up the bodies.

"She'll be dead. It won't make any difference."

"It'll make a difference to Joe."

And it did. When he thought about it later, Joe was moved that so many white men stayed to dig for his daughter. He wondered when they found the last white child whether everyone would go home. He wouldn't blame them if they did. There was no hope, and the night was bitter cold. The men had been digging for hours in snow that was heavy and compacted, like sludge. He didn't expect them to stay, but they did.

The men urged Joe to stop for a moment to rest, eat a bite of food, because he had not stopped digging since he reached the snowfield only minutes after the slide. But he wouldn't. He dug through the night and into the morning, and it was nearly noon the following day by the time someone took the shovel from his hands and told him to go home. "There's no hope, Joe. And there's danger of another avalanche." There was no more danger than at any other time, but it was the only way the men could persuade Joe to stop, by telling him he shouldn't risk the lives of others.

Joe did not go back to the mill that day, or the next. Instead, each day at sunrise, he walked to the snowslide and dug, worked until sundown. It got to be a regular thing to see Joe Cobb digging in the snow—a week, two, then a month.

"You ought to wait till spring thaw, when the snow melts. You'll find her then," someone told Joe, but he couldn't do that. He owed it to Jane, to Orange, to all of those he had left behind. He could not let his daughter melt out in the spring like some dead porcupine.

CHAPTER EIGHT

The Swandyke church could not hold all the mourners who attended the funeral for the five children killed in the snowslide. Although Jane Cobb's body had not been found, everyone agreed that she should be mourned with the others, and so her empty coffin was lined up with the caskets containing the bodies of her dead schoolmates.

The little caskets were mismatched, because they had come from different funeral parlors in Denver. The two Turpin children, Jack and Carrie, rested in the only two coffins that were alike, fancy coffins, metal, with brass handles. Emmett lay in a pine box that Minder had chosen because it reminded him of the coffins he'd built for dead soldiers during the war. Sophie's casket had a glass top and sides, and, dressed in the white gown that Essie had whipped up on her fingers, the girl was clearly visible as she lay against the white satin lining, her dark hear spread around her pale face. The fifth child's coffin had not arrived, so the one waiting for Jane was full-sized, black, with silver trim. Like the others, even Emmett's, Jane's casket was open, displaying the vacant pillow, as white as the snow that still encased the girl, waiting for her. The dead children, clad in their best, lay rigid, their white faces waxy in the winter light. "They look as if they're sleeping," one mourner said, and others murmured their agreement, although Grace Foote thought they all looked dead.

The terrible tragedy had been front-page news in Denver, and a mention of it had even made the papers in New York City and Washington, D.C., so the service attracted the governor, a congressman, and one of the senators from Colorado, along with officials of the company that owned the Fourth of July Mine, because the slide, after all, had started on the mine's property. There were, as well, a handful of journalists and the curious, who, because the weather was good that day, took the train to Swandyke to gawk at the bereaved and bask in their grief. And, of course, everyone in Swandyke turned out. Few in that town did not know at least one of the families whose children had been caught in the slide.

No building in Swandyke was large enough for all those who came to the funeral, so the service was held outside.

The best place for such a large crowd would have been the open area below the Fourth of July Mine, but of course that was inappropriate, not to mention dangerous, because with the freezing and thawing in the past few days, the snow was as unstable as it had been the afternoon of the avalanche. In fact, there had been subsequent snowslides, small ones, none to compare with the one on April 20.

So the funeral was conducted at the Meadowbrook Cemetery, in an open area on one side of the graves, where no one had yet been buried. Usually, folks stood at such services, but chairs had been set out for the dignitaries and for the families of the students caught in the slide, both the children who had survived and those who had not, because as the minister said, they were gathered to rejoice in the lives saved as well as to mourn those that were lost. But of course, no lives were really *lost*, because the dead were innocent children who had gone to be with the Lord, gone to a better place, he added. Some believed him, but not many.

The woman from the governor's office who had called to say the state's chief official would attend had asked where the service would be held if it snowed, which made the people in Swandyke shake their heads. They were used to inclement weather and thought the governor should be, too. The service would be held in the cemetery even if there were a willow bender, as the thick spring storms were called. The minister probably would call such a blizzard cleansing, but the mourners would see it as God's poor joke, because snow was what had killed the children. Many who were there that day were not pleased with God. But He did not cause it to snow at the service. In fact, the sun shone so brightly that some in the crowd got sunburned.

The front row was reserved for the elected officials as well as for the representatives of the Fourth of July, who had come out from the East. Grace did not want to sit with them. She would rather have been with the other parents, but as her husband was the mine manager, she had no choice. The officials seemed ill at ease, as if they didn't want to mix with the mourners, but Grace insisted on introducing them to each of the parents, who were a little in awe. They had never met anybody higher than the local manager. Later on, it was remarked with some satisfaction that Grace knew each of the parents' names and those of their children.

People were surprised, because Grace had never noticed them before. They did not know that she had studied the two lists of children that Essie Schnable had compiled. She had called on not only the other family members whose youngsters had been caught in the avalanche but also the parents of the children who were safe on the other side of the slide, taking cookies, a cake, a jar of jam ordered from some far-off store. It was as if she'd been born and raised up in Swandyke. She'd written condolence notes to those whose children had died as well as letters of thanks to the women who had helped her at the manager's house that awful day, written them on creamy white paper almost as thick as cardboard, with her name, Grace Schuyler Foote, engraved at the top. The recipients kept those cards, because they were moved by them. They'd never in their lives received such letters. One woman who had brought a plate of snickerdoodles to the manager's house following the avalanche put her note in a frame and hung it in the living room. Now Grace stood with the officials, greeting the parents and presenting them to the officers of the Fourth of July and the governor, who said again and again how sorry he was.

The Bibbs and the Turpins had been the first families to arrive. They sat in the second row with their children, the women next to each other. Dolly, her hair brushed back under a hat instead of hanging down in long curls, stared hard at the two coffins with the placards JACK and CARRIE on them, began to cry, and clutched her sister. Ted was next to his wife, his face puffy, his eyes red, but he did not smell of liquor. The two Bibb children sat between their parents, and on the other side of Henry Bibb was Joe Cobb. Henry had seen Joe standing at the back of the crowd, dressed in his work clothes, and had taken his arm.

"I ought to be looking for Jane," Joe said. "Besides, I haven't got a funeral suit."

"You ought to be here, and no mistake. Jane deserves to be mourned with the others."

"I'll stay in the back."

"You do that, and you'll bring disrespect to your girl. I

believe you think she's as good as any of the other children. Am I right?" And so Joe followed Henry to the seats, and nobody remarked that the Negro sat in the second row, just behind the senator.

Before he went to the funeral, Minder Evans, a little hunched over, walking with the aid of a cane that day, trudged the trail connecting the Civil War graves. He did not know why he needed to visit the war dead just then, but they seemed to call to him, as if they were old friends offering comfort. He could not shake the thought that Emmett was dead because of Minder's own transgressions and that these veterans of that long-ago conflict understood. The old man sweated a little from the exertion of walking from grave to grave, brushing snow off the stones, removing leaves, and he knew he would not have many more years. He was glad of it. What reason did he have to live? He wondered about that. For what purpose did he stay on this earth?

He approached the crowd of people standing behind the chairs, some stamping their feet or coughing, wishing the service would start, because they did not want to be there. Nobody did. Several nodded at Minder, held out their hands, and told him they were sorry. One woman said it was God's will, and Minder feared she was right, that God's will was to punish him for the rest of his life, maybe into eternity.

He saw the prostitute Essie standing to one side, a little apart from the crowd, with the other hookers. Minder remembered her from the Pines. He'd gone there from time to time, not for the reason other men did, but just to sit and talk to a woman. He paid, of course, and went to the room with the girl. Once he'd gone to Essie's room and asked her to tell him about her life. She'd said she was French and had been seduced by a prince, who paid her enough money to move to the United States. Minder'd known all that was a lie, but he'd pretended to believe her. He had not known she had a daughter.

Someone tried to steer Minder to the front row, said he ought to be there with the mining officials, since he had once been an owner of the Fourth of July. But he looked over at Essie and wondered why she wasn't sitting with the other parents. So he went to her and offered his arm. "Mrs. Schnable, I believe it is. May I escort you to your seat?"

Essie looked surprised. "I'll just stay here."

"No, you ought to be with the other parents."

A man overheard and said, "She can't sit with decent folks. It's not fitting."

Minder stared at him, a black look on his face, and the man's wife muttered, "You never know which way a cat's going to jump. She might raise revolution. After all, she's a . . . she's a . . ."

"She's a what?" Minder asked, staring down the woman. "I believe she's a mother, and a bereaved mother at that."

The woman would not be bested. She might not tell it out loud that Essie was a whore, but she would say the next best thing. "She's a Jew."

"Well, what of it?" Minder asked. "So am I."

Essie was startled, but she took Minder's arm and the two walked to their seats. Essie walked proud, holding her shoulders back, the way she'd once moved as a dancer. The minister went to each parent and shook hands, patted shoulders, offered a word of condolence or a blessing. He did not hold back when he came to Essie, which pleased Minder. Then he thought that perhaps the young man, new to Swandyke, did not know Essie's occupation.

When he had finished with the parents, the minister went to a pulpit set up in front of the coffins and began the service with the Lord's Prayer. The people repeated the prayer, all except for Essie, who didn't know it. A few said the word *trespasses,* but most said *debts.* The governor gave a little talk. He told the mourners how sorry he was. He wasn't eloquent. In fact, his words did not inspire the people or lift their burden, but they were gratified that he cared to be there. That was enough.

Jim Foote spoke for the Fourth of July. The mourners knew that another company, long gone, had done the hydraulic mining that denuded the slope below the mine, making it dangerous for snowslides. Besides, the slide had been an act of God. Nobody could have prevented it if the Lord wanted to send that avalanche. So they didn't blame the mining company. Still, the tragedy had taken place on property owned by the Fourth of July, and the company wanted to show its compassion. So Jim told the mourners the mining company would erect a monument to the dead children, to be placed in front of the new grade school. It would honor them, make sure they would never be forgotten. People murmured and nodded their approval, because there were not statues in Swandyke.

Jim didn't mention that the statue had been Grace's idea. The mining executives who had gathered at the Footes' dining room table the night before thought they might put up a plaque. But Grace said the parents would want more than that, suggested a statue depicting each of the five children who had died. When one of the men remarked about the cost, Grace pointed out that labor agitators were moving into Swandyke, and that the statue would bring goodwill. After all, she'd lived in Swandyke for almost eight years and knew the people, knew they wouldn't organize a company that made such a gesture. Of course, Grace made all that up. She didn't know any more about labor relations than a trout, but the mining officials did, and they knew she was right.

There was singing at the service, of course. You couldn't have a funeral in a mining town without singing "Going Home," and there were other favorites, such as "The Old Rugged Cross" and "A Mighty Fortress Is Our God."

Then it was the minister's turn. "Almighty God in His wisdom . . ." he said, then stopped and stood a long time looking at the coffins, rubbing his fingers together. As a young man fresh out of seminary, he had never conducted a funeral before. It was clear to the parents of the dead children that the man had been sorely taxed by the avalanche and his inability to comfort his flock. "It will always be remembered," he said, beginning again, then was still. He wiped his forehead with the back of his hand while people fidgeted, the women nervous, swishing the air in front of them with paper fans that bore the name of the mortuary. They expected some word of explanation from him. They expected the man of God to know the reason the slide had taken place, to explain away their grief. The minister appeared to know it, too, as he looked out over the upturned faces. The mourners felt cheated.

He sighed deeply, and then he uttered in a voice that some later said sounded like the voice of God Hisself, "The stones should cry out . . ." He burst into tears and could not continue. The bereaved, who had not been touched by the minister's earlier attempts to comfort them, were satisfied then, overcome by his words, and many who had not cried before shed tears now.

The minister sat down, drained, and then at the last, Jim Foote stood and ended the service, inviting the mourners to the Woodmen's Hall for coffee and cake. The crowd broke up, some heading for the Woodmen's, others going home. Many stopped to say a word to the parents or to greet the governor, not that they admired him much, but they wanted to be able to tell others that they had shaken the hand of the governor of the state of Colorado. It did not take long for the burial ground to empty out, because despite the sun, the day was cold. Pine trees shaded the cemetery now, and the wind had come up. Over on the side, men hired by the cemetery waited with shovels. They would have to move the coffins to family plots and put them into the ground, all except for Jane's. Her casket would be loaded onto a hearse and taken back to the undertaker's, where it would wait until her body was found.

"You want to go to the Woodmen's? You can come with us. I expect you need to get caught up with your eating," Lucy told Essie, but Essie shook her head. The funeral had been strange to her. She didn't know the feel of being a Christian, and instead of sitting placidly through the service, she had wanted to cry out and rend her garments, but she had kept still and made only a little tear on the left side of her dress. She did not know what was expected of her now. Besides, she was afraid she would be shunned, that her presence would make people remember Sophie as the daughter of a hooker, and as she had protected her daughter from disgrace in life, Essie would protect her in death.

"I'll see you home," Minder said.

"All right," Essie replied.

The other hookers had left by then, and Essie's friend Martha, the woman who had raised Sophie, had already deserted Swandyke, saying that with the little girl gone, she didn't see any reason to remain in a place where it snowed twelve months of the year. "I got disappointed in this town a long time back. I ain't never had nothing here after Sophie got taken, and I won't ever have nothing again. You got to study and contrive so hard. I wouldn't have stayed except for Sophie." She hadn't even waited for the funeral, explaining to Essie that looking at the coffins "wouldn't be no good for me." So Essie did not have even Martha's comfort.

They were the last to leave, Essie and Minder, because he wanted to walk the war graves again. He'd never taken that path with another person, but Essie didn't seem intrusive. She asked if he'd been in the war, and he replied, "Yes, and it cost me right sharp, cost me Emmett."

Minder didn't know why he said that, because he thought the girl would ask him to explain. But she didn't. Instead, she said, "God alone knows life brings a lapful of troubles."

They walked slowly back to town, passed through it, and came to the place where the slide had been. Off to the side, Joe had already begun to dig. He'd be able to get in an hour or two before nightfall, shoveling the snow, which had become compacted and was as hard as granite. "That man gets along slim," Minder observed. They continued on to the edge of the snowfield, and Minder stopped then, resting on a boulder that had been loosened in the avalanche. "I've got a proposition for you," he said to Essie. He was a little surprised that he told her like that, because it was not a thing he had thought through, and he wondered if he should have waited, if he would be sorry later. But it seemed like he should ask.

"I don't want you to trouble me," Essie said, her voice edged with disappointment that the man who had been so kind to her was fixed up now to pay for her services. Or maybe after he'd been so nice, he'd want to visit her for free.

She took a step toward the Pines, but Minder held out his hand and said, "Now don't get up and git. It's fruitless for you to worry about me. I'm no rascal. Besides, as you know, I'm ill off in that way. What I've got to say to you is to offer you a job."

"Doing what?" Essie asked suspiciously.

"I'm not asking you to make a penny dishonest." Then, instead of answering her, Minder asked his own question. "Do you want to go back to hooking?"

"I could possibly be a dressmaker in Denver."

"Then maybe you ought to do that."

"How can that be? I saved up to get me and Sophie a start—you have to keep yourself until the women get to know about your sewing. But I didn't have burial insurance, and every little money went for the coffin." She shrugged. "So what is it I can do?"

"What about Sophie's father?"

"A mutt. A dirty, rotten bum. He already had a wife when he married me. I was a dope." She hadn't intended to make such an outburst, and Essie took a deep breath to calm herself.

"Sounds like there wasn't any other place for you to go. Well, I've got a choice you can consider," Minder said. He patted the flat space on the rock next to him, and Essie sat down, her back to the man. "My trouble is I've lived too long. I got to find somebody to keep me, to do various pieces of work for me. With the rheumatics in my legs, I can't walk as good as I should, and I can't cook anymore. Somebody's got to fix my meals, fix them careful, on account of I can't eat much grease. And before long, somebody'll have to take me to the cemetery to walk the graves. Now, I'll pay you good to tend me, and you'll have your own room. There's even a room for your sewing machine. It's a big house."

"You offer me this with an open hand?"

"I do."

Essie thought over the offer. Then, remembering back to when she was a girl with her sister, she said, "You have a big house. Have you got a chandelier?"

"Two of them."

"Two chandeliers. Such a wonder!" Essie exclaimed, wishing she could write to her sister and tell her that, then deciding maybe she could. She thought a moment and asked, "What would people say?"

"Nothing good, most likely, but it'll be no worse than what they'd say about you if you went back to the hook-house."

"You, I mean. What would they say about you?"

Minder held his cane between his hands and bumped it up and down on the packed snow, chuckling. "I stopped worrying about that a long time ago."

"You've got nerve. I'll give you that." Essie looked out

over the snowfield, over to where Joe was breaking up ice with a pick. She'd already given some thought to what she'd do after the funeral. As she'd told Minder, she didn't have the money to set up as a dressmaker, and there weren't any dress factories in Colorado where she could get a job. As for dancing, Essie had come to understand that she was not so good at it as she'd once thought, that Max had led her on when he'd told her she could be a Ziegfeld Girl. She burned with embarrassment to think she had believed him. So her only choices were to stay on at the Pines or go on over to the Blue Goose in Breckenridge, and while she hadn't minded hooking so much before, she thought that after what had happened, it was time to get out of the life. It seemed disrespectful to Sophie's memory. Now this old man was offering her something else. It might not be a flowery bed of ease, but then, what was? She wouldn't mind keeping house, not in a place with two chandeliers.

"You could visit your daughter's grave every day when I go to the burial ground," Minder told her.

"What the earth covers must not be forgotten," she said solemnly.

"Why don't you rest your hat at my house for a week or two, see if we suit each other. I'm not pert, but I'm not fractious, either. I'm trusty." He stood and held out his hand to help her up, although Essie was steadier on her feet than Minder was. "You think it over."

Essie studied the man for a moment, then said she'd

already had time to think it over. "A good heart you have, Mr. Evans. I'll try it a little." She frowned and pursed her lips. "But I'll be just frank. A lie should not come between us." She waited until Minder nodded at her to continue. "I'm not French."

"That's all right," Minder said solemnly. "I'm not a Jew."

Lucy and Dolly walked hand in hand a little ahead of their husbands as they made their way toward the Woodmen's Hall. Their three children scampered in front of them, the girls stopping to make angels in the snow. Charlie pelted his sister and his cousin with snowballs, but the girls only laughed and chased him, pushing him into a snowbank.

The children, even Lucia, who had lost both a brother and a sister, did not yet understand the finality of death, Lucy realized. That was good. Lucia's playfulness would help Dolly. She squeezed her sister's hand, and Dolly looked up at her, eyes dry. "When he's better seasoned, that man will make a good minister," Lucy observed.

"He has heart," Dolly said. "He'll make it."

"So will you, Doll. You'll be all right."

"I lost them. But I got you."

Lucy thought that wasn't much of a trade, but she didn't say so. "We wasted a lot of years."

"We'll make up for them. We already have."

Indeed, the day after the avalanche, Lucy had fixed a pot

roast and potatoes and taken them, along with a bottle of green beans, to her sister, and the two sat down beside the cookstove in Dolly's kitchen, Lucy on a straight chair, Dolly in the rocker, and they talked. They caught up on each other's lives and the children's, laughing at the antics of the little ones that they had never shared with each other. They spoke about everything except for what hung over them, what had driven them apart. And then Dolly said, "It wasn't worth it, Lucy. Ted. He was never worth you."

"Hush," her sister told her.

"No, it has to be said. I betrayed you, just like they talk about betraying in the Bible. I ask you to forgive me."

"You've paid for it," Lucy said.

"And so have you."

"No. I married the man I was intended for. Henry's a good husband. He suits me."

"You must have hated me." Dolly got up from the rocker and went to the stove, where water in the teakettle was steaming. She measured tea into an old pot that was cracked, its spout broken, and poured in hot water. Then she sat down without looking at her sister. "You must have hated me," she said again.

Lucy was about to deny it, but now was a time for truth. "I did at first. And then I stopped, but I didn't know it. The hate became a habit. It hurt me as much as you."

Dolly nodded. "Ted still loves you. I think he does. He never loved me, not after a while."

"No. Ted loves himself." The two sat there, silently for a minute. "And I don't love Ted anymore. I haven't in a long time." Lucy did not realize that until she said it, and she paused a moment in wonder. Then she turned to her sister. "But I love you."

"It upholds me," Dolly said, and she went to fetch the tea.

The evening of the funeral, after Schuyler was asleep and Jim was at the depot with the departing Fourth of July officials, Grace went into the fireplace room with a pad of paper and a fountain pen and stood looking out at the snowfield illuminated by the moon. She looked for the figure of Joe Cobb—she looked for him every day, the black man against the white snow, and watched him dig—but he had gone home. She did not turn on a lamp, because the moon made the room almost as bright as day, but sat down on a footstool by the window and put the soft wool throw over her shoulders.

She wondered if it would bother the two women to sit in that room, where they could see all the way down the slope to the spot where the avalanche had buried their children. Grace had liked Lucy the best of the women in her kitchen that night, and so after the funeral, she'd said, "Come for tea." And Lucy had asked if she could bring her sister. Grace said, "Of course," remembering that Dolly, having lost two children, had suffered more than any of the other parents. Grace had thought they'd be more at ease in the kitchen over coffee and gingerbread, but then she decided she ought not to look down on them. In the morning, she would bake a cake and make tea sandwiches, because the two had agreed to visit that day.

She sat in the moonlight for a time, wondering if the women would become her friends. She rather hoped so, because she liked them. And then she set aside thoughts of the sisters and turned to the pad of paper and unscrewed her fountain pen, holding it poised over the paper. In a moment, she wrote the first lines: "It was very little of pretty things they had."

She had intended just to put down the experience, to write about the avalanche so that Schuyler, when he was grown, would know what had happened. And then she thought she might write a magazine story, explaining how people in a mining town high in the Colorado mountains had come together when tragedy hit them. But when she wrote, the words of a novel came out.

And so Grace Foote told the story of the avalanche at the Fourth of July Mine. It was not a best-seller, like her later books, because, frankly, people on the East Coast did not care much about a little mining town in Colorado. There were a few good reviews, however, and later on, several literary critics believed that Grace Foote's first novel, which had come out of her own experience as the wife of a mine manager in Colorado, was the most moving of all the books she wrote. It was always Grace's favorite—and Jim's, too. She dedicated it to him.

The book became a classic among folks who lived in mining towns along the spine of the Rocky Mountains, and there was not a house in Swandyke that didn't have a copy, most of them autographed by the author, back when she lived there. After she moved away, people in the town did not recall her as the famous author, however. They remembered her as the mine manager's wife, the woman who had opened her house to the town on the day of the April avalanche, who had asked that the bodies of the dead children be laid out in her home, who had taken in the prostitute mother and let her sleep in Grace's own bed.

Minder Evans finished his tour of the graves and stood beneath a jack pine, looking out over the burial ground. He thought he was alone in the cemetery, but now he saw the figure of a man in the distance, squatting beside a grave. The man was Joe Cobb, the Negro, whose daughter had been killed in the avalanche along with Emmett. Her body had finally been found.

Joe had dug in the snow for Jane every day following the slide, churning up tons of snow in his search, but it was a miner, walking home from the Pines one evening, who had seen the hand sticking out of a drift that was slushy from spring melt. He went for the sheriff, and the two of them thought to dig up the girl and take her to the funeral parlor, but after some consideration, the sheriff said he believed Joe would want to do it. So he'd gone to Joe's cabin and told him Jane's body had been uncovered.

Joe did not care who had found his daughter, only that the search was over. He didn't take a shovel to the snow-slide. Instead, he dug up his daughter with his bare hands, saying now that she'd been found, he didn't want to hurt her none by hitting her with a shovel or a pick. And so he'd slowly loosened the ice around Jane, and the people who had come to watch were humbled to see how lovingly he scooped away the snow from the peaceful body, which lay sprawled in the white. Joe carried his daughter to the under-taker and sat beside her through the night and into the next day and night, until the body had thawed enough to be fit-ted into the coffin. Then he himself placed the girl inside the box and closed the lid.

He did not want a service. Joe said Jane wouldn't care to have people gawking and crying, and newspaper folks set-ting off their flashbulbs as they had at the earlier funeral for the dead children. But the real reason was that he was afraid nobody would show up to honor a Negro girl who had been dead for weeks. He didn't want to let the town disre-spect Jane. And so, accompanied only by Mittie McCauley, he stood at the edge of the grave under a pine tree as the preacher said a prayer. And then Joe, who had dug the grave himself, shoveled the dirt over the casket. Mittie and the preacher left him alone then. They knew he wanted to grieve by himself.

That had been a week earlier, and Minder knew all about how the body had been discovered. People were glad for it, because it meant the avalanche had come to an end and they could put it in the past. There were some who thought it odd that Joe had not wanted a service, but others were relieved, because they did not know what would be expected of them at a Negro funeral. Still, there was compassion for Joe. The women left cakes and bread on the table in Joe's cabin. Essie herself asked Minder if it was all right to make an extra portion of stew so that she could take it to the grieving man.

It was a good thing, Minder thought, that he had employed the young woman. He was glad that she cooked and cleaned the house for him, glad that she kept company with him, and gladdest that others were beginning to accept her. The Patch sisters, as they were called again, Lucy and Dolly, had invited her to stitch with their little group of quilters, and Essie said she would, although she had not yet felt comfortable enough to attend.

Joe was welcomed back to his job at the mill, which was unusual for any worker who had been away so long. The mill rarely held a job open for more than a week. Men, who were not much at expressing sympathy, slapped him on the back and said they were glad he was there. Joe only nodded.

He'd always been an accommodating fellow, but now he was aloof. He brooded. But then, grief brought strange changes. Just look at how Ted Turpin had stopped drinking and who knows what else, and had started going to church. So no one wondered about the change in Joe.

Nobody knew better than Minder what grief could do. The old man studied Joe's bowed body as he stood in the graveyard. Joe might have been praying, or he could have been crying, or perhaps he was just leaning over to brush the leaves off the grave. Minder couldn't tell at that distance. It wouldn't do to bother the man. Minder'd never been much good with words anyway and wouldn't have known what to say to Joe even if Joe'd been a white man.

The old man started to turn away then. The day was cold, and he had finished his rounds and was anxious to go home, because Essie made tea in the afternoons and the warmth of it seeped into his bones. But for some reason, he stayed. Maybe he was just curious, but it seemed as if something wasn't right, and it got on his mind. After all, it was strange that Joe wasn't at work at the mill. With all the time he'd taken off to search for his daughter, he ought not to miss work to go to the cemetery. It was an odd thing, a man going off like that in the middle of the day to visit a grave, even if he was filled with grief.

So Minder stood in the cold, with the wind whipping up the leaves and blowing them across the graves, and watched. And he saw Joe pick up a bag he'd laid beside the grave and take out a rope, a long one and thick. Minder knew then what Joe had in mind to do. He knew because he had thought a hundred times to do it himself. But he'd never had the courage.

Minder thumbed Kate Forsythe's worn Bible in his pocket and wished that he'd gone on home, that he hadn't discovered Joe's intent. It wasn't just because Joe was a Negro and Minder didn't like Negroes. He wouldn't have wanted to come between any man and what the man had to do. But Minder knew in his heart that he had to stop the black man, knew at that moment that this was the reason he'd lived so long, knew that this was his chance to redeem himself for what had happened to Billy Boy.

Minder stepped out from behind the old graves just as Joe threw the rope over the limb of a pine. The old man walked slowly toward the new grave, because he had dropped his cane, and quietly, because there was still snow on the ground and the wind in the trees made a soft moan that covered up the sound of footfalls.

He came up close to Joe and said, "Trouble's come on you all at once."

Joe had not heard the old man approach, and he whirled around. He didn't attempt to hide the rope or the purpose for which he intended to use it. "No," he said after a pause. "I've never been out of trouble. It's been with me my whole life."

"It comes pretty high, the cost of life," Minder replied. "Sometimes you wonder if it's worth it."

"Sometimes you know it isn't." Joe looked down at the fresh pile of dirt covered with a wash of white snow that had fallen the night before.

Both men were silent for a moment, then Minder asked suddenly, "Are you acquainted with the Lord?"

"I was. But He taken everything I had. I thought He'd leave my girl, but He didn't."

"He's a hard one to understand. I haven't made His acquaintance again myself, but I might this day."

Joe felt the rope in his hand, the rough surface gripped in the hard, calloused fingers of his right hand. "How come you're to be here?"

"Because I'm somebody who's wore your shoe."

"You're the one with the grandson that got taken," Joe said. He had not recognized Minder at first. "But that doesn't mean you know me."

"I've been to hell myself."

"Well, I'm sorry for it, but you don't know what it's like to have nothing left to you. My life's been so fetched mean. I've stepped in every trap the devil's set for me. All my life I've been a white folks' darky. They worked me up like a mule. My wife died 'cause it was suppertime for a white doctor. I had to leave my farm behind, run off with Jane. Now she's gone, I got no reason to live anymore." Joe coiled and uncoiled the rope, then made a circle, the beginning of a noose.

Minder raised himself up and looked the colored man

in the eye. "You've had it mighty bad, but you don't have the corner on hard times. I won't historize on you, but there's others been mighty ill off. It's root, hog, or die for a good plenty of them."

"They're not my business, and I'm not yours, old man."

"You are," Minder said, "because maybe you're my retribution. Maybe if I keep you from doing this fool thing, the devil will call it quits on me. I got to save you to save myself." Minder was never a big talker, and the words surprised him. It seemed as if they were someone else's words, and he wondered where they'd come from, but he knew they were true, knew if he saved Joe's life, the grief he'd carried for more than fifty years might let up on him, Billy Boy might forgive him.

"There is nothing wrong about it, what I'm doing. Jane's waiting for me, waiting the way a dog waits for a bone. I got to go to her."

"I guess it slipped you by that this is no decision for you to make. It's up to the Lord."

"I thought you weren't acquainted with Him."

"Maybe I met up with Him just now." Minder thought hard. "Besides, how do you know you'll go to heaven with Jane? Maybe you haven't done enough good to deserve it. Have you thought of that?" Minder hadn't thought of that, either, until he said it. He wondered again where his words were coming from.

"What do you know about it?"

"I know a good plenty. I used to think hell was too good for me, but now maybe I've been kept alive this long for a chance to go to heaven myself." He paused and watched Joe twist the rope around the loop. "You want to risk it, do you?"

"You're a plainspoken old man, aren't you? You think you know every little thing, do you?"

The shift whistle blew then, and the two men were still until the sound died away. Then Minder said sadly, "No, I don't know so much. I'm an evil man. I've done wickedness you'll never know. I let my friend die because I was a coward. And maybe I couldn't kill myself like you're trying to do because I'm a coward."

Joe thought that over and said slowly, "Living's not a thing for cowards."

"Maybe not. It does have its joys, and you don't want them to slip you by. If I'd killed myself way back then, well, I wouldn't have had Emmett. And it was better to have him for a little while than not at all." Minder looked off toward the Fourth of July, but he could see neither the mine nor the slope below it. "I believe you think the same about your girl."

"You think if you stop me from stringing myself up, it'll make up for that boy you killed?"

"Not make up for it. No, not a tidbit, I don't suppose. But you'd be doing me a favor. I'd feel better about it if you wasn't to kill yourself."

Joe shook his head. "I don't know. You wouldn't stop me, would you? You couldn't, a puny old man like you."

"No, I wouldn't. You'd just slap me down." Minder thought a moment. "I'll tell you what, though. I'll ask you to wait a day. Would you do that for me? After all, there's no hurry, is there? If tomorrow you still want to do it, I won't say a word to stop you. I'll even hand you the rope. Just give me one day." And the next day, Minder thought, and the next, but he didn't say that.

Joe looked at the rope in his hands and then at the limb of the jack pine. He took pity on Minder then, or maybe it was that he really didn't want to die. Whatever his reason, Joe slowly began to pull at the rope. When it was off the tree, he coiled it and put it back into the bag. "You're a troublesome old man."

"I am that." Minder stood a little apart then as Joe knelt beside the grave. Minder waited until the man stood up, and then he said, "Mrs. Schnable makes tea every afternoon. Her daughter was another one got killed in the slide. There wasn't anyplace for Mrs. Schnable to go, and so she tends to me now, and she's a kindly lady. She'd be pleased if she had somebody to talk to besides me. She needs it. So I'd consider it a kindness if you'd come along home with me for a hot drink. You could doctor it if you like."

The sun was starting down behind the mountains, and Joe shivered, because he hadn't taken a coat with him. A man planning to kill himself did not need the encumbrance of a coat. He'd been at the grave for a long time, and he wondered what harm it would do to warm himself, what harm to wait a day. So he nodded, and the two men walked through the Meadowbrook burial ground, walked slowly, because Minder didn't have his cane and had to hold on to Joe's arm.

They were silent for a time, until Joe said, "It troubles me, Mr. Evans, that one day I'll forget about her, that she won't live anymore in my heart."

"You don't have to worry about all those things like that. You won't forget. Never did I ever disremember my friend Billy Boy. There's not a day I don't think about him, don't remember how much I cared about him."

Joe thought that over as they walked down the road in the late afternoon, Joe holding on to Minder now, keeping the old man steady. He nodded.

"Mrs. Schnable'll have enough supper for three of us," Minder said. "But it won't be pork. She won't eat pork. You couldn't hire her to pass it."

"Won't eat pork. I never heard of such a thing."

"Women are funny, but I guess you already know that, 'cause you've been married. What was your wife's name?"

"Orange. Her name was Orange."

"Why, that's as pretty a name as I ever heard, a sign better than Minder." He chuckled.

The two continued on through town, nodding to the men they passed, lifting their caps to the women. A woman wearing an old-fashioned cloak stopped and took Joe's hands, which were hard and calloused and stained with dirt from the grave, and said she was sorry, real sorry. She was a teacher, and Jane had been a good student. Smart. And sweet. He'd raised a real sweet girl. Joe nodded his thanks, because his throat tightened and he couldn't speak.

The two men trudged on in the dying winter light toward Minder's home. It was the ending up of one day. Minder knew there would be another.

Join Sandra's *Piecework* subscriber's list for her quarterly
newsletter and information on her appearances.
Go to www.sandradallas.com and click on "Newsletter."

And welcome!